RAVES FOR JAMES PATTERSON

"THE MAN IS A MASTER OF HIS GENRE. WE FANS ALL HAVE ONE WISH FOR HIM: WRITE EVEN FASTER."

—Larry King, *USA Today*

"WHEN IT COMES TO CONSTRUCTING A HARROWING PLOT, AUTHOR JAMES PATTERSON CAN TURN A SCREW ALL RIGHT."

—*New York Daily News*

"JAMES KNOWS HOW TO SELL THRILLS AND SUSPENSE IN CLEAR, UNWAVERING PROSE."

—*People*

"PATTERSON HAS MASTERED THE ART OF WRITING PAGE-TURNING BESTSELLERS."

—*Chicago Sun-Times*

"PATTERSON KNOWS WHERE OUR DEEPEST FEARS ARE BURIED...THERE'S NO STOPPING HIS IMAGINATION."

—*New York Times Book Review*

"JAMES PATTERSON WRITES HIS THRILLERS AS IF HE WERE BUILDING ROLLER COASTERS. He grounds the stories with a bare-bones plot, then builds them over the top and tries to throw readers for a loop a few times along the way."

—Associated Press

"A MUST-READ AUTHOR...A MASTER OF THE CRAFT."

—*Providence Sunday Journal*

16TH SEDUCTION

BOOKS BY JAMES PATTERSON

Featuring the Women's Murder Club

15th Affair (with Maxine Paetro)
14th Deadly Sin (with Maxine Paetro)
Unlucky 13 (with Maxine Paetro)
12th of Never (with Maxine Paetro)
11th Hour (with Maxine Paetro)
10th Anniversary (with Maxine Paetro)
The 9th Judgment (with Maxine Paetro)
The 8th Confession (with Maxine Paetro)
7th Heaven (with Maxine Paetro)
The 6th Target (with Maxine Paetro)
The 5th Horseman (with Maxine Paetro)
4th of July (with Maxine Paetro)
3rd Degree (with Andrew Gross)
2nd Chance (with Andrew Gross)
1st to Die

A complete list of books by James Patterson is at the back of this book. For previews of upcoming books and information about the author, visit JamesPatterson.com, or find him on Facebook or at your app store.

16TH SEDUCTION

JAMES PATTERSON
AND MAXINE PAETRO

VISION

NEW YORK   BOSTON

Copyright © 2017 by James Patterson

Hachette Book Group supports the right to free expression and the value of copyright. The purpose of copyright is to encourage writers and artists to produce the creative works that enrich our culture.

The scanning, uploading, and distribution of this book without permission is a theft of the author's intellectual property. If you would like permission to use material from the book (other than for review purposes), please contact permissions@hbgusa.com. Thank you for your support of the author's rights.

Vision
Hachette Book Group
1290 Avenue of the Americas, New York, NY 10104
grandcentralpublishing.com
twitter.com/grandcentralpub

Originally published in hardcover and ebook by Little, Brown and Company in May 2017
First oversize mass market edition: March 2018

Vision is an imprint of Grand Central Publishing. The Vision name and logo are trademarks of Hachette Book Group, Inc.

The publisher is not responsible for websites (or their content) that are not owned by the publisher.

The Hachette Speakers Bureau provides a wide range of authors for speaking events. To find out more, go to hachettespeakersbureau.com or call (866) 376-6591.

Women's Murder Club is a trademark of JBP Business, LLC.

ISBNs: 978-1-5387-4441-3 (oversize mass market), 978-0-316-55345-2 (ebook)

Printed in the United States of America

OPM

10 9 8 7 6 5 4 3 2 1

For Harry Cronin

PROLOGUE

THE MAN KNOWN AS J.

ONE

THAT MUGGY MORNING in July my partner, Rich Conklin, and I were on stakeout in the Tenderloin, one of San Francisco's sketchiest, most crime-ridden neighborhoods. We had parked our 1998 gray Chevy sedan where we had a good view of the six-story apartment building on the corner of Leavenworth and Turk.

It's been said that watching paint dry is high entertainment compared with being on stakeout, but this was the exception to the rule.

We were psyched and determined.

We had just been assigned to a counterterrorism task force reporting back to Warren Jacobi, chief of police, and also Dean Reardon, deputy director of Homeland Security, based in DC.

This task force had been formed to address a local threat by a global terrorist group known as GAR, which had claimed credit for six sequential acts of mass terrorism in the last five days.

They were equal-ethnicity bombers, hitting three holy places—a mosque, a cathedral, and a synagogue—as well as two universities and an airport, killing over nine hundred people of all ages and nationalities in six countries.

As we understood it, GAR (Great Antiestablishment Reset) had sprung from the rubble of Middle Eastern terror groups. Several surviving leaders had swept up young dissidents around the globe, including significant numbers of zealots from Western populations who'd come of age after the digital revolution.

The identities of these killers were undetectable within their home populations, since GAR's far-flung membership hid their activities inside the dark web, an internet underground perfect for gathering without meeting.

Still, they killed real people in real life.

And then they bragged.

After a year of burning, torturing, and blowing up innocent victims, GAR published their mission statement. They planned to infiltrate every country and bring down organized religion and governments and authorities of all types. Without a known supreme commander or national hub to target, blocking this open-source terrorism had been as effective as grasping poison gas in your hand.

Because of GAR's unrelenting murderous activities, San Francisco, like most large cities, was on high alert on that Fourth of July weekend.

Conklin and I had been told very little about our assignment, only that one of the presumed GAR operatives, known to us as J., had recently vaulted to the number one spot on our government's watch list.

Over the last few days J. had been spotted going in and out of the dun-colored tenement on the corner of Turk and Leavenworth, the one with laddered fire escapes on two sides and a lone tree growing out of the pavement beside the front door.

Our instructions were to watch for him. If we saw him, we were to report his activities by radio, even as eyes in the skies were on this intersection from an AFB in Nevada or Arizona or Washington, DC.

It was a watch-only assignment, and when a male figure matching the grainy image we had— of a bearded man, five foot nine, hat shading his face—left the dun-colored apartment building, we took note.

When this character crossed to our side of the street and got into a white refrigerator van parked in front of the T.L. Market and Deli, we phoned it in.

Conklin and I have been partners for so many years and can almost read each other's minds. We exchanged a look and knew that we couldn't just *watch* a suspected terrorist pull out into our streets without doing something about it.

I said, "Following is watching."

Rich said, "Just a second, Lindsay. Okay?"

His conversation with the deputy was short. Rich gave me the thumbs-up and I started up the car. We pulled out two car lengths behind the white van driven by a presumed high-level terrorist known as J.

TWO

I EDGED OUR sharklike Chevy along Turk and turned left on Hyde, keeping just far enough behind J.'s van to stay out of his rearview while keeping an eye on him. After following him through a couple of turns, I lost the van at a stoplight on Tenth Street. I had to make a split-second decision whether or not to run the light.

My decision was *Go*.

My hands were sweating on the wheel as I shot through the intersection and was blasted by a cacophony of horns, which called attention to us. I didn't enjoy that at all.

Conklin said, "There he is."

The white van was hemmed in by other vehicles traveling at something close to the speed limit. I kept it in our sights from a good distance behind the pack. And then the van merged into US Route 101 South toward San Jose.

The highway was a good, wide road with enough traffic to ensure that J. would never pick our Chevy out of the flow.

Conklin worked the radio communications,

deftly switching channels between chief of police Warren Jacobi and DHS deputy director Dean Reardon, who was three time zones away. Dispatch kept us updated on the movements of other units in our task force that were now part of a staggered caravan weaving between lanes, taking turns at stepping on the gas, then falling back.

We followed J.'s van under the sunny glare on 101 South, and after twelve miles, instead of heading down to San Jose and the Central Coast, he took the lane that funneled traffic to SFO.

Conklin had Jacobi on the line.

"Chief, he's heading toward SFO."

Several voices crackled over the radio, but I kept visual contact with the man in the van that was moving steadily toward San Francisco International Airport.

That van was now the most frightening vehicle imaginable. GAR had sensitized all of us to worst-case scenarios, and a lot of explosives could be packed into a vehicle of that size. A terrorist wouldn't have to get on a plane or even walk into an airline terminal. I could easily imagine J. crashing his vehicle through luggage check-in and ramming the plate-glass windows before setting off a bomb.

Conklin had signed off with Jacobi and now said to me, "Lindsay, SFO security has sent fire trucks and construction vehicles out to obstruct traffic on airport access roads in all directions."

Good.

I stepped on the gas and flipped on the sirens.

Behind us, others in our team did the same, and I saw flashing lights getting onto the service road from the north.

Passenger cars pulled onto the shoulder to let us fly by, and within seconds we were passing J.'s van as we entered the International Departures lane.

Signs listing names of airlines appeared overhead. SFO's parking garage rose up on our right. Off-ramps and service roads circled and crossed underneath our roadway, which was now an overpass. The outline of the international terminal grew closer and larger just up ahead.

Rich and I were leading a group of cars heading to the airport when I saw cruisers heading away from the terminal right toward us.

It was a high-speed pincer movement.

J. saw what was happening and had only two choices: keep going or stop. He wrenched his wheel hard to the right and the van skidded across to the far right lane, where there was one last exit to the garage, which a hundred yards farther on had its own exit to South Link Road. The exit was open and unguarded.

I screamed to Conklin, *"Hang on!"*

I passed the white van on my right, gave the Chevy more gas, and turned the wheel hard, blocking the exit. At the last possible moment, as I was bracing for a crash, J. jerked his wheel hard left and pulled around us.

By then the airport roadway was filled with law enforcement cruisers, their lights flashing, sirens blowing.

The van screeched to a halt.

Adrenaline had sent my heart rate into the red zone, and sweat sheeted down my body.

Both my partner and I asked if the other was okay as cop cars lined up behind us and ahead of us, forming an impenetrable vehicular wall.

A security cop with a megaphone addressed J.

"Get out of the vehicle. Hands up. Get out now, buddy. No one wants to hurt you."

Would J. go ballistic?

I pictured the van going up in a fiery explosion forty feet from where I sat in an old sedan. I flashed on the image of my little girl when I saw her this morning, wearing baby-duck yellow, beating her spoon on the table. Would I ever see her again?

Just then the white van's passenger door opened and J. jumped out. A voice amplified through a bullhorn boomed, *"Don't move. Hands in the air."*

J. ignored the warning.

He ran across the four lanes and reached the concrete guardrail. He looked out over the edge. He paused.

There was nothing between him and the road below but forty feet of air.

Shots were fired.

I saw J. jump.

Rich shouted at me, *"Get down!"*

We both ducked below the dash, linked our fingers over the backs of our necks, as an explosion boomed, rocking our car, setting off the car alarm, blinding us with white light.

That sick bastard had detonated his bomb.

THREE

RICH AND I sat parked in the no-parking zone outside the terminal, still reeling from what had happened an eighth of a mile from the airport terminals.

We had seen J. jump from the departures lane to a service road and knew that he had detonated his vest before he hit the pavement.

We had tried to guess what he had been thinking. Our current theory was that he hadn't wanted to be captured. He didn't want to talk.

Conklin said, "Maybe he figured jumping off the ramp, he'd land safely on a passing vehicle, like he was in a Jackie Chan movie."

I jumped when someone leaned through the car window. It was Tom Generosa, counterterrorism chief, keeping us in the loop.

He said, "Here's what we know so far. The guy you call J. had a plan to kill a lot of people inside a crowd, that's not in doubt. His vest was of the antipersonnel variety. Packed with nails and ball bearings and rat poison. That's an anticoagulant. The explosion was meant to propel the shrapnel, and it did. But the only casualty was the jumper."

I nodded and Generosa continued.

"The nails and shit shredded his body and any information he may have been carrying on his person. He left a crater and a roadway full of human tissue and shrapnel."

"And the van?" I said.

"Bomb squad cleared it. The FBI is loading it onto a flatbed, taking it to the crime lab. For starters, J. stole the van from the market on Turk. Maybe his prints will be on the steering wheel, but I won't be surprised if he can't be positively ID'd."

Generosa told us that federal agents as well as SFPD's Crime Scene Investigation Unit were at the site of the explosion now, that the CSI was processing it, and that after it was measured and photographed, the remains of the man known as J. would be transported by refrigerated van, along with explosive samples, to the FBI's and the SFPD's forensics labs.

Of course we knew that J.'s bomb had shut down SFO.

All airline passengers had been bused to other locations. Outbound flights had been grounded, and incoming flights had been rerouted to other airfields. We could see for ourselves that the terminal buildings were crawling with a multitude of law enforcement agents from CIA, FBI, DHS, and airport security, as well as their bomb-sniffing dogs.

Generosa couldn't estimate with any certainty how long SFO would be out of commission, but as bad as that was for the airlines, their passengers, and traffic, GAR hadn't scored a hit in San Francisco today.

We thanked Generosa for the report.

He told us, "Take good care," and walked over to the next car in the line behind us. We were about to call in for further instructions when our radio sputtered and Jacobi's voice filled our car. Both Conklin and I had partnered with Jacobi before his promotion to chief. It was so good to hear his voice.

He said, "You two are something else, you know? You cut J. off from his target. Thank God for that."

I said, "Man, oh, man. I can't stand to imagine it."

But I *did* imagine it. I pictured an airport in Paris. I pictured another in Turkey. I could easily see what might have gone down at SFO if J. had gotten into or even near a terminal. When I first started in Homicide, an airport bombing had been inconceivable. Now? These horrifying bombings were almost becoming commonplace.

Jacobi's voice was still coming over the radio.

He said, "Effective as soon as you turn in your report, you two are off duty. Boxer. Conklin. I'm proud of you. I love you both.

"Thanks from me and from Deputy Reardon and a lot of people who've never heard of you and never will. Many lives were saved. Stand down. Come home. The Feds are going to take it from here."

I was shaking with relief when I turned the car keys over to Conklin. I got into the passenger seat. I leaned back and closed my eyes as he drove us back to the Hall.

PART ONE

ONE MONTH LATER

CHAPTER 1

IT WAS OUR wedding anniversary, also our first date night since Joe and I separated six months ago. Joe had surprised me, calling me up as I was leaving work, saying, "I reserved a window table. Say yes, Lindsay. I'm parked right outside."

I'd given in and now we were at the Crested Cormorant, the hot new seafood restaurant on Pier 9, with a front-row seat on San Francisco Bay. Candles flickered on tables around us as a pink sunset colored the sky to the horizon, tinting the rippling water as the mist rolled in.

Joe was talking about his youngest brother.

"So, at age forty, Petey finally meets the love of his life at a fire department car wash." He laughed. "Amanda was power-washing his whitewalls, and, somehow, that jump-starts his heart."

"You think her T-shirt got wet?"

Joe laughed again. I loved his laugh.

He said, "Very possibly. We're invited to their wedding in Cozumel next month. Think about it, okay?"

Looking into my husband's eyes, I saw how

much he wanted to bring us back to our wedding in a gazebo overlooking Half Moon Bay. We'd vowed in front of dear friends and family to love each other from that day forward.

It had been a promise I knew I could keep.

But I hadn't been able to see around corners, not then. Now, in this romantic setting, Joe was hoping for magic to strike again. As for me, my innocence was gone.

I wished it weren't so.

I was conflicted. Should I reach across the table, squeeze Joe's hand, and tell him to come home? Or was it time for us both to admit that our Humpty Dumpty marriage couldn't be put back together again?

Joe lifted his wineglass and said, "To happy days."

Just then there was a sharp sound—as if the world had cracked open—followed by the boom of rolling thunder and a bright flash on the neighboring pier.

I screamed, "Nooooo!"

I grabbed Joe's arm and stared openmouthed across the water to Pier 15, the site of Scientific-Tron, a science museum, called Sci-Tron for short. It was a massive, geometric glass-and-steel structure designed for human interaction with the past and especially the future. The structure was unfolding like a bud bursting into bloom right in front of my eyes. Metal panels flew toward us, a mushroom cloud formed over Pier 15, and an overarching hail of glinting glass shards fell into the bay.

Joe said, *"Jesus. What the hell?"* His expression perfectly mirrored the horror I felt. *Another bomb.*

Sci-Tron was open to the public seven days a week but to adults only on Thursday nights. This was Thursday, wasn't it? Yes. People were inside the museum.

Was this a GAR attack? Had to be.

Joe threw down a credit card, then stabbed at his phone and called his job. Similarly, I called SFPD dispatch and reported what looked to be a mass casualty incident.

"There's been an explosion with fire at Sci-Tron, Pier 15. Send all cars. FD. Bomb squad. Ambulances. And find Lieutenant Brady. Tell him I'm on the scene."

Joe said, "Lindsay, wait here. I'll be back—"

"You're kidding."

"You want to get killed?"

"Do *you*?"

I followed Joe out of the restaurant onto the walkway that ran the length of the pier. We stood for a long moment at the railing and watched Sci-Tron's two-story metal-frame structure crumple as the roof caved in.

The sight was devastating and almost impossible to believe, but it was real. Sci-Tron had been blown up.

Joe and I started running.

CHAPTER 2

JOE WAS IN the lead as we headed along the pier from the restaurant to the Embarcadero, the major thoroughfare that bordered the waterfront on the western side of San Francisco Bay.

When we reached the sidewalk, we turned right and ran another couple hundred yards, past the historic pier bulkhead, stopping short of the entrance to Pier 15. Flames leapt above the smoldering carcass of Sci-Tron.

On our left traffic was going berserk on the Embarcadero. The terrifying sight and sound of the disaster had slowed vehicles to a crawl, causing others to swerve into adjacent lanes, while screaming, freaked-out pedestrians fled from the pier and dashed into the road. Brakes squealed and horns blared like it was the biblical end of the world.

Explosions have a shattering impact on all your senses. The cracking and ripping sounds, the stink of explosives, the terror on human faces. I knew this from firsthand recent experience, and still I found it hard to comprehend how a calm and beautiful night had twisted inside out into mayhem and inexplicable destruction.

Joe pulled me from the walkway to the railing on the bay side and kept his arm around me as crowds stampeded away from the bomb site and past where we were standing.

As I watched the movement of the chaotic scene, I was struck by an anomaly. A man was standing motionless in the middle of the sidewalk like a boulder in the raging stream of terrified pedestrians.

I'm trained to take note of anomalies, and I noticed everything about him. He was white, brown-haired, midforties, average height and weight, and wearing jeans, a blue flannel shirt, and wire-framed glasses. A scar cut through his upper lip, drawing my eyes to his thin smile.

He was *smiling*.

Was he shell-shocked? Having escaped the blast, was he trying to understand what had happened? Was he transfixed by the explosion itself?

Whatever he was thinking or feeling, I was having a cop reaction. In the midst of everything imaginable going wrong, he stood out. I waded across the oncoming rush into his line of sight, flapped open my jacket to show him my badge and to get his attention. Joe was on the phone, but he ended his call and joined me.

We stood close to the man in blue, and speaking loudly, I said, "Sir. I'm with the SFPD. Did you see what happened here?"

His expression was one of pure, wide-eyed

pleasure. He said, "Did I *see* it? I *created* this—this magnificent event. This is my *work*."

This was his *work*? He was claiming credit? I glanced at Joe like, *Did you hear that?*

"What's your name, sir?"

"Connor Grant. Citizen, genius, artist par excellence."

I said, "I don't understand, Mr. Grant. Are you saying that *you* bombed Sci-Tron?"

"Exactly."

I was already on adrenaline overload and it took all my will not to shout, *Are you batshit crazy? There were people in there.*

Grant was manic, or drugged up, or something, because he kept on talking at high speed.

"Good job, don't you think? Did you see the entire display? The mushroom cloud? Oh, my God. It was better than I had even hoped. I'm awarding myself an A-plus with extra points for the sundown sky. You want to know why, and I say, 'Why ask why?' Beauty doesn't need a reason."

Yes, it was a confession, but was it for real?

I asked Grant again if he had actually bombed the museum, and again, smiling like a child on Christmas morning, he confirmed *emphatically* that he had.

"You did this alone?"

"I told you," said the ordinary-looking man in blue. "This is my work. I did it and I did it perfectly."

"Are you feeling all right, Mr. Grant?"

"Yes, I *am*. Why do you ask?"

Was Connor Grant, citizen-genius-artist, insane? I didn't know what to believe.

Joe had his gun in hand and kept it pointed at Grant as I told him to put his hands on his head. He obeyed me while staring at the destruction, still wearing a beatific glow. I patted him down, found nothing but keys, coins, and a wallet. His ID confirmed his name, and now I had an address and his credit cards.

I cuffed the smiling psycho, arrested him for the destruction of public property, which would hold him, and read him his rights.

Squad cars were screaming up to the curb, and I marched Grant over to one of them. I knew the uniformed cop who scrambled out of the passenger seat.

I told young Officer Einhorn and his partner, "Mr. Grant claims that he blew up Sci-Tron. I'm calling Lieutenant Brady now, asking him to meet you at booking. Do not let this man out of your sight until you transfer custody to Brady. I mean, do not take your eyes off him for a second. Any questions, Marty?"

After the squad car had pulled out, I speed-dialed Brady and briefed him on Connor Grant, saying that he had taken credit for blowing up Sci-Tron.

"I don't know what to make of him, Lieu. He says he did it. I'll be coming back to the Hall as soon as I can."

Joe had been taking photos of incoming law enforcement and activity around the pier. He put his phone away and said, "Wait here, Linds. I'm going to assess the scene real quick before the fire department tramples it. Be back in five."

With that, Joe ran toward the wreck of Sci-Tron. I didn't like it. The structure was still smoking and was unstable. Joe was alone.

I shouted after him, but it was so loud on the street I honestly don't think he heard me.

CHAPTER 3

JOE CROSSED THE threshold of what only a few minutes before had been a futuristic science museum.

Now it felt as though he were entering a rain forest.

The sprinkler system poured water down and the air smelled of rotten eggs. That meant natural gas, maybe propane, and he picked up other odors: burning plastic, hair, flesh.

Clouds and fog blocked out the waning light.

Looking up, Joe saw only the twisted tracery of trusses and tubular superstructure. Water collected on the floor, which was littered with overturned exhibits and displays torn from the walls. And there were the lumpy shapes of the victims.

Aiming blindly, Joe took photos of the debris.

The blast had blown out the glass but left the interior standing, so the explosive device had probably not been a manufactured bomb. It seemed likely that the device had been improvised, a compression bomb, a gas-filled container wired with an explosive charge. The attendant flash fire had consumed available combustible materials until the heat had set off the sprinklers.

What remained of Sci-Tron was a hazardous obstacle course of smashed glass and sheared-off metal tubing, overturned exhibits and exposed wiring. Joe carefully picked out a path through the pile of rubble by the light of his phone and the low-burning fires.

He called out, "Hellooo. Can anyone hear me?"

There was an answering moan ahead to his right. Joe called out, *"I'm coming,"* and headed toward the sound, when something snaked around his ankle. Reflexively he kicked his leg free, then made out the pale hand, the arm, the upper torso, of a woman lying facedown on the floor, half buried under a display case.

She said, "I can't...move."

Joe stooped to see her.

"I'm going to help you out of this. What's your name?"

"Sophie Fields."

"I'm Joe. Sophie, are you in pain?"

"I feel numb."

"Looks like an exhibit fell on you. I'm going to try to move it. Hang on."

"Tell my husband...Robbie...I love. Him. The key is in the tackle...box."

"You get to tell him yourself, Sophie. Listen. We're a team now. I'm going to try to move this junk off you. The visibility in here really sucks. If anything hurts you, shout out."

Sophie moaned and then she was quiet again.

Joe sized up the six-by-six-by-twelve-foot case, which was part metal, part glass, with jagged edges and what looked to be a heavy steel base. If he could get a decent angle and a good grip…if he could lift and shove at the same time…if Sophie weren't pinned by something he couldn't see underneath the display cabinet…a whole lot of ifs.

He at least had to try.

He told Sophie what he was going to do on the count of three, and then, hoping to God he could do it, Joe got his arms around the plastic backing, bent his knees under the base, and heaved.

There was a good deal of creaking and rocking, but the exhibit shifted off the woman's body and then stabilized. Joe was pretty sure Sophie should be able to move if her back wasn't broken.

He asked her, "Sophie, can you roll onto your side so that you're facing me?"

Joe never got an answer.

There was a small blue flash up ahead, like an arc of electricity, followed immediately by a concussive boom. Something heavy struck the back of Joe's head. Sparks flashed in front of his eyes as, weightless, he fell through the dark.

CHAPTER 4

I WAS IN a state of high anxiety as I stood up-stream of the exodus from Pier 15, with a clear view of the halogen-lit incident scene.

Uniformed cops moved barricades into place on the Embarcadero, closing it off from Bay Street to Market, shutting down local traffic.

The incident commander, wearing a neon-yellow vest, directed ambulances toward the internal parking area inside Pier 9, which had now become a staging area for medical units.

Fire trucks with lights flashing and sirens on full blast drove over the sidewalk and up to the entrance gate. Men and women wearing EMT vests gathered and stood ready as the firefighters went in.

Joe had said, "Back in five."

Time was up. When he said that, had he truly believed that a quick look at the scene would take only five minutes? His estimate was off, but I resisted the fierce temptation to call him, telling myself that he was working hard and fast and couldn't take time to call me. Still, I was in tremendous conflict. Was Joe in trouble? Had something happened to him inside that bomb site? Should I just stand here? Or should I get help?

I looked at my watch. He'd been gone for twelve minutes. Now thirteen.

I phoned Mrs. Rose, my neighbor, my friend and babysitter. I yelled over the noise that I was near Sci-Tron. That I wouldn't be home until late. I was calling Brady when, as if tapping the keypad had triggered it, another bomb went off.

The force of that explosion obliterated every other sound, including my own voice screaming, *"Joe!"*

I broke for the entrance to the pier, but before I reached it, I was stopped by three firefighters, who blocked my way and pulled me off to the side and out of harm's way.

I fought back.

"Jesus *Christ*. I'm a *cop*. My husband's in there. Give me some help, would you please? I have to find him."

One of the firefighters said to me, "Officer, you can't go in, not now. Please stand back. Stand there. We'll get him out as soon as we can."

The firefighters were doing their best to control an unstable situation, and I didn't hold it against them. I stood where I'd been directed to stand, out of the path of the rescue squads and with a pretty good view of what had been Sci-Tron's entrance. I prayed that Joe would walk out onto the sidewalk.

Please, God. Let Joe be safe.

That's what was in my mind when the medical

examiner's refrigerated trailer rumbled through an opening in the barricades and parked on the trolley tracks that ran down the middle of the Embarcadero.

I turned away from the mobile morgue and looked out over the bay as I called Joe's number again and again, hitting the Redial button incessantly and getting no reply.

Since Joe wasn't answering, I called my friends and my partner, and I know they heard the terror in my voice. They could do nothing but say, "How can I help?"

I said to each, "I'll call you later."

And then I was fresh out of lifelines.

For the next hour in that horrible, stinking night I watched as EMTs ran empty stretchers through the museum's shattered entrance and carried bagged bodies out to the sidewalk. There the dead were lifted into the medical examiner's van.

As for the living, firefighters helped some of the blast victims walk out of the museum. Others were carried out on stretchers.

I dialed Joe's number.

Joe, answer your phone.

This time I thought I heard his ring tone, five familiar notes, getting louder as EMTs rolled a stretcher through the gate and out toward the curb. I ran toward that stretcher, feeling hopeful and terrified at what I might find. I heard the ring tone again.

"Joe?"

The face of the man on the stretcher was horribly swollen, bruised, and smeared with blood. His left arm rolled out from under the blanket that covered his body, and I saw the wedding ring I had placed on his finger when we were standing together inside a gazebo facing Half Moon Bay. We'd vowed to love each other in sickness and in health.

I gripped his shoulder and said, *"Joe. It's Lindsay. I'm here."*

He didn't answer. Was he alive?

I ran alongside his stretcher, stayed with him in the triage area, where he was swiftly assessed and lifted through the open doors of an ambulance.

I fumbled for my badge and said hoarsely, "That's my husband. I'm his wife."

An EMT nodded and offered her hand and forearm. I got a good grip and she pulled me inside.

CHAPTER 5

I HELD JOE'S hand as the EMTs gave him oxygen, and I answered their questions about Joe's age, blood type, and occupation. "Private security contractor."

Despite the police barricades and traffic jams, it was a short, wild ride to the hospital. Joe was brought directly from the ER into surgery, and I took a seat in the waiting room. It was filled with people who had emergencies unrelated to the blast, and there were also friends and the families of those victims who'd been caught in the explosion.

The overhead TV in the corner was muted, but there was closed-captioning and a crawl at the bottom of the screen.

Bomb blast destroys Sci-Tron.

Death toll rises to 20 dead, 30 injured.

No comment yet from police or Homeland Security, but GAR is suspected as the terrorist organization responsible for this bombing.

No one has claimed responsibility.

There were video clips of the blast, of the crowds, of the traffic, of the EMTs racing toward the disaster. The clips were horrific, and they triggered my own vivid memories of the explosion I had seen and felt, images that were playing on a closed loop inside my mind.

I was watching the TV when another clip came on. A microphone was put up to the incident commander's face. A reporter shouted a question, and the IC agreed to speak to the press.

He gave his name and spelled it, said that he was the commander in charge of managing and coordinating personnel across the board, across several disciplines.

He said, "Fire, medical, and law enforcement are on the scene. It's much too early to arrive at any conclusions as to what exactly happened here, to identify the victims. We've got great people here. The best. I've got to get back to them. The public will get an update as soon as we have something to report."

Next came a clip of the mayor speaking from outside Pier 15.

He was in shirtsleeves and wearing a hard hat. He said, "This is a terrible day for our city and for the United States. We grieve with the families of the deceased and we pray for the injured. We ask for your patience as we get to the bottom of this savage act of terrorism. Federal agencies have joined with our brave emergency responders and the SFPD. We will get whoever is responsible for this tragedy. You can count on it."

People sitting around me in the waiting room collapsed into the arms of their family and friends and wept.

Connor Grant had told me, "I *created* this—this magnificent event."

Someone called my name.

I jumped to my feet and saw the doctor, a dark-haired surgeon in blue scrubs, mask hanging loosely around her neck. I searched her face for reason to hope for good news, but all I saw was sadness.

She introduced herself as Dr. Janet Dalrymple. I walked with her into the hallway, and she told me that Joe had an acute subdural hematoma that was rapidly expanding, that it was putting pressure on his brain.

"I put in a shunt to drain the fluid buildup," she told me. "He's on medication to keep the swelling down. What we'll do now is watch him closely, keep checking the pressure."

I had to ask. "What are his chances, Doctor?"

"I don't operate on chances, Lindsay. Every patient with a head injury responds differently. I don't want to give you false hope. His injuries are serious. Still, he could be past the worst in hours. We're taking him now to intensive care."

I returned to the waiting room thinking about the bombshell that had broken up our marriage.

Six months ago I'd learned that my husband had been lying to me for—I had no idea how long. When I confronted him, he admitted that he'd been keeping things from me and he said that he couldn't tell me what he was doing. That it was all strictly classified. He said that he had to put country first.

Although I maybe still loved him, the words "country first" changed so many things that I had believed in without question. While I had thought my husband was a work-from-home dad, he had actually been working for the CIA. There was a woman involved. I wasn't sure what they had meant to each other, but it wasn't casual. I was married to a *spy*. And that meant that I hadn't really known Joseph Molinari—ever. And that I could never truly trust him.

Despite how angry I had been with Joe, right now I would do anything if he would survive his injury with his mind intact. I made deals with God and I waited for news.

CHAPTER 6

NEWS DID ARRIVE, but it was not the news I was hoping for.

The TV in the soothing ICU waiting room cut away from a rerun of *The Big Bang Theory* to a bright-red BREAKING NEWS card that spiraled and filled the screen. Then Channel 5's Susan Margules Steinhardt appeared on set, looking as though she'd just bolted from her bed, put on her lipstick while driving to the studio, and gone directly on-air.

"We've got breaking news," she said.

She read from a sheet of paper in front of her.

"GAR has taken responsibility for the bomb that blew up Sci-Tron, resulting in twenty-five deaths and forty-five injuries, by recent count."

I had been slumped and dozing, but I shot upright and gripped the arms of the chair.

The anchorwoman went on. "KPIX 5 *cannot* verify the authenticity of this video message that was posted on the internet moments ago."

A silhouette of a man appeared on-screen. His face was in deep shadow and there seemed to be a circle behind his head, almost like a halo. His voice was unaccented, digitally altered, could have been completely fabricated by a synthesizer.

The man with the distorted voice said, "GAR is proud of our devoted soldier SF65 in the Great Antiestablishment Reset. He has shown true courage in bringing down Sci-Tron, a frivolous endeavor fed by corrupt corporate and university sponsors.

"GAR works in secret and explodes in public. And we will continue our work until all people around the world have achieved authority over themselves."

The video went to black, and Ms. Steinhardt reappeared on-screen.

She said, "This is all we have at the moment, but we will continue to update our viewers as new information comes in. And now we are suspending our scheduled programming and taking you to our studios in New York for commentary on the news as it unfolds."

Six people in the ICU waiting room were watching this jaw-dropping news along with me.

"I knew it," said one. "Had to be GAR."

"Evil bastards," said another.

On the TV the scene cut away from the small local station to a slick set in New York. Images of the blast were displayed on large screens behind an angular table seating news correspondents and terrorism analysts familiar to everyone with access to a TV.

News anchor Dallas Greer asked the opinions of the experts, and the majority accepted GAR's statement as true.

Roger Watkins, CBS's crusty international cor-
respondent, was the dissenting voice. He said,
"Although Sci-Tron was funded by corporate
donors, it was managed by an ecumenical group of
educators. See, that doesn't jibe as I see it. Sci-Tron
was not authoritarian in any way. It's a museum
that was principally designed for kids. Blowing it
up sends a very confusing signal and is off message
for GAR."

Alexander Carter disagreed. He had been analyzing and reporting on domestic terrorism since
McVeigh bombed the Alfred P. Murrah Federal
Building in Oklahoma City, killing 168 people in
1995.

Said Carter, "Roger, with all due respect, are
you suggesting that GAR is taking credit for someone else's bomb? Or could this be more likely?
GAR is known for ditching the traditional terrorist
playbook. They don't have a headquarters, nor a
spokesperson or leader. They thrive on their open-
source recruitment and management. Equal
bombs for all.

"How can anyone, without certain knowledge,
say that Sci-Tron was a random act of terror unrelated to GAR?"

Both men had made good points, and I was
weighing their arguments against what I knew of
Connor Grant.

Was he a partner in GAR? Was he a lone wolf
who had been inspired by GAR? Or, if he was in
fact the bomber, as I believed, had he acted entirely
by himself for his own sick reasons?

Or was he innocent of all charges and just a lying piece of crap?

I pictured him in a small cinder-block interrogation room contemplating a possible death sentence. I thought I could get him to tell me the truth again.

CHAPTER 7

IT WAS ALMOST midnight when Rich Conklin found me in the waiting room outside the ICU.

He sat down beside me and I updated him on Joe's condition.

"They put him into a coma to stop him from thrashing. Along with the bleeding around his brain, he's got a lot of broken bones. Right leg is fractured in two places, right arm burned and snapped just above the wrist. He's got three or four cracked ribs."

Richie is more than a partner. He's like a sibling with no rivalry between us. A couple of years back he fell in love with and is now living with Cindy Thomas, one of my dearest and closest friends. He is family.

Now he walked with me to the glass-walled intensive care unit down the hall, where Joe lay in a hospital bed, tubes going into and out of him. He was wired up to monitors, with his leg in traction, bandages around his head.

I said, "Why did he have to go inside that place? Why?"

"I know. I know," Richie said.

We both knew. We'd both gone into no-win fire-fights with eyes wide open, gotten shot, and gone back for more.

Richie put his arms around me and I cried against his chest. He said all the right things: that Joe was strong, that he was in great hands, that he was going to live to kick ass. "With his broken leg."

And then he said, "You heard that GAR took credit?"

"I heard."

"We should go, Linds. Brady is waiting for your debrief."

I left my number with the nurses' station and followed Richie back to the Hall of Justice, a gray granite building that houses the criminal court, the DA's offices, a jail, and the Southern Station of the SFPD.

We parked on Gilbert Street and entered the building through the main entrance, a set of double glass-and-steel doors leading to a marble-lined lobby. We cleared night shift security and headed up the back stairs to the Homicide squad room, on the fourth floor.

The squad room was a fairly grim place on the best of days, but at night it was like a crypt. The lighting was stark, the green walls looked gray, and so did the dear old-timers and rookies and guys on their second shift sharing desks to answer the incessant ringing of the tip lines. Some of them looked up and said, "Hey, Boxer. You okay?"

The bull pen was gritty, but there was no place on earth I'd rather work.

At the back of the room was a glass-walled office with a princely view of the interstate. This was the lieutenant's office and he was there now.

Jackson Brady, formerly of Miami PD, had transferred to our Homicide Unit a few years back. It hadn't taken long for him to earn his promotion to lieutenant and become the boss. I'd had issues with Brady at first, but despite his no-frills style, I had come to like *him*.

He was fearless. He was tough. He was loyal to the max and he was a decider. You couldn't ask much more from your commanding officer. Last year Brady had married Yuki Castellano, another of my closest friends. Welcome to the family, Brady.

He stood up when I entered his small office. He came around his desk and hugged me. He patted my shoulder and asked after Joe. I told him what the doctor had said: "We have to wait and see."

When we were all seated, I asked about Connor Grant.

"He's in a cell by his lonesome, round-the-clock guard," said Brady. He raked back his longish white-blond hair with his fingers and took a long, cold pull from his coffee mug.

Then he said to me with a voice still faintly colored by a Southern drawl after all these years, "Git talkin', Boxer. Don't leave anything out."

CHAPTER 8

IT WAS ALMOST two in the morning when I came through the front door of the apartment I used to share with Joe. It's a roomy space in a former commercial building. The ceilings are high, and the kitchen is open to the main room, which is furnished in leather and neutral tones, and has tall windows west and south, facing Lake Street.

Tonight home sweet home never felt so good.

Martha, my longtime border collie best dog friend, charged across the floor, her barking waking Mrs. Rose, our saintly nanny, who'd been asleep in Joe's big chair.

Martha also awakened Julie Anne, age twenty-two months, who called out for me.

"Mommmmeeeeeeeeeeeee."

"Be right there, sweetie," I croaked.

"You need some honeyed tea for that throat," Mrs. Rose said. I followed her into the kitchen, and as I washed my hands and face I told her that Joe's condition hadn't changed.

She said she would pray for him, and after she made tea and assured me that both baby and dog had had their needs addressed, I walked her through my front door and across the hall to her own domicile.

We hugged, and I said, "See you in the morning. Um. See you in six hours."

Back inside, I went to Julie's buttercup-yellow room. My dark-haired, blue-eyed girl was standing up in her crib with her hands up for a hug—which I gave her in full.

We have a big, JFK-style rocking chair with a cushion and a view. I lifted my sweetie and pulled her into my lap. I rocked as I cuddled with her. I smelled her hair, kissed her fingers, listened to her breathing lengthen, before I settled her back down into her bedding. I whispered, "I love you soooooo much. Sweet dreams, babycakes."

I checked my cell phone to see if I'd missed a call from San Francisco General. I had not.

Martha joined me in the bathroom, watching over me from the bath mat while I showered and scrubbed off the grit and stink of diesel fuel that had glommed on to me that night. As the spray beat down on my back and shoulders, I thought of my poor Joe with his gashed, shaven, and drilled head, his eyes swollen shut, his broken bones.

Please, God, don't let him die.

I don't remember getting into bed with my best dog friend, but she woofed me awake and then my phone buzzed.

Joe!

I grabbed it from the nightstand and saw *San*

Francisco Hospital on the caller ID. I jammed down the green button and said hello to Dr. Dalrymple.

She told me, "Joe's condition hasn't improved to my satisfaction. We're going into surgery right now," she said. "I'm putting in a second drain."

"Oh, no, no."

"It's okay, Lindsay. I'll tell you when to get worried. I promise you. Okay?"

The doctor did her best to assure me that this second drain wasn't a bad thing and that I should call her later. When I'd clicked off with Joe's surgeon, the phone buzzed in my hand.

Brady was calling.

"You planning on coming in?" he asked me.

It was Friday, right?

"What time is it?"

"Time to interrogate the pris-nah," he said.

CHAPTER 9

BRADY AND I huddled in his office.

He gave me the official body count, just tallied.

"Twenty-five people dead. Forty-five injured. Some of them critical, with low to terrible odds of survival."

He handed me a list of the casualties. I skimmed it for Joe's name. Then I folded the paper into thirds and stuffed it into the inside breast pocket of my everyday blue blazer.

"You sure you're up to this?" he asked me.

I was mad. I was hurting. I was worried about Joe, sleep deprived, and still in shock from last night's horror show, which would very likely stay with me for the rest of my life. I was stressed to the bone and I knew that it showed on my face.

Still, that Brady even questioned my ability to do the interrogation pissed me off.

"Who can do this interview better than me? I was *there*. He talked to *me*."

Brady said, "Okay. I was being considerate. *Trying* to be considerate. So look, Boxer. Here's what we know about Connor Grant."

Brady makes lists. Whenever possible, he writes them in red grease pencil on a yellow legal pad. I looked at the pad. What I saw was a very short list.

Said Brady, "He's forty-five. Drives a late-model Hyundai. Never married, no kids, no family we could find, but there are a lot of Grants in this country. Anyway. He teaches ninth-grade science at Saint Brendan High School. Been there for about five years. Science teacher blows up a science museum. That's interesting, right? His reviews on Rate My Teachers are good. The kids like him."

"He doesn't have a sheet?"

"Nope. He's clean as a nun's habit. A solid citizen. Pays his taxes. Obeys traffic laws. Colors within the lines."

"Humph. I find this hard to believe."

Brady went on. "Parisi will be observing. Jacobi, too."

I wasn't surprised that the DA and the chief of police would be watching our interrogation. We had an admitted mass murderer in the box.

I asked Brady, "What else do I need to know?"

"You take the lead. Be nice. The tape could be used in court. If nice doesn't do the job, I'll step in as badass."

Brady handed me a folder of eight-by-ten photos. I flipped through them, then looked back into Brady's ice-blue eyes. All we had in the way of leverage was Grant's on-the-scene admission. We didn't have it in writing.

Brady said, "Boxer. Don't worry about the big

picture right now. I don't care who he knows, what he hates, et cetera. If he's talking, great. We want it all. But right now, this morning, be his friend. We just need him to say, 'I did it.' Anything else is gravy."

CHAPTER 10

BRADY AND I left his office and walked the short length of corridor to Interview 2. He held the door open and followed me inside.

Connor Grant was seated at the table wearing a bright-orange jumpsuit and a smirk. His hands were cuffed, ankles shackled. He looked happy to see me, and oddly, I was happy to see him, too.

I nodded to the two guards standing in the corners and shot a glance at the red blinking camera eye in the ceiling. Then I looked at the two-way mirror. I was glad that Parisi and Jacobi were behind it. Top brass on deck.

Brady had given me a clear-cut assignment: Get Grant's confession on the record. Get it to stick. After that Len Parisi could negotiate with this monster for convincing details, names of others involved, then either make a deal or prosecute him to the full extent of the law for killing more than two dozen human beings.

I took a seat in one of the straight-backed aluminum chairs across the table from Grant, and Brady did the same.

To the "pris-nah" I said, "Hello again, Mr. Grant. How are you this morning? Sleep okay?"

"Not bad. I forget. How do I know you?"

"Last night at the pier. I arrested you, remember?"

"Oh. Right. For destruction of property? I still don't get that."

I opened the folder full of photos and started laying them down on the table. The pictures were post-explosion: the fire licking the foundation of the museum, the emergency vehicles, the stretchers coming out of Sci-Tron, the double lines of body bags. And then there were shots, from different angles, of the museum's metal framework looking like the skeleton of a large, prehistoric animal kneeling down on the pier.

"Oh, wow," said Mr. Grant. "These are great pictures."

"Aren't they? If you like, I'll get you copies."

"Sure. Thanks a lot."

I smiled at this wretched specimen of a human being.

"If you could help me by thinking back…," I said to Grant, leaning in, crossing my arms on the table, doing my best to look nonthreatening, not like a cop at all.

I said, "Do you remember last night when I asked you if you knew what happened at Sci-Tron?"

I pushed one of the photos toward him. It was time-stamped 7:23 p.m. Smoke was still coming off the rubble heap on the pier.

Grant said, "No. What did I say?"

"You said to me, 'Did I *see* it? I *created* this.... This is my *work*.'"

Grant was shaking his head no throughout.

I kept my voice soft and pressed on.

"You know what really got to me, Mr. Grant?"

I tapped my chest somewhere near my heart. "When you told me you wanted to create beauty. You were so happy about the sunset-lit sky. Gave yourself bonus points for the color of the sky. Too bad we don't have a picture of that, right?"

"Well, that's just *crazy*," said Grant with a laugh. "How could I take credit for a sunset?"

I was prepared for total denial even though he'd freely offered his confession in the immediate aftermath of the explosion, while glass was still falling from above. For a second I flashed on Joe. I saw him standing with me, covering Grant with his gun. Joe looked solid, intelligent, brave. This freak, the one with the smirk, had brought Joe down.

Grant said, "Oh, I get it now. You're saying that *I* actually told you that I blew up Sci-Tron? That's hilarious. You must have misunderstood me, Sergeant. Or the explosion affected your hearing. That's possible, isn't it?"

He kept talking.

"What I must have said was that I *saw* the explosion, but honest to everything, I had nothing to do with 'bombing' that place."

He made awkward air quotes when he said "bombing."

I nodded politely.

"I think I know that this wasn't your doing, Mr. Grant. Not alone, anyway. You had help from a terror network. Maybe they instigated bombing the museum. Maybe they planned it all. Why should you take the heat yourself?"

He shook his head, said, "Nope. I know nothing about who bombed the museum. It wasn't me."

Had Grant played me *then*? Or was he playing us *now*? Was he GAR's "devoted soldier"? Or here was an idea: Was he teeing up his insanity defense?

Brady tensed up beside me.

Fifteen minutes ago Brady had told me, "Be his friend. We just need him to say, 'I did it.'"

What would it take to push that button?

It felt to me like Grant had taken a position before we walked into that room and then he'd dug in. He was entrenched. And he was happy and secure in his foxhole.

CHAPTER 11

GRANT'S FOXHOLE WASN'T going to protect him or stop me.

He had totally denied his confession, acted as though I were the crazy one, and that was infuriating. Still, I couldn't show him my anger. I had to stop thinking that this jerk was making a fool of me and that Brady was sitting next to me. The tape was rolling. All I had to do was get Grant to repeat three of the roughly one hundred words he'd spoken to me just before I'd arrested him. All I needed him to say was "I did it."

He'd been proud of himself when he took credit for the blast, no doubt in my mind about that. I would appeal to his vanity. I moved my chair to the corner of the table so that it wasn't between us and I was sitting closer to him. I made a conscious effort to relax the muscles in my face, and I smiled again at my dear friend Connor Grant.

"People misunderstand each other all the time. You're upset. Who wouldn't be? You're worried, of course."

"Nope."

"Mr. Grant, I saw the museum *explode*. I was right there when it *happened* and it was really…just *awesome*. That's why I'm so interested, and when you told me you'd blown it up—"

"Nope."

"I'd really love to know, how did you do it? You're a science teacher, aren't you? Maybe if you just use layman's terms, so I can understand you—"

"Well, I don't understand *you* at all."

Brady got up from his seat. He's powerfully built, and just his *standing up* shifted the atmosphere, like when a rodeo bull explodes out of the chute.

He spun the chair away from him. It scraped the floor, toppled over, clattered. I bit my lip as Brady slammed both hands down on the table. It shook. As promised, Lieutenant Badass was stepping in.

He said, "No more games, sir. We have you at the scene of the bombing. You confessed to Sergeant Boxer and also to Joseph Molinari, who happens to be a former government agent and the former deputy director of Homeland Security. These two unimpeachable witnesses corroborate each other's statements, and they will testify against you."

Grant tilted his head back and just looked up at Brady. Like he was fascinated.

"Your blood test came back, Mr. Grant. There were no drugs or alcohol in your system. You were flat-out sober when you told this officer of the SFPD that you bombed Sci-Tron. That was yesterday.

"Now we have a search warrant and we're going to take your house apart, board by board, until we find evidence. When that happens, you're cooked, and I think you know it."

Brady retrieved his chair and sat back down.

"Now look," he went on. "Twenty-five people have died, man. As soon as we charge you with twenty-five counts of murder, your name is gonna get out, and the entire city and the whole country are going to be calling for your blood.

"You want to live, Connor? You help us, we help you. If you come clean, Sergeant Boxer and I will see if we can get the DA to waive the death penalty. No promises, but this right here is your last best chance."

Grant's cuffs clanked as he shrugged. I knew what was coming. I wasn't wrong.

"I want a lawyer," said Connor Grant, the madman who no longer appeared insane. He looked me in the eye and smiled. He was still smiling when his guards yanked him out of his chair and took him back to his cell.

CHAPTER 12

BRADY AND I returned to the squad room, both of us looking like we had been knocked out in the first round.

I was mortified. I thought Brady felt even worse.

He said, "I shouldn'ta lost it."

"Nothing would have worked."

"*Something* has to."

He stomped off to his office. I stopped at the front of the room and looked up at the TV hanging from the ceiling, tilted so that everyone in the squad room had a good view. Even though the sound was off, the pictures spoke without using words.

Thousands of people were banked outside the barricades on the Embarcadero that had been set up to preserve the crime scene. Some in the crowd held up hastily scrawled drawings of broken hearts. The camera panned across the grieving faces to the charred remains of Sci-Tron. The headline across the top of the screen was ANOTHER GAR STRIKE?

Was GAR responsible? Or were they taking responsibility for a bomb not their own? Had GAR inspired Connor Grant? Or did we have the wrong freaking freak in a cell in the sixth-floor jail?

I left the TV and walked toward the corner Rich and I had co-opted, equidistant from the entrance to the squad room and the window with its view of Bryant Street. Our desks faced each other, and Rich looked up when I slung my jacket over the back of my chair.

He was on the phone, but he said, "Hold on, please," and put his hand over the mouthpiece.

"You okay?" he asked.

I shrugged, said, "Be right back," and headed into the break room. When I looked up, Rich was standing with me at the coffeemaker, watching me pour a mug of mud with a shaky hand.

"What happened in there?" he asked.

"Typical dirtbag," I told him. "He recanted his confession or whatever you call what he told me and Joe. Said I needed to clean out my ears. He didn't do it, didn't bomb anything, of course. And he lawyered up. The bastard."

Conklin said, "You sure you want coffee?"

"I want *something*," I said. "I'm going to run over to the hospital for a couple hours. Two of Joe's brothers are just coming in from New York. I'm going to meet them there."

"Stay as long as you want," he said. "We can't get into Grant's place until after the bomb squad clears it."

I took three sips of coffee, dumped the rest into the sink, and rinsed out the cup. I said, "Rich, what if I hadn't seen Grant standing there on the sidewalk beaming at his masterpiece? We'd have less than nothing, and the Feds would be working this case."

"True."

"Is Grant having a good laugh at the SFPD? Or is he for real? I'd really like to know."

"If he did it, we'll *nail* him," Conklin said. Then, "Linds, did you see the message from Claire? She wants to see you ASAP."

"Did she say why?"

"Hell no."

"Okay, then."

I got my jacket and headed out.

CHAPTER 13

DR. CLAIRE WASHBURN is the city's chief medical examiner and my closest friend. I needed to see her, too.

The most direct path from Homicide to the ME's office is out the lobby's rear entrance and a hundred yards down the breezeway toward Harriet Street. I was on total autopilot until I opened the double doors to the ME's office.

I didn't recognize the guy behind the reception desk. This wasn't so unusual. On account of overexposure to death and no opportunity for advancement, Claire's receptionists tended to turn over every couple of months of their own accord.

The new receptionist was middle-aged, male, wearing a jacket and tie. He had folded a sheet of paper into a nameplate and written GREGORY MARK PETERS.

I badged Gregory, introduced myself, and said, "Dr. Washburn asked to see me."

There were about eight cops and as many civilians in the waiting room, all of them waiting to see Claire.

Gregory said, "She's awfully busy right now, Sergeant. Why don't you take a seat."

I gave him a look that could bore through stone. "Hit the buzzer," I said.

He did it. I strong-armed the glass door, marched past Claire's office, and went directly into the autopsy suite.

I found Claire gloved up, gowned, masked, and bloodied, leaning over a body on the autopsy table. She dropped her scalpel into a bowl, stripped off her gloves, and said to her assistant, "Bunny, I'm taking a five-minute break."

She put a hand on my waist and walked me to her office, then settled in behind her desk as I took the chair across from her. Claire is African American, bosomy, and warmhearted, although how she manages warmth when she performs or oversees twelve hundred autopsies a year is kind of a mystery.

She said, "I can't stop thinking about Joe. How's he doing?"

I had called her while I was waiting for Joe to reappear from his trip into Sci-Tron and again from the hospital, but I updated her now.

"His doctor tells me it's still too soon to know."

"I'm so sorry about this, Linds. But he's going to pull through. It's *Joe* we're talking about."

I took a deep breath and said, "One minute he's raising his glass to 'happy days.' Next minute…"

I put my hands over my eyes, breathing deeply, willing myself not to cry. When I looked up, my friend was watching me with deep concern.

She reached over the desk and grabbed my hands. "Let me know how I can help. I can call the doctor. Look at film. Go with you to the hospital. Whatever you need. Anything."

"Thanks, Claire. Very much."

I gave her Dr. Dalrymple's card and she put it next to her phone.

I said, "You wanted to talk to me?"

"Yeah, well, obviously we're full up here and overflowing. But something rare came in last night. And I need to tell you about it."

"Go ahead."

"A forty-year-old white woman in nice clothes was found in the street just off the Embarcadero and brought in with the blast victims. She had some bruises that make me think she was hit by a car, but not the kinds of lacerations people got who were inside Sci-Tron or close to it.

"Her handbag was missing," Claire said, "so no ID. I thought she'd died from cardiac arrest. That scene last night could cause some people to have a heart attack, you know?"

"Don't I ever."

"I did the post. Her heart was perfect, Lindsay."

"She had a stroke maybe? Or an aneurysm?"

"Before I went there, something was nagging at me. I gave her another external exam. Found something that reminded me of a case that came in a few months back."

"Don't stop now," I said.

"She had a nice bruise on her left hip and a scrape on her arm, probably got bumped by a car.

This wasn't fatal. But there was a puncture wound on her right buttock centered on a bruise the size of a quarter. I have seen a nearly identical puncture and bruise once before."

Claire had my attention, but I felt urgently that I had to get into my car and switch on the sirens. I needed to get to the hospital. I had to meet with Joe's brothers. I had to see Joe.

I said, "What are you saying, Claire?"

"I've sent out the victim's blood. I'll know more soon. Right now I'm calling her manner of death undetermined. But what I'm thinking is that this nice-looking lady was killed. That her death was a homicide."

CHAPTER 14

AFTER AN EMOTIONALLY wrenching meeting with Joe's brothers at my husband's bedside, I cried all the way back to the Hall. I washed my face, reset my ponytail. Then I joined Conklin for a meeting in Brady's office.

It was a tough transition.

I was still with Joe, not knowing if he would slip away before I saw him again. At the same time I was needed *here* and *now*.

Brady was keyed up and focused. He had taped up an enlargement of Sci-Tron's final moments on the wall facing his desk, where he could see it all the time. He offered us chairs, booted up his computer, and pulled up the video of our interrogation of Connor Grant that morning.

The three of us watched it together, looking for something we'd missed. Something we should have asked. We strained for something useful or revealing. Straining through the nothing Grant had given us for any kind of lead.

Brady said, "One more time."

He reversed the video, hit Play. We watched again.

Then we kicked it around for a while, concluding that, based on our combined decades of cop experience and gut instinct, the science teacher was not a team player. He was a textbook megalomaniac working alone.

That said, we'd all been wrong before.

Did he do it?

No idea.

Meeting over, Conklin and I headed out at high speed through Bayview, a gentrifying, mixed-use area that was once home to Candlestick Park, currently home to Connor Grant, our suspected mass murderer.

I hardly spoke as Rich drove us toward Grant's house on Jamestown Avenue. I was thinking about having seen Joe, being with his devastated brothers. We had tried to buck one another up, but it hadn't worked. Joe was still deep in the woods without a compass. He could die. Our daughter would lose her father. And I would never be able to forgive myself for not making peace with my husband while I had the chance.

Conklin's voice broke into my thoughts: "Linds, up ahead on the right."

Behind a thicket of law enforcement vehicles, positioned between two old cinder-block buildings and sitting far back on its lot, was a tidy blue wood-frame house with white trim.

Conklin parked in the midst of the cruisers, and as he turned off the engine, there was a knock on the glass. CSI director Charlie Clapper was standing between his car and ours, bending down to say hello.

Clapper is a former Homicide cop and one of SFPD's most valuable players. As always, he was well dressed—jacket, no tie, his salt-and-pepper hair slicked back—and his expression showed that he was itching to get into the house.

The three of us stood in the sunshine as the bomb squad did their work, and we talked about the monstrous incident on Pier 15, the numbers of dead and seriously wounded—including Joe. I told Clapper that Joe was still in a medically induced coma but holding his own in the ICU.

A door slammed and I looked toward the house to see three bomb squad techs in full protective gear come outside. One of them pushed up his face shield and signaled a thumbs-up.

"All clear," said Clapper. "Let's go."

CHAPTER 15

GRANT'S HOUSE WASNT a crime scene, but Clapper's techs treated it that way. It was a potentially invaluable source of evidence, and they would be comparing traces from the house with whatever they could scrape off Pier 15. They took pictures, lifted prints, and swabbed hard surfaces. When they'd covered a room and moved on to the next, Conklin and I stepped in.

We were looking for something tangible that would crash Grant's cat-and-mouse game—a manifesto, a foreign flag, GAR-related or any radical literature, a blueprint of Sci-Tron, a thread to follow, proof of something either to force a confession out of Grant or to blow up his fanciful story.

Conklin went upstairs, and I went through the cramped living room, frisking the TV console and the bookshelves. Grant had the complete DVD collections of *Law & Order* and *The Sopranos*. His books were nonfiction, subjects ranging from ancient civilization to law, architecture, art history, military weapons, and of course, everything you ever wanted to know about bombs. He also had about fifty biographies of artists, writers, and politicians, none of them seditious.

The guy had a wide range of deep interests.

The laptop in the office would be taken back to the forensics lab, but meanwhile, I checked out his stack of unopened mail on the credenza with my gloved hand. I found bills, flyers, assorted catalogs for school chemistry supplies. I flipped through the catalogs and saw only consumer-grade beakers and microscopes for sale in bulk amounts.

Conklin came down the stairs, saying to me, "Second floor has two bedrooms and a bath. One of the bedrooms is in active use, the other is a spare. I tossed the hell out of both of them. He's a neat guy. No weapons. No bombs. No clutter. Nothing under the mattresses. I didn't find anything stronger than Advil in the medicine chest."

He shrugged and turned his attention to the fifties-style kitchen. I watched from the pass-through as he removed the pots and pans from the cabinets, and looked under the range hood and inside the stove, fridge, freezer, and drawers. Everything looked dull and old and normal.

I went into the half bath next to the kitchen. The medicine cabinet had a half-used container of Tums, a pack of razor blades, and a bottle of expired antibiotics. I made note of the doctor's and pharmacist's names, checked the cabinet to see if it was possibly a door to a stash hole. It was not. The trash can held an empty bottle of Listerine, used dental floss, used Q-tips.

More work for the crime lab and maybe a lead to DNA in a database.

Conklin and I went to the basement with a CSI, who passed an ALS wand over every square foot of the walls and floor, finding no blood or organic trace. After that we examined the tools, paint cans, canned food on neat wire shelving, but found no secret doors or hidden rooms or 3-D models of the science museum.

Overall, my impression of Connor Grant's small, dark house was that the man was bookish, organized, isolated, without a speck of whimsy. There were no weapons, no sign of a woman's presence, nothing to point to Grant being an anarchist or a murderer. And there I was again, still wondering if we'd arrested the wrong man, if Connor Grant had been delusional or a jackass when he told Joe and me that he'd blown up the science museum for artistic expression.

I shared that thought with Richie.

"Actually, delusional jackass is a definite possibility."

We took a last look around the house, Conklin snapping pictures to take back to Brady and Jacobi, and we left by the back door. Clapper was standing outside waiting for us.

He pointed at the wood-frame garage at the end of the driveway adjacent to the house and at the three-person bomb squad standing outside the roll-up doors.

Clapper said, "Well, my friends, wait'll you see this."

CHAPTER 16

IT WAS ALMOST five when Rich Conklin said to Lindsay, "I'll call you after the meeting," and dropped her at her car in the All-Day lot across from the Hall. He parked the squad car in front of the building, then headed inside and took the elevator to the fifth floor.

Brady was already waiting in Jacobi's corner office.

"We might have found something, Lieu," Conklin said.

He had just taken a seat next to Brady on the tufted leather sofa when Chief Jacobi came in, straightening his gray hair with both hands, wincing from an old gunshot injury to his hip as he angled his body and dropped into the chair behind his big cherrywood desk.

Jacobi's new assistant, Toni Reynolds, breezed in with her coat buttoned and told Jacobi that Boxer called to say she couldn't make the meeting.

"You've got approximately two hundred e-mails, Chief, and too many calls to count. Mostly journalists and TV people. You're gonna be famous. Here are the calls and e-mails I marked *urgent*."

She handed Jacobi a sheet of paper and asked if he needed anything else. "Speak now. Otherwise, I'm going home to my hubby."

When Toni had gone, Jacobi told Conklin and Brady about his day.

"FBI section chief Gerson Oliver came here first thing. He's got one objective. If Grant threatened to kill folks, it's domestic terrorism and the case goes to the FBI.

"If Grant blew up the big glass building all by himself—as he told Boxer—the case is ours."

Brady and Conklin nodded. Jacobi continued.

"Oliver shared his info and it's next to nothing. All the FBI could dig up on Grant is job history and some small-town newspaper and internet stories, mainly about science programs he ran in high schools in three states since the time he graduated from the University of Miami in '93."

"That's all they've got?" Conklin said.

"Wait. There's more. After our talk Oliver and another agent asked Grant for a chat. He agreed, rather happily. They interviewed him for about four hours. They did all the talking, with Grant saying 'I don't know what you're talking about' and 'I got nothing else to say.'

"So the Feds wanted to take Grant to the bomb site, and I thought, *Okay. We've got nothing to lose except maybe this giant headache gets handed off to the FBI.* I tagged along, hoping the science teacher would show us something, *say* something."

"Fifty cents says he didn't say a thing," said Brady.

Jacobi rocked in his chair. "You're close. He stood in one place and looked around, saying, 'Oh, wow. This is just amaaaazing.' He said several versions of that. Like it was an outing and he was happy for the day off."

Jacobi shook his head in disgust. "Divers are going into the bay tomorrow. The bomb is still missing."

Conklin said, "Chief, Grant has a chemistry lab in his garage."

Jacobi stopped rocking. "No shit. Really?"

Conklin summarized in a few words what had taken hours to analyze from Grant's Bayview property, and then he homed in on the lab in the garage.

Said Conklin, "It's like what you might see in a high school classroom. One side of the garage has got a sink and shelves of chemicals and all the fixings: beakers, Bunsen burners and microscopes, some stainless steel equipment, I don't know what to call it.

"CSI cataloged everything and took samples."

Brady said to Conklin, "You were about to say something to me when the chief came in?"

"Right. I found this inside his lab."

Conklin took out his phone and pulled up a photo of a notebook lying on a stainless steel table. He said, "This could be a book manuscript."

He read the title out loud: "'How to Make a Bomb.' Subtitle says, 'For Twenty-Five Dollars in Twenty-Five Minutes,' and here, lower right corner, 'by Connor A. Grant.'"

Conklin walked his phone over to Jacobi, who slapped his hands on his desk and said, "Thank you, Rich, and thank you, God."

He picked up his desk phone, punched out some numbers.

"Len," he said to DA Leonard Parisi. "We got something useful on the science teacher. Conklin is forwarding a photo to you now."

CHAPTER 17

AFTER CONKLIN AND I said good night in the parking lot, I pulled the car out onto Bryant and made my way to Harrison, then took Tenth toward the hospital.

Traffic was thick and maddeningly stop-and-go, but I resisted the urge to hit the siren. The normally ten-minute drive took twenty, during which time my mind was flooded with images of Connor Grant, the way he'd looked Thursday night in front of Pier 15. He'd been awestruck, and yet his expression when Brady and I interviewed him this morning had been mocking.

Now we had a little more circumstantial evidence against him: his laboratory and his unfunny manuscript on how to build a bomb at home in your spare time for pocket change. It wasn't *proof,* but it was enough to charge him. At least I thought so.

Even if Joe couldn't hear me or answer me, I wanted to tell him all about it, just like I used to do.

I turned into the hospital parking area and found an empty spot outside the ER. I took that to be a good sign. I threaded my way through the lobby, to the correct elevator bank, and reached the ICU without a hitch.

I introduced myself to the nurse at the desk and asked how Joe was doing.

"We're weaning him off the medication to bring him out of the coma," she said. "It's not a sudden waking up, more like slow-w-w-ly coming back into consciousness. I think he'll know you're here even if he seems to be out of it."

She walked me to the glass-sided stall where Joe lay swaddled in bandages.

"I'll be back in a few," she told me.

There was no chair, so I stood right next to the bed and looked down at my battered husband. His head was wrapped, and tubes ran from somewhere inside his skull, looping under a flap of skin in his neck, and from there emptied into his abdomen. His face was bruised purple. His right forearm was in a cast and his right leg was in traction. He was breathing regularly. He was alive.

In my mind I replayed images of the explosion and the immediate aftermath, the shocking remains of the museum, the body bags lined up on the sidewalk, and the families of the dead and injured both outside the tape and inside the ER waiting room. I was so grateful for Joe's life.

I covered his hand with mine.

"Joe, it's me. Lindsay. You are doing really well. Dr. Dalrymple is going to put you in a private room tomorrow. With a window. And a chair."

Joe's eyes fluttered open.

Oh, my God. He was awake. *"Joe!"*

I squeezed his hand and his fingers moved. Tears ran out of my eyes and dropped onto the sheets.

"What happened?" he asked me.

I hurried to say, "You're okay. Everything's okay."

I cleared my throat and, striving for a calm tone, I told him about the explosion, that something had fallen on his head, that he'd had surgery.

"Your doctor, Joe, she's great. And you remember that guy who said he set the bomb? We might have evidence against him."

Joe closed his eyes, and a moment later he opened them and said, "Sophie? Sophie Fields?"

"Joe, it's *Lindsay*."

I flushed. Who was Sophie Fields? A childhood sweetheart whose name had gotten knocked into the present? Maybe she was a partner in one of the clandestine services Joe had worked for. Or was she a current girlfriend? We were living separately, so a girlfriend wasn't actually any of my business, right?

Joe had never explained about the mysterious spy, a femme fatale, who'd been part of his life and possibly the true root of our split-up. Those raw feelings of betrayal rushed in as I sat with my husband, holding his hand. I didn't like the feelings. Joe didn't owe me an explanation. But why had "Sophie Fields" been the first name out of his mouth?

"What happened?" he asked me again.

Oh, Joe.

Of course I told him...again.

CHAPTER 18

WHEN I WENT to bed on Friday night, my Saturday was well planned. I would sleep late, spend quality time with Julie, take a long nap after lunch, and go to the hospital to see Joe. Then my phone rang at 5:00 a.m., Jacobi saying, "Boxer. It's me. A number of tips have come in regarding the GAR video, and you're on deck with the task force."

"The video?" I asked. My voice was gravelly and my eyes were glued shut with sleep.

"The GAR video, Boxer. The one taking credit for Sci-Tron. Overnight there was internet chatter of the 'Yay, we freaking did it and posted it on Facebook' variety. The Feds traced the video to an IP address with a physical address in Ingleside."

"No kidding. This is for real?"

"Let's hope so. There are four men living at the address I've just texted you. On the face of it, looks like a self-radicalized terror cell. They have no record, federal or otherwise, so for now they're ours."

Martha got up, circled a couple of times, dropped back to the bed with her tail over her nose. Lucky dog.

Jacobi was saying, "SWAT has federal warrants and orders to secure the premises. Niles is commander. He and the tac team will meet you and Conklin in Ingleside. Three of our teams in the task force unit are on the way. Boxer, you're point man. Get up. Get dressed."

I said, "Yes, boss."

I blinked at the clock, with its second hand audibly clicking around the dial. I was thinking that being on this task force had exposed me to a high probability of bombs.

I had only just gotten over the car bomb brought to us by the letter *J* when Sci-Tron blew up exactly thirty-six hours ago. I had a new, heightened reaction to sharp, unexpected sounds; door slams, for instance, or a glass clattering in the sink doubled my pulse rate. I wanted to say to Jacobi, *Look. My husband is in the ICU. I have a baby. I've done enough.* But Joe's famous punch line came into my mind: *Country first.*

Jacobi said, "Boxer? You there?"

I grunted and swung my legs over the bed.

He was still talking.

"I sent you some background on these men. Be careful."

With gross misgivings, I phoned Mrs. Rose and begged her for the favor of helping me do my job for the USA. Part of me wanted her to say no.

Conklin arrived outside my door in his Bronco at 5:20. I had brought bottled water for two, as well as my charged phone and my Kevlar vest, which was zipped up and ready to go. If I'd had a lucky rabbit's foot, I would have brought that, but Julie's finger puppet of Hello Kitty would have to do. I had tucked the puppet into my shirt pocket under my vest, silently promising her I would bring it home by dinnertime.

There was a coffee container with my name on it in the beverage holder. I tasted it. It was hot, three sugars, just the way I like it.

"You're a good pal," I said to Conklin.

"None better," he said, cracking his famously great grin.

I gave his arm a little shove, and then, as I strapped in, Rich set course for Ingleside, six miles away.

Our task force had a dedicated radio channel, and one after the other, the three squad cars in our team checked in with their current locations. One team was from Narcotics, another from Robbery, one from Vice. Conklin and I knew these cops and had worked with them all.

As my partner drove us south on Route 1, we talked over our assignment in shorthand snippets. We were facing something that might turn out to be as easy as calling your dog, or it could be a hellacious firefight. DHS said that shutting down this cell had to be done.

By the time we got to Ingleside, we had our firefight faces on and were ready to do whatever it took to end this clear and present danger.

CHAPTER 19

FOR MOST OF my life Ingleside had been a drive-through working- and middle-class community on the way to the beach. Now, like the rest of San Francisco, it was gentrifying above the middle-class ability to buy.

At five thirty a.m., streetlights lit Ocean Avenue, the main artery of the business district, which had light-rail tracks down the center of the road. There was very little traffic, and no cars at all in the parking lot behind Bank of America.

We pulled in, and the SFPD squad cars arrived right behind us. Car doors opened and thunked closed, and we greeted one another, gathered around the hood of Conklin's Bronco, where we discussed our briefing. Namely, that the video purportedly produced and disseminated by GAR had been tracked to a group or cell of four young men living here in Ingleside, not far from the SFSU campus.

These young men, who ranged in age from twenty to twenty-four, were renting a house that had once been their frat house, now banned from the school because of an alcohol-related death not attributed to these four.

Jacobi had sent photos of the men in alphabetical order to our phones. We checked out the suspects: Neil Elverson, who had been three-quarters of the way through a degree in chemistry before flunking out his senior year; Bruce McConnell, a theater major; Mac Travers, who had a bachelor's in political science; and Andrew Yang, who was a computer science whiz.

They looked like kids. Regular, cute kids who, when combined, happened to have a powerful skill set that could be used to disrupt and terrorize and kill. Individually, they had a history of posting angry screeds and radical comments on antigovernment message boards.

Until a few hours ago, nothing any of the four had said or done was illegal. They hadn't threatened attacks. They were on no watch lists. However, when one or more of them posted a video as GAR and took credit for an explosion that had killed twenty-five people, they crossed the line.

The GAR video had gone supernova overnight, accruing millions of hits on all social media. It was not a stretch to say that the "kids" we were going after this morning fit the profile of self-radicalized, homegrown terrorists to a tee.

Had this group of angry former frat boys been instrumental in blowing up Sci-Tron? Were they affiliated with Connor Grant? If so, had they been the planners and Grant the doer? Or were these four young men, exactly the type GAR recruited, angry, disaffected young men, depressed or disappointed or both, armed and looking for glory in this life and the next?

My attention was drawn to two camouflage-green assault vehicles, as sturdy as tanks, that entered the parking lot and stopped. A man got out of one of the vehicles. He was tall, wearing tac gear from head to toe, and had the bearing of a man who'd been in the military for most of his life.

He came toward me, calling my name. We shook hands and I introduced SWAT commander William Niles, a.k.a. Billy Bob Niles, to my seven task force cops, several of whom had worked with him before.

We pulled maps up on our phones, and Niles assigned the task force to points around the target as our perimeter.

I checked in with Jacobi, and then our caravan pulled out.

The sun hadn't yet come up.

Conklin asked, "What are you thinking?"

I shook my head. I didn't want to say I'd been asking myself and God if I would see Julie and Joe again.

CHAPTER 20

NILES'S ASSAULT VEHICLE was leading our caravan as we sped up Ocean Avenue at sunup.

The military-style vehicles, the train of police cars, couldn't be more inappropriate in this very sweet-looking, all-American neighborhood.

Niles pulled to a stop at the intersection of Ocean and Plymouth. I saw the craftsman-style house we were targeting, two doors down from the intersection. It was white stucco with a green roof, sitting on an unmown lawn. An expensive SUV, a couple of years old, was in the driveway. Plates registered to MacCord Travers, one of the presumed terrorists.

The house was dark. No lights and no sign of activity.

I called Jacobi.

"Thanks for doing this. Come home safe," he said.

Copy that.

Per the plan, three cars in our team blocked off the streets around the subject house, forming our perimeter. SWAT poured out of their vehicles and broke into their well-practiced maneuvers, four men covering the back and side doors, four getting into position on either side of the front entrance.

Niles pointed to me and then to the Honda SUV in the driveway. Conklin and I left the Bronco and used the Honda as a barrier twenty yards from the front door.

On Niles's signal the tac team stove in the green door and flashbangs were tossed. Conklin and I took cover behind the Honda as the blinding, deafening grenades went off.

I looked up, saw the tac team storming the house, leaving Rich and me to wait while they cleared the scene. I knew well that the grenades had no shrapnel, were meant only to blind and stun the occupants of the house, but tell that to my startle reflex.

I held on to the side of the Honda, shaking like a baby mouse in a cat's paws. This would not do. This would not do at all.

I looked over the hood, and beside me, Rich did the same. I heard the word "Clear" shouted repeatedly from inside the house as the teams went from room to room and up to the second floor. Only five minutes later Niles came out to the porch and shouted, "Boxer, we're all clear. You're up."

I said to Rich, "Ready or not, here we go."

CHAPTER 21

RICH AND I and the rest of the SFPD counterterrorism task force thundered into the bomb-cleared
house.

It actually looked as though a bomb *had* gone
off; clothing and garbage and bedding were strewn
everywhere. After a second look I realized this was
not explosive fallout. This was frat-house living.

Niles called me into a ground-floor bedroom
where two of the suspects and a naked woman
were rolling around on the bed and floor, crying
and moaning. Sergeant Mal Reigner, Vice, cuffed
the two males to the bed and, after covering her
with a blanket, Flex-Cuffed the young female by
the wrists and took her out to his cage car.

The two other boys were in the living room,
both on the floor, sobbing and cursing. The flash-
bang had disabled their equilibrium and scared the
hell out of them. Making this a good time to sepa-
rate and question them.

Conklin took the one who appeared to be Elverson, the former chem major, and I grabbed Yang,
the computer guy, and set him down in a tattered

chair. His nose was running. His eyes were red. He looked pitiful.

I said, "Mr. Yang, you're under arrest—"

"What did I do?"

I said, "You're under arrest for threatening communications."

"What? What is that?"

"For putting out a terror message. It's a federal offense."

"I didn't do anything like that. You're crazy."

"Mr. Yang. Listen to me before you start claiming your innocence. I'm Sergeant Boxer. I am with the SFPD, working with Homeland Security. I'm arresting you for blowing up Sci-Tron—"

"What?"

"Or for saying you did. That's threatening communications, specifically disseminating the video claiming credit for the GAR attack on Sci-Tron."

"I didn't—"

"That video has been traced to a computer inside this house. That's why I'm reading you your rights."

This twenty-two-year-old was watching and listening, but from the look in his eyes I couldn't be sure that he was following me.

I called out to Inspector Ronnie Burke, a good guy in Robbery I'd known for a couple of years, and asked him to witness my conversation with Andrew Yang while I recorded it on my phone. I wasn't repeating the Connor Grant confession/no-confession error twice.

Burke leaned against the wall and I showed Yang my phone. I pressed Record.

I said my name, and the date, time, and address, and then said, "Andrew Yang, you have the right to remain silent. Do you understand?"

He said, "Say it again."

I complied. And then, "Anything you say can and will be used against you in a court of law. Do you understand?"

After I took him through his rights and he answered that he understood them, I asked him to tell me what part he'd had in the bombing of Sci-Tron.

He shook his head no, while casting his eyes toward Neil Elverson, who was being half dragged out of the house in cuffs.

"Please take me seriously, Andrew. One of your friends, or maybe that young lady, is going to cut a deal with the police and confess to this crime in exchange for lighter time.

"If I were your mother, I'd tell you that the one who talks first wins. You should listen to me. I'm telling you the truth."

CHAPTER 22

DYLAN MITCHELL WAS a fit, fifty-two-year-old internet cult figure, operating as a member of GAR, who went by the name Haight. He lived in and podcast from a former bicycle factory in Dogpatch, a neighborhood on the eastern shore of San Francisco.

The open-space building had a tin ceiling and twenty-foot-high walls, with a catwalk halfway up the walls that wrapped around three sides. At one end was a computer studio, which was where he was sitting now.

Powerful industrial ceiling fans blew a benign breeze over the platform bed on wheels and the wide-plank floors below.

Haight was frugal. He dressed simply, in loose clothing, and kept his possessions to a minimum. But when it came to electronics, he had the best. He accepted donations to keep himself alive, which freed him to put his energy into producing his podcasts and posting the videos and protest speeches that he'd archived from the sixties and seventies, beginning with those his mother had given before he was born.

Haight, a.k.a. the redheaded stepchild of the sixties revolution, was the son of Erin Mitchell, the famously brave extremist who had founded Youth for a Democratic Society, a group of radicals that had forever shifted the consciousness of a complacent America.

Haight had never discovered the identity of his "father unknown."

Momma had told him at various times that his father might be Jerry Rubin or Jerry Garcia, or even Bob Dylan. She never swore to the truth of his paternity, but it was probably because she didn't know. By the time she died of ovarian cancer, Haight no longer cared who his father was. He had formed his own ideology and his manifesto was online worldwide.

Haight drafted alongside the GAR movement. He believed what they believed, but his methods were hands-off. He didn't recruit. He wasn't a technical adviser. He was a spokesman for the overturn of corrupt governments, and he spoke of revolution. He believed that all politics should be local and fully participatory. This left him both anti-state and anti-corporate. His major demons were the US government, the West in general, the IMF, Big Oil, Wall Street, central banks, and the various US bloodsucking cartels: defense, Big Pharma, agribusiness, and higher education.

Along with GAR, he was inspiring the lone wolves and stray-dog rebels, the angry underclass around the world yearning to break free. His podcasts were reports from the new front of terror without borders that was breaking out all over the world.

Violence was a way of cleansing humanity of its statist and corporatist sins and ushering in a new world in much the same way the Russian Bolsheviks did. It boiled down to an old slogan, simple and moving: POWER TO THE PEOPLE.

He was also Machiavellian and he knew it.

Any means to the correct end.

Haight was active in many twisting corridors on the dark web. He gathered and disseminated news from the underground and produced his own commentary. People wrote to Haight. He didn't write back, but through an encrypted app he could pop into friendly computer stations at will, and so his friends could talk to him anytime. And they did. J. had chatted with him before he set off for his sadly failed mission at SFO.

Still, J. had made his mark and, in so doing, had fueled the revolution.

This morning Haight was sipping his homemade peppermint-leaf tea while browsing the open transmissions from web friends, donors, and acolytes when his monitor went sharp white, accompanied by two consecutive booms that shocked the high right out of him.

What had to have been an explosion had come from the house rented by the four in Ingleside. When the picture cleared, he was looking at Andy Yang's face as a woman cop with a ponytail shouted, "Mr. Yang. Wake up. This is the police."

Haight watched what he could see of an

emergency response team sweep through the house in Ingleside. Then he disconnected from the net.

He thought about those kids for a few minutes. They knew nothing about him that wasn't common knowledge. He had a law degree from Columbia. He exercised his free speech rights, knowing how to keep himself safe from complicity in acts of treason.

Haight selected a favorite album from his playlist, *L.A. Woman,* the Doors, 1971, and turned on the speakers. He stepped into a pair of sandals and took the spiral staircase to the roof deck. There he turned on the hose, and as he watered the tomatoes, he sang "Riders on the Storm" along with Jim Morrison. And he pictured those brave kids in Ingleside. He looked forward to a time when all people would be free.

CHAPTER 23

THAT MORNING, YUKI went to the third floor of the Hall and checked in with Marie Fanucci, DA Len Parisi's personal gatekeeper.

She took one of the chairs in a row along the wall and waited to be called. As she sat there, ADAs came one after the other into Len's area. Some paced like soon-to-be fathers with wives in the delivery room. Others stood, pensive, avoiding eye contact with everyone until the previous ADA left and Marie told the next in line to go right in. Five minutes later the ADA would leave Len's office at a smart pace, eyes straight ahead, mind clearly on the case at hand.

Yuki found it disorienting, both familiar and strange, to revisit a past that she'd thought was securely behind her.

Yesterday while she was driving home from work, Len had called. She let the call go through to voice mail, then thumbed the keys until it played back.

"Yuki, it's Len. Parisi. Uh...Yuki, I have to talk to you. Call me."

He left his cell and home numbers.

Having worked under Len Parisi for four years, Yuki had to fight her powerful reflex to call him right back.

She thought about how much she had loved working for Len, prosecuting bad guys, becoming an ace litigator in the nuclear-charged atmosphere of the DA's office.

Then, a year ago, after a near-death experience, Yuki had a change of heart and mind about her career with the DA. She wanted to give back, use her skills to do good works for less fortunate people who couldn't afford a lawyer.

She expected Len to understand, but she misgauged his attachment to her. She was his protégé, and he didn't take her resignation well. In one short meeting she lost him as a boss, as a mentor, and as a friend. That had hurt. Bad.

It had been a year since she took the job with the not-for-profit Defense League, and she hadn't spoken with Len in that time. What could he possibly want to discuss with her now?

She pulled off Highway 92 onto an overlook and hit Return Call. She pressed her phone hard to her ear and listened to it ring. Then Parisi was on the line.

"Yuki?"

"Len."

They exchanged a very short volley of awkward pleasantries, after which Parisi got to the point.

"We have a suspect under arrest on the Sci-Tron bombing."

"I heard. The science teacher."

"I need a lead ADA who thinks like I do to work with me on the trial. Look, Yuki. Will you come back? I need you. The city needs you. Tell me what you want and I'll break down doors to get it for you. How's that for an easy-breezy negotiation?"

Pro: Len was going to make her lead ADA, second chair to him, on this enormous and very important trial.

Con: it was going to be unrelenting, exhausting work. There were so many victims and intense public scrutiny and everything at once—the good, the bad, and the ugly. Bottom line, it would be a return to a life not her own.

This morning, as she waited in the hectic area outside Len's office, Yuki silently continued to debate the possible outcomes of this meeting. After hearing Len out, would she be even more determined to stay in her job at the not-for-profit Defense League? Or was helping Len Parisi put a mass murderer away just too challenging an opportunity to turn down?

The frosted glass-panel office door opened, and the large, rough-looking man came toward her.

She stretched out her hand to shake his, and he bent to her, hugging her so hard that her feet almost left the ground.

"So good to see you, Yuki," said Len. "Please come home."

CHAPTER 24

THREE DAYS AFTER we pulled in the Ingleside Four, they were arraigned and remanded to a federal jail, awaiting their hearing by a grand jury. Their video taking responsibility as GAR had been seen throughout the USA, and therefore, their crime of threatening communications was the first charge against them and enough to hold them during further investigation. Now, all four were fully in the hands of the federal judicial system and not in ours at all.

Several rough versions of the GAR video had been filed in a folder on Yang's computer, but to date the government techs had found nothing about explosives on any of the kids' computers.

Red Dog Parisi saw nothing to indicate that those kids had actually been involved in the Sci-Tron bombing.

But he felt otherwise about Connor Grant.

Yuki was waiting for me at MacBain's, the designated Hall of Justice watering hole conveniently located across Bryant and down the street, wedged between two bail bondsmen's storefronts. As usual, the homey bar and grill was loud, and customers had packed it to the walls.

We hugged, pulled our chairs up to the little table at the front of the room. She looked beautiful. Her straight, dark, shoulder-length hair with a blue streak in front framed her face. She was wearing a perfect size-two midnight-blue designer suit with excellent accessories.

Best of all, she was beaming.

"How'd it go with Red Dog?" I asked, referring to her meeting three days ago with San Francisco's larger-than-life, red-haired, no-holds-barred district attorney.

"I'm back on the city payroll," she said, "with a two percent increase, and they gave me a one-time exemption. My benefits are restored. Plus, I get reimbursed for overtime parking and two full weeks of vacation, circumstances permitting."

I laughed along with her.

"So no vacation, right?"

"I pretty much got my old work-till-you-drop job back."

We ordered BLTs with steak fries and near beer, and then Yuki got into it.

"We've got an arraignment in Judge Rabinowitz's court tomorrow at three," Yuki told me. "I've got some paperwork from Parisi, but you were the arresting officer. Tell me everything."

Lunch was served. Yuki ate and I just talked and talked. She was not just my friend and member in good standing in the Women's Murder Club, she was responsible now for getting

Connor Grant officially charged and remanded without bail.

I told Yuki that I didn't even want to think of him getting bail and walking free. And then I told her everything else, including date night at the Crested Cormorant, the sunset-lit explosion, the arrest of the bizarre Mr. Grant, quoting his comments to me in front of Pier 15. And I answered her questions about the evidence we had found in his house.

"CSI is still hacking into his computer, but apparently, he has all kinds of hack blockers in place. Conklin and I are going through reams of school papers he thoughtfully boxed up and stored in his lab," I told her. "The FBI checked him out. As Grant says, he's been a science teacher for over twenty years. He's been written about in local papers for his science projects, et cetera, but this unpublished how-to book was all we found related to bombs."

I asked, "You think this book could give you enough to make the charges stick?"

"I'm going to reserve my opinion until I see the book."

We finished lunch, returned to the Hall, and went directly to the property room, where Yuki checked out Connor Grant's manuscript on how to build a bomb cheap, fast, and well.

"It's not proof of anything, but it goes to intent," she said cautiously.

I had hoped for more enthusiasm, but Yuki was right to have low expectations. The manuscript was circumstantial at best.

Yuki said, "The book might incriminate him, but we need Joe's testimony to corroborate Grant's confession. That's critical. But even that doesn't guarantee a slam-dunk conviction."

Joe was no longer comatose, but his consciousness was impaired. It was impossible to know what he would recall when or if he recovered from his traumatic head injury.

Yuki and I talked about Grant's computer, our hope that the explosive material in Grant's house would be found at the bomb site. Then we split up. She went down one floor to Len's office, and I worked with Richie in the squad room for the rest of the day.

We were thorough, but slogging through half of Connor Grant's hundred-plus boxes of tests and term papers was exhausting and fruitless.

When the day was finally done, I called home and spoke to my little Julie and my dear, lifesaving Mrs. Rose. Then I drove to the hospital.

Joe had a new room with a chair and a window and a whole lot of flowers. I taped an abstract crayon drawing to the window, signed by the almost-two-year-old artist in residence on Lake Street. I told Joe about Yuki, and Grant's arraignment, and then I watched TV in Joe's room for about an hour.

He never opened his eyes, and he never spoke a word about Sophie Fields, me, Julie, or anyone else.

He slept.

CHAPTER 25

CONKLIN AND I sat in the back row of Judge Steven Rabinowitz's arraignment courtroom in the San Francisco Superior Court, located on the second floor of the Hall of Justice. We were there to support Yuki and to see for ourselves that Connor Grant's attorney didn't Houdini him out of our jail with a low bail.

The blond-wood-paneled courtroom was standing room only. The victims' families filled the rows, wanting to see the killer in the flesh and to help the judge understand the depth of their horror and loss.

Yuki was ready when Connor Grant's case was called and his lawyer walked him to the bench.

Grant turned to look at the gallery full of people. I don't think he saw me, but I got a look at him—a man who had spent five full days in jail, sleeping with his eyes open, standing with his back to the wall. He wore a classic orange jumpsuit, clanking bracelets and shackles, and a chain belt hooking all his metallic restraints together.

I had met his attorney, Elise Antonelli, a four-hundred-dollar-an-hour lawyer who, my guess, had taken this appalling case because of the career-building opportunities in criminal defense.

She was about five two, fair skinned, and brown eyed, and she had an easy smile. She was also sharp and, in my opinion, eager to join the battle.

The charges were read—twenty-five counts of murder two—and the deceased were named in alphabetical order. Every time a name was read, someone in the room moaned or cried out. Judge Rabinowitz threatened to clear the courtroom. I thought he didn't want to do that, but he would if the spectators in the gallery got out of hand.

Rabinowitz asked Grant, "Do you understand the charges against you?"

Connor Grant said, "Do I understand them?"

I sucked in my breath. What was the psycho killer going to say?

"No, I don't understand them," he said. "I was a passerby when Sci-Tron was detonated. I was a very *unlucky* passerby, Your Honor. I didn't have anything to do with that bombing."

Rabinowitz said, "Let me rephrase the question, Mr. Grant. Do you understand that you are being charged with twenty-five counts of murder in the second degree?"

"Well. I heard the charges."

"Good. How do you plead?"

"Not guilty twenty-five times."

Antonelli spoke up. "Your Honor, we ask that the charges against Connor Grant be dismissed. He had nothing whatsoever to do with bombing

Sci-Tron and, therefore, nothing to do with these tragic deaths."

Yuki said, "Your Honor, Mr. Grant confessed at the scene to Sergeant Lindsay Boxer of the SFPD, Homicide Division, and her husband, Joseph Molinari, who was injured in the secondary blast. We have bomb-making materials taken into evidence by Crime Scene Investigation from Mr. Grant's premises. These materials, plus written materials in the defendant's handwriting, go to show that Mr. Grant, a science teacher, is quite knowledgeable in the making of explosives. He also had the means and the opportunity to set off this blast."

Rabinowitz said, "Let's talk about bail. Ms. Castellano."

"We request that bail be denied and that Mr. Grant be remanded to the maximum security jail in the Hall of Justice."

The judge said, "Ms. Antonelli?"

"Mr. Grant is a law-abiding citizen with strong ties to the community, Your Honor. He is gainfully employed by Saint Brendan High School. He has no prior charges, nothing so much as a littering ticket in his life, and the evidence against him is completely based in police mistakes and hysteria. Furthermore, Mr. Grant has no passport and is not a flight risk."

Judge Rabinowitz glanced at Yuki, then at Antonelli. Last, he gave Connor Grant a good long look.

"Bail denied," said Rabinowitz. "Defendant is remanded to the custody of the court."

Bam.

It was clear to me what the judge had been thinking when he denied bail. A suspected terrorist was in custody, a man who had possibly killed twenty-five people, and if he was released and then disappeared, this one decision would be the only act Judge Rabinowitz would be known for. It would be paragraph two in his obituary. It would probably be chiseled on his headstone.

As his gavel slammed down, two court officers came forward and escorted Connor Grant out of the courtroom through the side exit that led into the back stairs, which were restricted to courthouse personnel.

As they reached the door, there was a struggle. Conklin and I were on our feet, hands to our guns.

But Grant wasn't trying to make a break for freedom. He turned to face the judge and shouted, "I'm being framed. I have a life and I want it back. I demand a speedy trial. That is my right. Short date, Your Honor."

The judge said to the court officers, "Please remove the defendant from the courtroom."

We waited for Yuki out in the hallway as the bomb victims' friends and families blew through the double doors. When the room was nearly empty, Yuki stepped into the corridor.

"Great job," I said to my friend.

"Terrific," said Richie. "You were brilliant."

"I felt…like myself," said Yuki. She looked surprised when she said, "It's good to be back."

CHAPTER 26

CLAIRE CALLED THE next morning as Conklin and I were going through ninth-grade science classwork on earth and life sciences.

"Lindsay," Claire said, "I got some info on that dead lady who came in with the bomb victims. You know who I mean? Presumed heart attack, but she had a needle mark in her posterior?"

"I remember. Puncture mark and a small bruise."

"Correct," said Claire. "Come on down."

"I'll be right there," I said. I pulled on my jacket and said to my partner, "Be back in a few."

"I know what you're doing, you know."

"Guilty of leaving you with dead dinosaurs, Inspector. I'll be back in ten minutes. Want to come with?"

He glared. "You go," he said. "You two have fun."

I grinned at him, and then I took off.

Claire was waiting for me in the reception area. We walked back to her office, and she opened a folder and spread eight-by-ten morgue photos across her desk.

"Meet Ms. Lois Sprague," she said. "I finally had

a minute to do a real thorough search for her, and guess what? Found her in a Washington State missing persons database. She was reported missing two days after Sci-Tron. I took the liberty of calling the Spokane police, and I have some information."

"Shoot," I said, sitting down.

I looked at the morgue photos of the dead woman, and she was as Claire had described. White. Forty. Caramel-colored hair, well nourished. Lacerations and abrasions on her legs from having been clipped by a car. And she had a round bruise, the size of a half-dollar, on her right buttock.

Claire said, "What I learned from Spokane PD is that Ms. Sprague was single, in private practice as a family lawyer. Her sister told the police that Lois was a workaholic, had social anxiety and a few cats. That's the worst that could be said of her."

"No enemies?"

"According to the sister, Lois was a peacemaker. No one threatened or stalked her. She was on vacation and had no friends here. It was a solo trip, a week-long change-of-scene type vacation."

"So what killed her?"

Claire went on. "Like I told you, I put a rush on the tox screen," she said, "and no drugs were found in her body. But you know, Lindsay, there are drugs that leave the system quickly. If you're not on it fast, and not looking specifically for that drug, you may not find a trace of it. I can't put on the death certificate that I'm one hundred percent certain that Lois Sprague was murdered, but in my opinion, it's the only possible cause of death.

"Remember I told you I'd seen something like this two months ago? Presumed heart attack? I chased down the death certificate and morgue photos of Anthony George, cabdriver, white, fifty-five years old, probable cause of death cardiac arrest. Dr. G. did the post, and the heart was healthy, but no one insisted on further investigation, and the puncture mark just seemed irrelevant. Look at the death certificate. Here. Manner of death: 'Undetermined.'"

Claire opened a second folder, took out a photo of the hind section of Mr. George, the dead cabdriver, and placed it beside a matching image of Ms. Sprague's derriere.

The puncture wounds and bruises looked the same, and both were located in an awkward place for a person to inject themselves.

"So that's two dead people, possibly killed the same way and with no known relationship to each other," said Claire. "I'm going to take a wild guess and say that someone is on a random-victim killing spree. And that victim number three is coming to a morgue near us real soon."

My phone vibrated and buzzed.

It was Conklin.

He said, "Clapper just called. The divers pulled something out of the bay not far from the piers. It's a large fire extinguisher with the ends blown off. Clapper says it may be what's left of the bomb."

CHAPTER 27

CLAIRE WALKED ME out to the front door of her offices and asked me, "Okay if I come with you to see Joe this evening?"

"Sure. Yes. Of course."

"Yuki and Cindy want to see him, too."

"Claire, he's nonresponsive."

"We're coming. Okay?"

We all met up in the lobby after work, and I drove us to the hospital, my car filled with my girlfriends and a whole lot of flowers.

The light was dimmed in Joe's private room and he was asleep, looking like he'd played chicken with a locomotive and lost. As my friends spoke encouraging words to my husband, I scrutinized his face. He showed no sign of hearing them. He just breathed in and out, while the vital-signs monitor registered the rhythmic beating of his heart.

The girls each patted his good arm, and I put my hand on his, and after a while we said good-bye and headed down to the cafeteria. We made hasty selections from the assorted hot trays and salad bars, and Cindy grabbed a booth for four.

Normally, it's kind of a party when the four of us meet for a meal. But not today. The bombing disaster had nearly crushed San Francisco and it also hit home.

I asked Claire for her professional opinion of Joe's condition.

She reached across the table and took my hands.

She said, "The shunts are out. He's not in a coma anymore, he's in a stupor. He's healing. He has spoken since the accident. His memory may be jumbled, but that he spoke makes me think he's doing a little better than could be expected."

The cafeteria was loud at dinnertime. The PA system crackled and squealed. Trays clashed in bins, and loud conversation burst from folks gathered at the small tables.

Cindy asked what I'm sure everyone was thinking.

"Linds, can you talk about the science teacher? Off the record—or on."

It's a long-standing joke that Cindy has to be warned and muzzled when we're talking shop. She's a crime reporter who has broken murder cases using grit, tenacity, and insight. Of course we all love those qualities in her, but still. Reporters report, right? If we don't say "off the record," it's our own fault if something said at the table appears on the *Chronicle*'s front page.

"Off the record, Cindy," I said over the din. "If Conklin didn't tell you, Grant compiled a book-length manuscript on Bomb Making 101, and one of the bombs he describes is a compression bomb. That's probably what was used in Sci-Tron."

Three asked as one, "What's a compression bomb?"

I said, "As I understand it, you fill a metal container with gas and a chemical that makes oxygen. You attach a detonator and maybe a timer, and when the gas ignites, the explosion changes the atmospheric pressure of, say, Sci-Tron, and that's what blows up the structure. It's called a hard-force explosion. The second blast may have been C-4, also triggered by a timer on a detonator. The pieces of that second bomb may never be found, but a fire extinguisher with the ends blown off has been dredged out of the bay. No prints on it, of course."

"It's better than nothing," Yuki said. "Grant *describes* a similar bomb in his manuscript and he made a few drawings. Plus, we have the remains of the exploded bomb. Too bad he didn't take a selfie of himself planting it in Sci-Tron."

Cindy asked, "So he just brought it in and left it there? How?"

"Don't know," I told her. "Maybe he came to the museum disguised in a service uniform, like he was there to replace the old fire extinguisher. Maybe he came in as a science teacher. There's an idea. He could have used his real ID to get in and inserted the canister into an exhibit. At the same time he slapped up a glob of C-4—anywhere. It's a plausible theory."

I went on, telling my girls that Grant's laptop had finally given in to our CSI, but what they found wasn't illegal or even incriminating.

"Yes, he did research on bombs, also nanotechnology, astronomy, the Dead Sea Scrolls, and the Entertainment section of the *Chronicle*.

"Forensics also went through his phone, read his texts, chased down his frequently called phone numbers. We've got names, school administrators, take-out pizza, utility companies. There were absolutely no calls to Syria or Pakistan or Brussels, or they were untraceable. No calls to known criminals, either," I said. "Needless to say, we also have no hits on his fingerprints or DNA in criminal databases."

"The guy is a closed book," said Cindy.

"A ghost," said Claire. "Or a wraith."

"A very dangerous person," said Yuki.

I asked, "So why did he leave that manuscript in his lab? Just an oversight?"

"Maybe it was his joke on law enforcement," said Claire. "A fake lead to make this even more exciting for him."

I nodded.

"That feels right, Claire. He's definitely screwing with us."

I know I looked defeated, and right then I felt that way. I said, "Cindy, you can't quote me on any of this, but I'll get you a one-on-one phoner with Jacobi."

"Excellent. Thanks, Linds."

"I owe you," I said.

Cindy asked Yuki, "You have enough to make a case against Grant?"

Yuki said, "Right now all we have is circumstantial evidence, but if Joe remembers what Grant said, that could be a clincher. Either way, I'm going to have to convince twelve men and women that that mild-mannered science teacher built a bomb capable of leveling a seventy-five-thousand-square-foot building, and that he set that bomb, ignited it, witnessed it, and left not a trace."

PART TWO

CHAPTER 28

YUKI FELT THE tension spanning courtroom 2A from corner to corner as Connor Grant's trial was about to begin.

The jury had been seated and Judge Philip R. Hoffman had taken the bench, where, flanked by Old Glory and the California state flag, he had instructed the jury. The eight men and four women and their alternates in the jury box looked expectant and dead serious.

This was a trial of a lifetime and they knew it.

Hoffman was in his midfifties, had thick hair and glasses, was well known in San Francisco for presiding over high-profile cases—notably, the trial of a teenage girl who had returned from college on spring break and gunned down her family of six.

Yuki had history with Phil Hoffman. She had gone up against him in two trials when he was a criminal defense attorney. She'd lost to him the first time, beat him the next, and in both cases thought Hoffman was a gentleman. And she admired his taut, no-frills style. As a judge, he was fair, and he didn't stand for what he called funny business.

Yuki had had moments of regret about leaving the Defense League, but today, sitting beside Len Parisi at the prosecution table, she felt fully satisfied with her decision. The opportunity to lock up Connor Grant was monumental. If ever there was a case for the death penalty, this was it.

She and Len had discussed every aspect of the case, the strengths and weaknesses, and now Len was very still, no doubt silently rehearsing his opening. Yuki used the pretrial moments to steady her nerves with an affirmation: *You're prepared. Len's the best. The case is solid. Trust the jury.* Repeat.

Yuki shot a quick glance across the aisle to the defense table, where opposition counsel, Elise Antonelli, sat with her unfathomable client, Connor Grant. She and Grant were speaking together behind their hands. Yuki read conflict in their expressions, but their voices never rose above a whisper.

The gallery, the rows of seats behind the bar, was full. The victims' families, survivors of the blast, and reporters waited expectantly for the trial to start.

At the bench, Judge Hoffman repositioned his glasses, spoke to the court reporter and then to the bailiff, who read the charges against Connor Grant, and called the court into session.

Hoffman looked to the prosecution table and said, "Mr. Parisi. Are the People ready?"

"Yes, Your Honor."

"Then let's proceed with opening statements."

Red Dog Parisi got slowly to his feet. He was six foot four, three hundred pounds more or less. His skin was acne-scarred and he had coarse, rust-colored hair. He wore a black suit, white shirt, and red tie. He'd once been described as looking like a cross between a yeti and a superpower avenger. When this large, homely man said that he was doing the People's work, it felt good to have him on your side.

Parisi lumbered out to the well of the courtroom and fixed his eyes on the jury. Their eyes were also fixed on him.

CHAPTER 29

PARISI WALKED TO the podium that had been set up in the well, halfway between the bench and the jury box, and addressed the court.

"Your Honor, ladies and gentlemen of the jury, it's been a while since I've personally tried a case. In my job as district attorney of San Francisco County, I am responsible for over one hundred attorneys and ADAs in my office, and I oversee dozens of cases and trials.

"So, why am I standing before you today? Because Connor Grant, the smiling man in the cheerful blue sports coat sitting at the defense table, is a mass murderer who deliberately, with malice aforethought and considerable skill, destroyed Sci-Tron, a science museum on Pier 15. In so doing, he killed twenty-five of the people who were inside."

Yuki felt a thrill as she heard Len's voice. He was keeping his anger to a slow burn. The jurors could hear the fury. They could feel the heat.

Parisi went on.

"Those twenty-five people—in fact, all of the

people who happened to be inside the museum that day—were of no interest to Mr. Grant. He never even thought about them. Mr. Grant simply wanted to blow the museum into billions of little pieces, and the living people were, as far as we can tell from Mr. Grant, utterly inconsequential."

Yuki watched the jurors, who had fixed their attention on Len. He swept his gaze across the length of the box, looking at each one, before he picked up the thread of his opening.

"Ladies and gentlemen, among the twenty-five deceased are three firefighters, three selfless men who were caught in the secondary blast. Some fifty other people were injured, maimed, traumatized. And then there are all of the unnamed friends and families of the victims, hundreds of people who are grieving, emotionally damaged, who will never be the same again.

"During the course of this trial, you will hear that Connor Grant confessed to the police that he had blown up Sci-Tron even as the aftershock of the bomb reverberated in the air and the sirens and the screams echoed along the Embarcadero.

"Later, when Mr. Grant realized that he had trapped himself and that he was going to be tried for this terrible crime, he recanted his confession. Too late. We will present witness testimony that Mr. Grant proudly admitted to perpetrating this conscienceless attack. He was bragging. He was self-congratulatory."

Parisi shook his head, conveying his disgust with

the defendant's actions. Yuki, having gone over his opening remarks with him, knew he was about to lay down the foundation of their case.

He said, "But even if Mr. Grant hadn't confessed, the proof against him is overwhelming. As you will learn during this trial, he had not only the means, but the motive and the opportunity to blow up Sci-Tron.

"Did Connor Grant have the means to make a bomb of sufficient size and force to blow up this large glass-and-steel building? Yes, he did. We will show you that Mr. Grant, a science teacher, had an unusual degree of interest in explosives, and all of the tools necessary to blow up…anything.

"We will show you photos of the bomb-making laboratory in the defendant's garage and his book-in-progress that describes in detail how to build bombs of all types with ingredients easily obtained in your local pharmacy and hardware store. He even described how to create the type of bomb that was used to take down Sci-Tron.

"He had the knowledge and the tools.

"Did Connor Grant have the opportunity to place this bomb and detonate it? Yes, he did. The museum was open seven days a week. He had a membership card, frequented this museum, and is familiar to many of the people who worked there. He could easily have brought in the bomb, which was disguised as a fire extinguisher, and armed it without alarming anyone. And after he left the building, the sight of a fire extinguisher wouldn't alert anyone to its real purpose.

"As to motive," Parisi went on, "that is complicated."

Yuki watched Len pause, reload, and fire.

"You do not have to buy into Mr. Grant's motive in order to convict him. But in the face of all this death, destruction, and traumatic injury, we do want to understand why this defendant did what he did. And he told us.

"Here's why Connor Grant blew Sci-Tron into smithereens. Because he wanted to do it. And we will prove to you that he could and that he did.

"At the end of this trial, we will ask you, the jury, to find the defendant guilty of murder in the second degree in the deaths of twenty-five innocent people, to guarantee that this man"—Len pointed at Connor Grant—"can never harm anyone ever again."

Len thanked the jury, and if Yuki could have applauded him, she would have done so.

Instead, she scrawled on her notepad, "Great job, Len. Tremendous."

CHAPTER 30

JUDGE HOFFMAN PEERED over his bench and exchanged a few words with the bailiff as Len Parisi returned to the prosecution table. Then he looked across his courtroom at attorney Elise Antonelli, who was seated at the defense table beside her client, Connor Grant.

Hoffman said, "Ms. Antonelli, are you ready with your opening statement?"

Elise Antonelli stood and said, "Sidebar, Your Honor?"

Yuki almost said, *What?*

What was defense counsel up to?

Hoffman signaled to the lawyers to approach, and the three of them walked across the well to the bench.

"What is it, Ms. Antonelli?" said Hoffman. "I can't wait to hear."

Antonelli said, "Mr. Grant just fired me. He says that he wants to represent himself."

Hoffman said, "*Fired* you? Okay, step back."

Then, to the jurors, he said, "I'm calling a ten-minute recess. Sit tight."

The court officers, guns on their hips, grouped behind the defendant. The judge opened the door behind the bench, and prosecution and defense counsel followed him down the corridor and assembled in his book-lined office. Parisi and Yuki took the brick-red love seat, and Elise Antonelli sat in the chair across from Hoffman's desk.

Hoffman asked Antonelli, "Why did he dismiss you? What did he give as a reason?"

Antonelli said, "Paraphrasing now, he said, 'I'm sure you're very good, Elise, but I'm the best person to take my case to the jury.'"

"Really?" the judge said. "While facing twenty-five counts of murder two? What took your client so long to arrive at this staggeringly stupid decision?"

"He never mentioned that he was thinking about this, Judge, until I brought him his wardrobe this morning. I guess he got some jailhouse advice, or maybe he thinks if he defends himself and he loses, he gets a mistrial on the grounds that he's got incompetent counsel."

"Is he delusional?" Parisi asked.

Hoffman said, "Elise, don't answer that. Well, let me ask you, Len. You want to go back to the table, try to negotiate a deal with the defendant?"

"Judge, I'm not opposed to his confession in open court in exchange for twenty-five life sentences served concurrently rather than consecutively with no possibility of parole. I offered this previously and was turned down."

Elise Antonelli leaned forward in her seat. She

said, "Judge, he won't take a deal. He wants a trial and he believes that he can win. He plans to walk free. That's what he said. That, and that he has a constitutional right for a pro se defense."

Yuki recalled only three mass murderers who had defended themselves. Ted Bundy was found guilty and had been executed. Colin Ferguson, also found guilty, was given six life sentences. Only Lee Anthony Evans had defended himself successfully against multiple homicide charges. Connor Grant's odds of winning were better if Antonelli defended him, and that would be better for the prosecution as well. Yuki knew that a pro se defendant was a prosecutor's worst nightmare. Juries tended to feel sorry for them because they were inexperienced. Accordingly, they got away with mistakes, misstatements, and meritless objections. Whether these missteps were calculated or not, they could influence the jury in the defendant's favor.

Hoffman said to Antonelli, "Oh, boy. I'll talk with him, alone, and see if I can get him to change his mind."

CHAPTER 31

YUKI AND LEN went upstairs to Len's office and tried to figure out what Connor Grant was trying to pull. Whatever it was, Judge Hoffman clearly wasn't going to tolerate it. Right?

Yuki fired off a text to her husband, Homicide lieutenant Jackson Brady, telling him in a few words the twist of events: *Grant wants to defend himself. Says he's best person for the job.*

Brady texted back, *Huge ego. No legal experience. Good for the white hats.*

Yuki hoped Brady was right.

Courtroom 2A was still empty when the prosecution team returned to their table. Moments later Elise Antonelli came in through the side door with the defendant.

Grant wore a very pleased expression and a different jacket. Apparently, Len's remarks about a "cheerful blue sports coat" had prompted his attorney to quickly find him a more subdued replacement. The bailiff opened the door for the twelve jurors and four alternates, who filed in and got settled, putting handbags under seats, coughing politely, crossing legs, and exchanging questioning looks when they realized that the gallery was empty.

They stood when the judge returned and took the bench, then sat again as he addressed the jurors, saying, "Ladies and gentlemen, there has been a change to the proceedings that I'm going to tell you about right now. We can deal with any questions before the public comes in."

Yuki said softly, "Uh-oh."

Hoffman said, "Here's the story. The defendant, Mr. Grant, is exercising his legal right to defend himself."

There was a gasp from some of the jurors, and Yuki felt her heart speed up. She had really thought the judge would convince Grant that he was going to hurt his chances by becoming his own counsel.

Hoffman explained that every defendant had a right to a pro se defense, that pro se meant "on one's own behalf." He told the jurors that he had questioned Mr. Grant and that he was convinced that the defendant could do an adequate job of presenting his case to the jury.

The judge went on.

"Ms. Antonelli is acting as Mr. Grant's standby counsel. *She* is well versed in this case and will guide Mr. Grant on points of law. Mr. Grant has assured me that he is of sound mind, that he understands what is at stake, and that he will not be given any breaks because of his lack of legal experience.

"Accordingly, the prosecution will treat Mr. Grant as opposing counsel. As for me, I'm going to make sure that this trial stays on track and that you receive the information you need to decide Mr. Grant's guilt or innocence.

"Are there any questions?"

Mrs. Schumacher, a retired librarian, raised her hand.

"Is there time for me to use the restroom?"

"Yes. Anyone else? No? Bailiff, please escort juror number four to the jury room. Any other questions?"

There were none. When Mrs. Schumacher returned to her seat, the judge asked the court officers to open the front doors. The gallery was filled noisily as people jostled for seats. Once the attendees were reasonably quiet, court officers formed a line at the back of the room, blocking the doors.

Judge Hoffman reprised the explanation that he had given to the jury and announced that court was now in session.

He said to the defendant, "Mr. Grant, if you're ready, please make your opening statement."

CHAPTER 32

GRANT PLACED A stack of note cards on the lectern and looked across the room toward the jury. He seemed utterly relaxed, appearing to Yuki every bit the schoolteacher in front of his class. When he spoke, his voice was clear and confident.

"Folks, I'm shocked to be in this courtroom. I've been charged with killing twenty-five people, and I had absolutely *nothing* to do with that terrible tragedy.

"You deserve to hear exactly what happened and I'm going to tell you. On the evening of August 3, I was walking northwest on the Embarcadero and was only a block or so away from Sci-Tron when it blew the hell up."

He threw his hands into the air by way of description.

"I was stunned, caught completely by surprise. I stood on the sidewalk, a bystander, an accidental witness to this enormous and violent explosion. I was dazed by the sound and the sight of what you have probably seen on television.

"*Only, I was right there while it was happening.*

"I should introduce myself. My name is Connor Grant and I am a science teacher. I have been a science teacher since graduating from the University of Miami in '93 and have been with Saint Brendan High School for five years now, teaching ninth-grade science.

"I often go to Sci-Tron. I've taken my classes there. It was a beautiful place, and my students and I have always found it inspirational to see the exhibits, hear the lectures, and talk to other teachers and guests.

"As I said, on the evening of August 3, I was walking along the sidewalk in the direction of Sci-Tron. Thursday night was adults only, and I wanted to stand in the observatory gallery at sunset. That's all that was in my mind.

"Then the shocking explosion seemed to break the sky. Glass went flying and I saw a mushroom cloud forming over the bay. The concussion of the blast seemed to make time stand still. It was like my shoes were bonded to that pavement when the bomb went off. Imagine being so close to a bomb that the sidewalk is shimmying under your feet."

The glow on Grant's face was riveting. He had brought the destruction of Sci-Tron right into the courtroom. He was there. And even Yuki couldn't look away.

Hoffman said, "Mr. Grant? Please go on."

"Sorry, Your Honor."

Grant focused intently on the jurors, saying to them, "At some point I became aware of the screaming. People were running from the pier where the museum had been standing, and still I could not move. This was living science, and I was trying to understand what looked like spontaneous combustion.

"Mr. Parisi has told you that I confessed to blowing up Sci-Tron to a police officer. I did no such thing. Did I comment on the explosion? Did I say that it was amazing or something? I do not know.

"I was in a state of shock. I was also a witness. I hope you understand that within those first moments after the blast, I wasn't thinking about people or panic or death. As a scientist with a laboratory mentality, I was mesmerized by what I had seen in the wild, and I was analyzing it, too. Trying to figure out exactly what had occurred in front of my eyes."

Yuki scanned the jurors' faces. They, too, looked mesmerized. Parisi was leaning back in his seat. Watching. No doubt learning from the defendant and making a plan.

Grant shuffled through his note cards, examined a couple of them. He seemed to be collecting his thoughts. A moment later he again addressed the jury.

"Ladies and gentlemen, the prosecution will tell you that the police discovered a science lab in my garage. That is correct, although neither the garage nor the lab was hidden. My garage is in plain sight. I do experiments in my lab, not in my house. I think that makes good sense. The police will tell you that they have found a book on explosives that I have been working on for years. That's true, but it's very boring, and I don't think it will ever be published, because it's not newsworthy. It's a notebook. That's how I think of it.

"So I have a lab that takes up half of a two-car garage and a collection of notes, but more to the point, there is no way the People can connect me to this explosion.

"I did not go into the museum the night of the explosion, and no one claims otherwise. Whatever took down Sci-Tron was a perfectly distributed blast. A highly professional job. If I had been *asked* to detonate that building, I couldn't have done it. The skill involved is just way beyond my abilities, and that is a fact.

"Here's the prosecution's total case: I may have said something to a police officer when I wasn't thinking clearly. And to that I might add that this police officer may not have been thinking clearly, either. I'd ask you to give everyone involved the benefit of the doubt; we were deafened by the blast, shaken up by it, and frightened almost to death.

"We'll never know how or why this misunderstanding between me and the police officer took place, because no record was made of any so-called admission. If I had been taken to the hospital, doctors would have said that my hearing had been affected or that I was in shock. But I was thrown into a squad car and brought into a police station, where I was locked up overnight in a cell full of dangerous strangers. The next morning, after a sleepless night, I was interrogated without benefit of counsel.

"Days later I was charged and held without bond.

"Think of that," said the science teacher. "The police had me in custody, an innocent man, a victim of circumstances, and because they had no evidence at the time that this tragedy was caused by a terrorist group, they never looked any further than me, although apparently, GAR has taken credit.

"So the prosecution has me and no one else. That's why they are desperate to pin the tail on the donkey. Me. Because it's better than having no donkey at all.

"Here's the simple, honest truth," Connor Grant said to the rapt jurors. "Something or someone blew up Sci-Tron. But I give you my word. I swear on the Bible, I didn't do it."

Grant returned to the defense table. Yuki lowered her eyes and made notes on her tablet so that no one, not the defendant and not, God forbid, the jury, could see how amazed she was by Connor Grant's opening remarks. He'd been unbelievably articulate. He hadn't whiffed a line. And he'd come across as truthful and sincere with just the right amount of indignation, so much so that Yuki could see on the jurors' faces that they were identifying with him.

And she was questioning her own certainty that he had bombed Sci-Tron.

She canceled the thought as she heard Parisi say to the judge, "The People call Sergeant Lindsay Boxer."

CHAPTER 33

THE INFLUX OF media was creating dangerous traffic conditions on Bryant Street. Satellite trucks from network, cable, and foreign news outlets were double-parked, blocking the grid and narrowing the lanes in front of the Hall.

Camera crews had set up on the sidewalk. Reporters sat in tall director's chairs under silk shades and spoke to their viewers. Others put microphones up to the faces of anyone who would stop, and they did impromptu interviews on the Hall of Justice steps.

I dodged the mob scene by using my customary route: on foot from Harriet Street, along the breezeway, and through the back door.

I'd taken time to look my professional best. I wore my gray Ralph Lauren blazer and blue trousers, a man-tailored white shirt, and sturdy, polished Cole Haan flats. My blond hair was pulled back in a pony, as usual, and I'd worn makeup for the occasion. My badge hung from a long ball chain around my neck. And I arrived ahead of time in the hallway outside courtroom 2A, where I waited to be called.

The testimony I was prepared to give against Connor Grant was pretty much the heart of the prosecution's case. I wasn't nervous exactly, but I was keyed up. A lot of people were depending on me.

The door to the courtroom opened, and the bailiff said to me, "Sergeant Boxer? You're up."

He held the door open, and I strode into the courtroom and up the aisle, passing many people who were turning to look at me as if there were music playing "Here Comes the Bride."

I nodded at Yuki as I went through the gate, then continued to the witness box, where I placed my hand on the Bible and swore to tell the whole truth, so help me God.

When I was seated, my dear friend Yuki approached me.

She asked me a series of questions, establishing my occupation and expertise: how long I had been with the SFPD, what department, how many commendations, and if I had arrested Connor Grant on the night in question.

Yuki is a fast-talker, but I'm used to her pace. She snapped out the questions, and I answered without hesitation or embellishment.

She said, "Sergeant Boxer, were you working at 7:23 p.m. on August 3, the night of the Sci-Tron incident?"

I said, "No, I was having dinner with my husband in a restaurant on Pier 9 directly opposite Pier 15. We had a clear view of Sci-Tron."

She asked me to recount the events, and I did so, starting with our window on the explosion, our departure from the restaurant, and our race to the scene a short way up the street.

I said, "Crowds were fleeing the site of the bomb, running past where my husband and I were standing at the edge of the sidewalk. My husband—his name is Joe Molinari—was calling for emergency support, and I was waiting with him when I noticed a man standing stock-still in the middle of the moving crowd."

"Do you see that man in the room now?"

"Yes. I saw the defendant."

"Okay," Yuki said. "Please tell the jury what happened next."

I recalled my very vivid memories of speaking to Grant, and I repeated what I had said to him, what he had said to me.

"I took him to be a witness and I asked him to tell me what he had seen. My husband was standing with me, and we both heard Mr. Grant take full and individual credit for blowing up the museum.

"He told me that he hadn't simply *witnessed* the explosion, he had *created* it," I told the court. "He said that it was beautiful and that he awarded himself an A-plus with extra points for the sunset."

"And did you find this answer believable?"

"I didn't know what to think at first. So I asked him to tell me again what had happened. He again insisted that he had exploded the bomb, and he elaborated on his original statement, essentially boasting about what a beautiful work of art he had created."

"What happened next, Sergeant Boxer?"

"I arrested Mr. Grant for destruction of public property. After I read him his rights, I brought him over to a squad car and gave one of the officers orders to take him to booking and to turn him over to Lieutenant Brady of Homicide, my CO."

Yuki asked, "And how did Mr. Grant appear to you?"

I said, "He was lucid. He seemed to have full awareness of the events and his role in them."

"Did you offer medical treatment?"

"I asked him how he felt. He said he was fine."

Yuki asked, "What happened after that?"

"The squad car left and my husband ran into what was left of Sci-Tron to see if he could help any survivors. He was hit by debris in the second blast."

"Sergeant Boxer, was he injured?"

"Yes."

"And did you interview Mr. Grant the next morning?"

"I did, along with Lieutenant Brady."

"Can you describe that interview for the court?"

"Yes. The defendant was uncooperative. He denied confessing to the bombing and refused to answer further questions."

"Thank you, Sergeant Boxer," said Yuki. "Mr. Grant, your witness."

CHAPTER 34

YUKI WATCHED AS Grant got up from his seat and approached Lindsay. He stuck his hands into his pant pockets, giving him the insouciance of a popular college kid. Yuki found his demeanor damned creepy.

Grant said, "Hello again, Sergeant Boxer. I have just a couple of questions for you, unlike the punishing drubbing I've suffered at your hands."

Yuki shot to her feet. "Objection, Your Honor."

Hoffman said, "Sustained. Mr. Grant, no personal comments to the witness. Just ask your questions."

"Sorry, Your Honor. Uh...Sergeant, did you see me coming out of Sci-Tron that night?"

"No."

"Did you find any bomb implements, control devices, or anything of that nature when you frisked and cuffed me?"

"No."

"Did you record my so-called confession when you questioned me on the sidewalk between Piers 9 and 15 that evening?"

"No. I didn't have to record—"

"No. Your answer is 'no.' You didn't record any so-called admission. You didn't see me in the building, and you found nothing bomb-related on my person, isn't that right?"

"Yes."

"Your Honor," said Grant. "I'm done with this witness."

Yuki saw the flash of anger in Lindsay's face and understood exactly how she felt. Furious because she had no opportunity to redress the insult.

The judge asked the prosecution if they had questions on redirect, and Len said, "No, Your Honor. But we reserve the right to recall this witness."

The judge asked Lindsay to step down, and once she had left the courtroom, he made an announcement.

"I'm sorry," he said. "I have to attend to some important court business. I'm calling a recess. Short one. Court will resume in one half hour."

Doors opened. The jury returned to their room. Some people in the gallery left their seats, and Parisi said he wanted to make some calls and he'd be back in a few.

Yuki stayed at the prosecution table, made notes, and thought about Joe. His recovery had been touch and go; she and Len had worried for weeks about his ability to testify. He was still weak and visibly changed from the way Yuki had always known him—physically strong, mentally sharp.

Could he retell Grant's confession convincingly now?

Yuki could only hope so.

If Joe failed to corroborate Lindsay's testimony, a canyon of reasonable doubt would open in their case, and it would be almost impossible for the prosecution to bridge it.

CHAPTER 35

AFTER MY TESTIMONY I left the courtroom and went to the fire stairs, taking a seat on a step about midway between the second and third floors. I got a pretty good signal here, and no one using the stairway ever bothered me.

I called Joe, listened to the phone ring through, counted the number of rings, hoping he would answer.

"Lindsay?"

"Hi. How are you feeling, Joe?"

"Good. Pretty good."

He sounded like he wasn't sure.

"Where are you?"

"We're on Seventh Street. About five minutes away, right, Kevin? We hit some traffic."

Five minutes away? He was cutting it very close. If Hoffman hadn't called a recess, Joe would have been a no-show, leaving Yuki and Len to tap-dance for more time. I flicked that disturbing thought away.

I asked, "Is Kevin your driver?"

"That's right. You okay, Linds? It's hard to hear you."

"I'm in the fire stairs. I don't want anyone to hear me. I just want to tell you, I just got out of court. Grant is a beast."

"Meaning what?"

"He cross-examined me with a scalpel. Or a chain saw. Not sure. But it was brutal."

"Yeah. Well."

Joe's voice sounded like he was floating away.

"Joe. Joe. Can you hear me?"

"I can now."

"Do you remember when we talked to him right after the explosion?"

"Sure. He said he did it. He had a cockeyed story."

I tried not to sigh loudly into the mouthpiece. A couple of people ran past me down the stairs.

"You still there, Joe?"

"Yep. We're on Bryant. I can see the Hall."

I said, "Is Kevin bringing you into the building?"

I heard Joe ask, "Kevin, you're taking me inside?"

Then Joe said, "It's the second floor?"

"Right. That's right. Court starts again in fifteen minutes."

The phone clicked off. I looked. I still had battery life. Joe's phone had disconnected, not mine.

I went online and looked up *Connor Grant* on the *Chronicle*'s website and read Cindy's update on the trial. She had written that the defendant was a pretty decent lawyer for a schoolteacher and that the witnesses for the prosecution would be questioned today.

She wrote, "The prosecution called their first witness this morning, Homicide sergeant Lindsay

Boxer. Sergeant Boxer testified that Mr. Grant confessed to her at the time of the explosion that he had bombed Sci-Tron. He denied this admission in his opening statement.

"Earlier, DA Len Parisi told this reporter that he is confident that the jury will find the defendant guilty. As in all trials, the burden of proof is on the prosecution, who must convince the jury of the defendant's guilt beyond a shadow of a doubt...."

As I sat in the stairwell, shadows of doubt in all colors and shapes crossed my mind. Most of them pointed to Joe.

Would he remember Grant's confession?

Could he stand up to Grant's cross-examination?

I wouldn't even be allowed in the courtroom to see and hear him for myself.

I called Yuki.

"You did fine, Lindsay."

"Hah. Let me know how it goes for Joe," I said.

"Will do," said Yuki.

CHAPTER 36

THE COURT OFFICER opened the doors, and Yuki watched Joe Molinari enter the courtroom in a wheelchair, pushing the wheels with his hands. When he reached the witness box, the bailiff brought the Bible to him and swore him in.

Joe asked for assistance.

He leaned on the bailiff's arm, pulled himself to his feet, and hopped a short way, then hoisted himself into the chair a step up from the floor.

Yuki thought that Joe truly looked like a victim of the explosion. Not only was he unable to walk, his hair had grown back enough to highlight the terrible scars on the back of his head.

She felt tears coming into her eyes as she looked at him.

Parisi approached Joe and thanked him for coming to court in person rather than being televised by closed-circuit TV.

Joe said, "No problem. Glad to do it."

Len asked, "Mr. Molinari, what's your occupation?"

"I'm an independent security contractor."

"What kind of work did you do before you went out on your own?"

Joe thought for a second and then said, "I was deputy director of Homeland Security, and both before and after that I was a senior agent with the FBI."

"How would you rate your observational abilities before your recent injuries?"

"I would rate them as exceptional." Joe hesitated a beat, then said, "And after my injuries also."

"You suffered brain trauma in the second blast at Sci-Tron, isn't that right?"

"Correct."

Yuki waited for him to continue. His memory was fine. He was articulate. But his responses were slow.

Joe said, "I've had several MRIs and a lot of testing, and my cognitive faculties are intact."

"Thank you, Mr. Molinari. Judge Hoffman, I wish to enter exhibits 1 through 9, medical documentation and certification by neurologists and psychologists that Mr. Molinari has no mental incapacity or defect as the result of his injuries."

"Go ahead," said the judge.

The material was entered.

Joe looked over at Yuki. Their eyes met. He smiled.

Parisi moved back toward Joe and asked him, "Do you remember the evening of the bomb incident on Pier 15?"

"Like it just happened."

"Do you remember hearing the defendant, Mr.

Connor Grant, describing his role in the bombing to your wife, Homicide sergeant Lindsay Boxer?"

"I do."

"Could you tell the court what Mr. Grant told Sergeant Boxer and yourself?"

"Yes. She asked him if he'd seen the explosion. He said, 'Did I *see* it? I *created* this—this magnificent event. This is my *work*.' Sergeant Boxer asked him his name, and he told us and he described himself as a genius, a creator of beauty. He asked if we had seen all of it. The mushroom cloud. The color of sundown on the glass. He said he gave himself extra points for that."

Parisi said, "Do you remember anything else he said?"

"I do. Sergeant Boxer asked him again, 'Are you saying you bombed Sci-Tron?' And he said, 'Exactly.' He was emphatic. And he added that if we needed to know why, he said that beauty didn't need a reason."

Parisi asked, "Did you believe this confession?"

There was a moment of silence. Yuki didn't breathe as she watched Joe disappear into his memory. And then he snapped his eyes back to Len's.

"Yes, I believed him. Mr. Grant confessed, confessed again, gave his reasons for blowing up the museum, and bragged about what a fine job he'd done, how proud he was that he had done it. He was convincing, and despite the fact that, in my opinion, what he did was crazy, he sounded sane to me."

"Thanks, Mr. Molinari. Your Honor, I have no more questions for this witness."

CHAPTER 37

YUKI SAW CONNOR Grant speak to Elise Antonelli from behind his hand, and after a moment
Judge Hoffman asked, "Mr. Grant, do you wish to
cross-examine the witness?"

"Yes, Your Honor. Yes, I do."

Grant got up, crossed the room to the witness
box, and said, "Mr. Molinari, first, I'm sorry that
you were injured. You must still be in a lot of
pain."

Joe said, "I can handle it."

Grant went on.

"Do you love your wife?"

Parisi yelled, "Objection, Your Honor. Irrelevant and out of line because it has nothing to do
with anything."

Grant said, "Goes to the veracity of his testimony, Your Honor."

"Overruled, Mr. Parisi. Mr. Molinari, please answer."

"Yes. I love my wife."

Grant said, "So if your wife said to you, 'Joe, this
is what Connor Grant said to me,' and you actu-

ally didn't remember hearing anything, you'd be inclined to support your wife, wouldn't you?"

"Are you asking me if I'm lying?"

"Are you?"

"I am not."

"Let me ask you this," Grant went on. "Did you record my so-called admission?"

"No."

"Did you see me run from the building?"

"No."

"Isn't it true that my so-called confession could have been the dazed mumbling of a stunned bystander—me? Is it possible that your wife made the confession up and you're just backing her to the hilt?"

Parisi roared his objection. The judge sustained it. Parisi moved to strike the defendant's last question, and Hoffman asked the court reporter to so strike. Connor Grant apologized and said that he had no more questions.

Grant looked quite smug when he returned to his seat, and Yuki understood why. He'd made his point. Then he'd drilled in on it. And he'd concluded his questioning with the simple message that Joe's corroboration was a feature of his marriage, not his memory.

Joe's testimony had been terrific.

Would the jury believe him?

Yuki's silent mantra started up without prompting.

You're prepared. Len's the best. The case is solid. Trust the jury.

CHAPTER 38

YUKI, LEN, AND I sat around the big man's desk with our sandwiches, accompanied by the sounds of traffic whizzing by on Bryant.

As a witness, I wasn't allowed inside the courtroom except to give my testimony, but Yuki filled me in on what I'd missed, crowing, "Linds, Joe was perfect. He got it all right, and being a victim of the blast added to his credibility. I wish you could have seen him."

Yuki was pumped. Len was confident. I was bummed that Grant had chopped my testimony into pieces with four short, sharp questions.

"Geez, that's great. What a relief. And by the way, I want a do-over."

"You were fine," said Red Dog. "You laid it out. The jury got you. Grant's cross didn't hurt you, Lindsay."

"No," I said. "So why am I worried?"

Yuki said, "You're worried about our lack of physical evidence. Can't be helped. God knows we turned over every stone—his house, his friends, his story, the pier. Still, if there hadn't been such a public outcry, if we'd had more time, maybe we could have found something physical in that vast pile of wreckage on Pier 15."

I nodded. I understood the pressure. The bombing of Sci-Tron had been worldwide news when it happened and was superheated now because of the trial. Reporters were ambushing court workers in the parking lot. Clogging the street with their satellite trucks. Calling us at all hours for quotes. Until a political or celebrity scandal or an even bigger tragedy pushed the bombing off the front page, the media would feed the beast at our expense.

And there was also internal pressure to move smartly ahead and get a conviction. Parisi was up for reelection this year. So was the mayor.

"You think we missed something?" I asked.

Parisi's brow wrinkled and he put down his grilled cheese to answer me.

"No. I don't, or I would have put the brakes on this thing. Lindsay, you know as well as we do, the city had to crash that crime scene quickly. Had to search for survivors and bodies. Had to re-open the piers and the street. Look, there's no way that nutjob committed the perfect crime. He's going away. For good."

"Better believe it," Yuki said.

When I'd handed Connor Grant off to the squad car in front of Pier 15 two months before, I'd been sure we had the right guy headed for a probable slam-dunk conviction. That was once upon a time, long, long ago.

Parisi chucked pickles and used paper goods

into the trash. He checked the time on the wall clock with the growling red bulldog graphic on its face, and then he addressed my concern again.

"Lindsay. Juries do what they do. Our case is good and it's the case we have."

"I know."

I believed in Parisi and Yuki. I also believed in Connor Grant's shrewdness. His audacious crime reminded me of the Boston Marathon bombing, with one exception. Connor Grant didn't run and hide.

It hit me for the first time.

Yuki read my expression.

"What is it, Lindsay?"

"New thought. Grant *wanted* to be caught. He *stood* there. He confessed to a *cop*. Maybe this trial is part of his 'magnificent masterwork.'"

Len said, "Then he's going to have a lot of time in a cage to think about what he did wrong."

CHAPTER 39

COURT RESUMED AND Judge Hoffman asked the People to call their next witness.

Yuki called Charles Clapper, director of San Francisco's forensics lab. After Clapper had been sworn in, Yuki asked him preliminary questions: his title, the scope of his job, his background in forensics. Then she asked him to tell about the defendant's garage laboratory.

Yuki asked, "Were there bomb-making materials in Mr. Grant's lab?"

"Yes. We found implements and chemicals that could be used to make explosives. Quarter sticks of dynamite, black powder, cardboard tubes, sealing wax, rolls of green stuff that's called rocket fuse, and chemical colorants often used for fireworks. Glass jars of BBs and nails. Assorted lengths of pipe."

Under Yuki's questioning, Clapper testified that in his opinion the principal bomb used in the museum was a compression bomb that had been made with a gas-filled container and ignited by a detonator, either remotely or with a preset timer.

He said, "It wouldn't take much exploded gas to change the pressure inside that building. That'll cause what's called a high-order explosion that will disintegrate glass, any kind of paneling.

"It brought the roof down," Clapper said, "and the bowstring trusses crushed those second-story pedestrian bridges. The smaller bomb was probably C-4 with a timer device, probably placed near one of the posts supporting the center dome in order to finish off that whole house of cards."

"Could that second bomb have been timed to kill fire and rescue?"

"Secondary blasts are often set for that purpose."

Yuki asked, "Were these two types of bombs described and illustrated in Mr. Grant's notebook?"

"Yes. Chapter 9 was about the use of C-4 and other plastic bombs. Chapter 14 was devoted to compression bombs."

"In your opinion, was Mr. Grant capable of building and setting such bombs?"

"In my opinion, he could have practically done it blindfolded."

Yuki asked if remains of the bombs had been found at the scene, and Clapper answered, "A fire extinguisher with both ends blown off was recovered from the bay off Pier 15. That would be the remains of a compression bomb. The C-4 would have vaporized without a trace."

Yuki thanked Clapper and turned him over to the defendant.

Grant stood, buttoned his jacket, and approached the witness. Yuki admired his composure. Honestly, if it weren't for his patchy shave, she could believe that he was an actual high-priced litigator.

"Director Clapper," said Grant, "did you find any kind of gas or gas containers in or around my house or car or lab?"

"No."

"Did you find *any* evidence—a cell phone with a record of an outgoing call that can't be identified, fingerprints at the scene, records of a fire extinguisher purchase, or *anything*—that linked me to that explosion?"

"No."

"Thanks, I have no other questions for this witness."

Yuki said, "Redirect, Your Honor."

The judge said, "Go ahead, Counselor."

Yuki stepped out from the prosecution table, walked to the witness box.

"Director Clapper, where could a person obtain a container for a compression bomb?"

"Any hardware store, home improvement store. You can get a fire extinguisher, big one, like the one that was used, for about fifty bucks. If you wanted to use a pressure cooker, every big-box store in the country sells them."

"And gas. Is that hard to get?"

"Nah. Bottled gas, natural, propane, argon, it's all available in those same kinds of outlets. The perchlorate, any chemical supply company has that."

"Could you buy these implements for cash?"

"Sure."

"So, no, there wouldn't be credit card records.

And if someone wanted to plant such a bomb any-time in advance of the explosion, hypothetically, would that be possible?"

"Yes. That building had no metal detectors. They couldn't. Exhibits were coming through the doors, being set up and changed out nonstop. Someone could have wired up the bomb, brought it into the building. Could have left a fire extinguisher anywhere it wouldn't have looked out of place, including as a swap for an active fire extinguisher. Easy enough to slap a glob of C-4 onto a girder.

"In fact," Clapper said, "hypothetically, if a person had a degree in science and a working knowledge of explosives, it would be ridiculously easy."

"Thank you, sir. That's all."

With a stern look the judge silenced the whispers that swept through the gallery. Then Connor Grant stood up and said to Clapper, "Just a couple more questions for you, sir. Hypothetically, you say, a person could have left a bomb in Sci-Tron. Ridiculously easy. The implication is that even you could do it, isn't that right?"

"Hypothetically," Clapper said drily.

"Did *you* plant the bombs in that building?"

"No. I did not."

"Well, *I* didn't do it, *either*. That's all I have for you, sir."

CHAPTER 40

AFTER CLAPPER LEFT the stand, Yuki called Margaret Callahan, a motherly-looking thirty-something woman in a peach-colored suit and tortoiseshell glasses. She told the court that she was a bank teller and had been on her way home from the Chase Bank at Embarcadero Center when she'd heard what she thought was a sonic boom and had seen the explosion of glass filling the sky. She'd taken a video with her phone.

Yuki asked, "Is there anyone in this courtroom you recognize from that evening of August 3?"

"Yes." She pointed to Grant. "I saw the defendant there."

Yuki teed up her video presentation. Len opened the screen, adjusted it so that the jury could see, and asked the court officers to dim the lights.

Yuki pressed the remote, and after the first frames appeared, Connor Grant objected and Yuki paused the video.

"Judge, this isn't fair. The video will only serve to prejudice and inflame the jury."

Yuki said, "Your Honor, this video shows the

scene at Sci-Tron in the immediate aftermath of the bombing. The jury needs to see the effects of this crime in order to render a verdict."

"Overruled, Mr. Grant. Let's see the pictures," said the judge.

Yuki turned her attention back to her witness and the frozen first second of the video, and asked, "Will you please describe this image?"

Callahan said, "That's the defendant in the left front section of the picture, facing what had been Sci-Tron. A few seconds later he turned for a moment toward where I was standing."

Yuki advanced the video, which revealed the defendant's face.

"How did he appear to you, Ms. Callahan?" Yuki asked.

"Delighted," said the witness.

"Could you narrate the rest of this two-minute video?"

Yuki started up the video again. Now the camera was pointing directly at the crowd that was racing away from the explosion and directly toward where Callahan stood with her phone.

The video was of medium-grade resolution, but even when the shot was marred by shaking or jostling, the image of the skeletal remains of the museum, the whooping sounds of sirens as ambulances and fire engines screamed up to the pier, the distant image of a survivor being pulled from the wreckage, brought the full horror of this scene into courtroom 2A.

Sounds from the gallery competed with the

audio. Cries were heard. An elderly man moaned loudly, then rushed from his seat and ran toward the exit. A woman followed him out.

Yuki asked for the lights to be turned up, and when the doors were again closed, she thanked the witness. A clearly angry Connor Grant stood and approached her.

He greeted her and then said, "Ms. Callahan, can you connect me in any way to that explosion?"

"You were standing on the sidewalk."

"And you? Where were *you* standing?"

"Behind you."

"And were you connected to the explosion?"

The witness stared at Grant until he said, "I guess that's a no."

The witness was dismissed, and as she left the courtroom, Yuki thought about Grant's astonishing skill in disabling witnesses without implicating himself.

Judge Hoffman said, "Will the prosecution call their next witness."

Parisi stood, saying, "The People rest."

The judge turned his eyes to the defense table and said, "Mr. Grant, are you ready to present your case?"

Grant said, "Your Honor, I'd like to add a witness to my list, Ms. Annalee Shaw."

Len Parisi got to his feet and said, "Approach, Your Honor?"

The judge beckoned to counsel on both sides, and when the four were in front of him, Parisi said, "This is very late for the defense to be coming up with a new witness."

Grant said, "Your Honor, I only became aware of this person's name yesterday, and it took our investigator until now to locate her. She can speak to my whereabouts and frame of mind before the bombing."

Parisi said urgently, "This is completely out of bounds. We haven't deposed the witness, Judge. We must have time to do that before she can testify."

Hoffman said, "Mr. Grant, make this witness available to the prosecution immediately. Mr. Parisi, take the rest of the day and all of tomorrow to check her out. We'll resume the proceedings on Thursday."

The judge adjourned the court, leaving Yuki to wonder about the open switch of this new witness. What the hell was Connor Grant pulling now?

CHAPTER 41

JULIE AND I were sitting together on a lounge chair beside the indoor pool at Pacifica Rehab Center, where Joe had been living since his release from the hospital.

The pool room was large, with many floor-to-ceiling windows, a huge aqua-blue pool with ropes separating the lanes, and a lifeguard perched in a tall chair mid-pool. Families grouped around small tables, and a half dozen swimmers did laps to the soft music coming through the speakers.

Julie-Pie was wearing a candy-striped tutu of a bathing suit, her dark hair in two little pigtails above her ears. I wore jeans and a white cotton blouse over my two-piece, not sure if I would swim or watch Julie and her daddy from the sidelines.

Julie shrieked.

I looked up and saw Joe rolling toward us in his chair, the scars showing vividly on his scalp and arm, his right leg still encased in a walking boot. I had been afraid of Julie's reaction to seeing Joe this way, but I'd worried for nothing.

She screamed again, this time, "It's Daddy," and

she ran across the tiles in her bare feet and into his open arms. She climbed onto Joe's lap, and he hugged her to him and rolled over to my chaise.

I got up and gave Joe a gentle hug.

"So glad to see my girls," he said, his voice breaking with emotion. Julie didn't notice. She was singing out, "Let's go. Let's go in."

Joe said, "Next time, sweetheart."

"Noooooo."

I watched and listened as Joe explained to our two-year-old that he still needed help getting in and out of the pool, but that he was getting better really fast.

He asked me, "Lindsay. You brought a suit?"

"I did."

I stood up and wriggled out of my jeans. I tried not to make a big production out of it, but I knew Joe was watching me undress. It had been eight months since we'd lived together, made love, had breakfast with the baby, been a family.

I turned away while unbuttoning my blouse, flashing on our last delicious romp before Joe went off the radar without warning, without sending even a text message. His voice mailbox had been full, his car had been gone. No one had seen him. Those lost days were agonizing. I'd thought he was dead.

By the time Joe resurfaced two weeks later, it was because our cases were entwined. Of course, I hadn't known he even had a case. He offered an explanation but not much of an apology. He expected me to understand that his secret assignment from the CIA was a duty and a sacrifice, and that when he said "country first," it didn't mean that I was second in his heart.

But his actions told the truth.

He *had* put me second, and there had been no hiding from myself what I'd started to piece together about a mysterious blonde, a double life in his past, and the real possibility of more of the same in the future.

So for my own protection I'd kicked Joe out and armor-plated my heart. Who could blame me?

Now I walked over to the curved tile steps and into the pool, and once I was seated there in the shallow end, I reached for Julie. My little girl, who looks so much like her father, toddled over to me and wrapped her arms around my neck.

I held her and danced with her and helped her swim with the noodle and the boogie board, while Joe cheered from his chair.

Once I was sufficiently wrinkled and cold, I took Julie and my bag to the dressing room to shower and dress. When we reemerged, our dear and precious child broke away from me and ran to Joe.

"Hey, Jules," I said, sitting down on the chaise. "Shall we have dinner with Daddy before we go home?"

Joe said, "Sorry, but I can't, Lindsay. I've got PT in a couple of minutes. Rain check?"

"Sure."

I tucked in my blouse, tied my shoelaces. Joe said my name and caught my eye.

He said, "I'm going to make everything right, Lindsay. I mean it."

I nodded. Could he do that? Was it possible?

"Mommy. Let's go. Okay?"

I kissed Joe on the cheek and said, "Take care."

I saw the question on his face as I picked up Julie and headed for the door. I understood the question. But I didn't know the answer.

I settled Julie into the car seat in back and saw a folded piece of paper on the floor. I knew it was the list of the dead and injured that Brady had handed me after Sci-Tron.

I opened it up and read the list. I found Joe's name on the injured list. And then I saw another name that I'd either not read two months ago or not remembered.

Sophie Fields was on the list of fatalities of the tragedy at Sci-Tron. Sophie Fields had died.

CHAPTER 42

IT WAS THURSDAY morning, the second day of Connor Grant's trial, and Yuki was very ready for it to begin.

The jurors were in their box. The judge was at the bench in conversation with his clerk. The gallery was full and the doors were closed. The court officers had formed a line blocking the door, and two others flanked the bench, guns on hips, eyes scanning the room.

Cameras rolled from the corners of the ceiling.

Yuki and Len had deposed the late-breaking witness, Ms. Shaw, the day before. Apparently, this recently added witness was Grant's idea, and in Yuki's opinion, he was taking an unnecessary risk. But Antonelli looked relaxed. No doubt, she was glad enough to shift the burden of the outcome to her former client. Win or lose, there would be plenty of media exposure for Antonelli.

Judge Hoffman spoke. "Is the defense ready, Mr. Grant?"

Yuki glanced at the defense table and saw that

Grant and Antonelli were conferring behind their hands.

Grant stood up. "The defense calls Annalee Shaw."

A court officer opened the door and a young woman entered. She wore a slim leather skirt, a tight knit top, and high heels, and her glossy auburn hair fell loose to the middle of her back. Ms. Shaw took the stand, and after she'd been sworn in, Mr. Grant began his direct exam.

"Ms. Shaw, what is your occupation?"

"I'm a graduate student, going for my doctorate in literature."

"Have you met me before?"

"Yes."

Grant asked, "Were we together the evening of August 3 between 6:00 p.m. and 7:30?"

Parisi said, "Objection. Leading the witness, Your Honor."

"Overruled. I'm going to allow it."

Grant repeated his question, and the witness said, "That is correct."

"Why do you remember the exact time?"

"Because," Ms. Shaw said quietly, "you hired me for an hour and a half starting at six."

The judge asked Shaw to speak up, and after she repeated her answer, Grant asked his next question.

"We spent this time together in the Hotel Slocum on Battery Street, a few minutes' walk from Sci-Tron, is that correct?"

"Yes."

"Was I carrying a bag of any kind?"

"No, nothing."

"How did I seem to you?" Grant asked.

"When we were together?"

"Let me be more specific. During the time we spent together, did I have an attitude that would suggest to you that I was going to blow up Sci-Tron? Was I nervous? Or agitated?"

Parisi rose ponderously to his feet.

"Objection. Mr. Grant is asking the witness to speculate."

The judge sustained the objection, and Grant said, "I asked for her interpretation of my behavior. But I'll rephrase. Ms. Shaw, did I tell you anything that would lead you to believe that I had plans to blow something up?"

"No."

"Thank you. I have no other questions."

Parisi got up, scraping his chair legs loudly against the floor, and approached the witness.

"Ms. Shaw, how do you know Mr. Grant?"

"A friend gave him my name."

"I see. For what purpose?"

Shaw said, "It was...transactional. I needed to buy books. Connor gave me five hundred dollars."

"I see. Do you have any knowledge of the defendant's whereabouts *before* he met you at the hotel at six o'clock?"

"No. I only met him the one time."

"So he could have rigged bombs to blow up prior to your...assignation?" said Parisi.

Grant stood up and yelled, "Objection."

Yuki knew the judge would sustain the objection, and he did. Connor Grant was...impressive.

Parisi said, "Thank you, Ms. Shaw. That's all."

The witness stood up, and Parisi, who had started back to the prosecution table, wheeled around.

"I'm sorry, I have one other question. You're still under oath, Ms. Shaw."

The witness sat back down.

"Ms. Shaw, you have testified that Mr. Grant paid you for your time. Did Mr. Grant also pay you for your testimony today?"

The witness recoiled. Then she said, "He only told me to tell the truth."

"Thanks, Ms. Shaw. No more questions."

CHAPTER 43

GRANT LOOKED QUITE at ease when he called his next witness. "The defense calls Lieutenant Jackson Brady."

Yuki was well aware that Brady was on the defense witness list, which was pretty outrageous and another of Connor Grant's risky moves. Still, it was a little shocking to see her husband come through the doors and walk to the witness stand.

After swearing to tell the truth, he took his seat in the box.

Grant said, "Just a few questions, Lieutenant. You head up the Homicide squad of the SFPD's Southern Station, is that correct?"

"Yes, it is."

"You and your team were responsible for finding and arresting the person or persons who blew up Sci-Tron, right?"

"That's right."

"Sergeant Boxer works for you, correct?"

"Yes."

"And you two were the members of the police department who interrogated me the morning after the bombing?"

"Correct again."

Grant shot a look at the jury, as if saying, *Get this.* He asked, "During that long interview did I ever say or indicate that I had anything to do with the Sci-Tron disaster?"

"No, you did not."

"But you investigated me anyway."

"Of course," Brady said evenly. "You were our primary suspect. You had told Sergeant Boxer that the bombing was your work."

"So she *says.* As a result of whatever she thought she heard, you went to my house, my place of business, spoke to my neighbors, my banker, my dry cleaner. The list is long."

Yuki could see the muscle in Brady's cheek twitch. She thought, *Please, sweetie, don't let him get to you.*

Brady said, "We spoke to anyone who might know your whereabouts before the bombing and anyone who might have insight into your character."

"Lieutenant, did you find any direct evidence linking me to the bombing at Sci-Tron?"

"We found circumstantial evidence, Mr. Grant. Your presence at the incident. Your avid interest and expertise in explosives. Your notes found in your laboratory."

"So to be sure we all understand, the answer is no. You found *no* physical evidence at the site of the bomb—*no* DNA, *no* fingerprints—and there were *no* witnesses who could connect me to the bombing, isn't that correct?"

"Most homicide cases are built on circumstantial evidence."

"Please answer the question, Lieutenant. Did you find any direct evidence connecting me to the bombing, yes or no?"

"No," said Brady. "But we have plenty of reason—"

"Your answer is no. You have found *no* direct evidence, right, Lieutenant Brady?"

"Right."

Yuki reminded herself to breathe. Brady was doing fine, walking a narrow line between answering the question and underscoring the truth. Grant pressed on.

"Lieutenant, did you have any other suspects?"

"No."

"None at all? No one who had a grudge of some kind? Maybe a terrorist group? GAR, for instance?"

"The video purporting to be from GAR was a frat-boy prank. So no."

"So you concluded that even lacking physical evidence against me, I was the person who perpetrated this horrible tragedy?"

Brady just stared at Grant.

"Answer the question, Lieutenant. Lacking physical evidence against me, did you have no other suspects but me, yes or no?"

"You admitted to the bombing before you claimed ignorance," said Brady.

Grant shouted, *"Your Honor."*

The judge asked the witness to answer the question.

Brady said, "We had no other suspects."

Grant put his hands in his jacket pockets, looked down, and seemed to be gathering himself for his next charge.

"You've stated that I was your only suspect, isn't that right, Lieutenant Brady? And still you charged me and are part of a conspiracy of law enforcement to tar and feather me on my way to the gallows."

Yuki stood, saying, "Objection, Your *Honor*. Mr. Grant is argumentative. Move to strike Mr. Grant's remarks."

Judge Hoffman said, "Sustained." He ordered the statement to be stricken from the record and instructed the jury to disregard Mr. Grant's characterization of the proceedings. "Don't do that again, Mr. Grant."

Grant said, "I'm sorry, Your Honor. I didn't realize that was against the rules."

The judge said, "Move on, Mr. Grant. Do you have any other questions for your witness?"

"Yes, I do." Grant asked, "Lieutenant Brady, are you related to anyone involved in this trial?"

Brady shifted in his seat. Yuki felt her heart contract and then resume beating with a hard, rapid patter. A dense silence pervaded the courtroom as everyone listened for Brady's answer.

Brady said, "ADA Castellano is my wife."

"I see," said Grant. He pivoted to look at the jury. A sunbeam came through the windows at just that moment, lighting his face. He went on. "So let me see if I've got this right. You're in charge of this one-suspect case, and your wife is prosecuting me. Is that collusion or something? I'm not sure of the term."

"It's nothing," said Brady. "My wife and I are professionals. We have never discussed this case together."

"That's what you'd like us to believe, but I think otherwise. We have the sergeant's husband, Mr. Molinari, backing up my so-called confession, and now—"

Parisi was on his feet, yelling, "Objection," and Grant shouted over him.

"You and your wife are nailing me to the cross. What would you call that, Lieutenant? Conspiracy? Railroading?"

"I call it *bullshit,*" said Brady.

The judge banged his gavel and admonished counsel and instructed the jury to disregard. He then told the gallery to quiet down immediately or people would be removed from the courtroom.

Yuki was watching Connor Grant. For the first time she saw rage cross his face, and he was transformed from the mild high school teacher to something twisted and monstrous.

Grant shouted at Brady, *"One suspect. No evidence."*

Judge Hoffman slammed down his gavel and shouted back at Grant.

"Sit down, Mr. Grant. Speak out of turn again, or cause any disruption at all, and you will be watching this trial on closed-circuit TV. Do you understand me?"

Grant apologized to the court and said, "Judge, I ask that this be stricken from the record."

"No, there's no reason to strike that, Mr. Grant. Is the prosecution ready for cross?"

Parisi stood.

"Lieutenant Brady, have you colluded with ADA Castellano?"

"No. We have a Chinese wall at our house, and we respect it."

"Please tell the jury what a Chinese wall is."

"We don't discuss the case together. Ever. Period."

"Lieutenant, thank you," said Parisi. "Now here's a hypothetical question. If you were going to destroy evidence—DNA, fingerprints, video cameras, et cetera—would blowing up the crime scene with a hard-force explosion accompanied by a flash fire do the job?"

"Absolutely. There was nothing left of Sci-Tron but six tons of granulated rubble."

Parisi thanked Brady and told him that he could step down.

CHAPTER 44

AFTER THE LUNCH break, as everyone resumed their places, Yuki took her seat at the prosecution table. Len sat down heavily beside her.

Len seemed to have recovered his composure, but Yuki was still reeling from the accusation that she and her husband had colluded. The worst part of the assault on Brady's credibility was how Grant had brilliantly summarized his defense in four words.

One suspect. No evidence.

If Antonelli had coached him to do this, kudos to her.

Antonelli sat quietly by as Grant introduced his character witnesses: his priest, his banker, and last, Kenneth Evan Miller, an eighteen-year-old student at Saint Brendan who was president of the senior class.

Kenneth Miller had close-cropped blond hair and horn-rimmed glasses and wore a forest-green blazer with the school logo on a patch over the breast pocket.

Miller testified under Grant's questioning: "You

are a very devoted teacher. I'd say you have a warm relationship with your students, and I personally learned a lot from you."

Yuki was watching the young man closely. When she had deposed him, she'd felt that Kenneth Miller was holding something back. She was going to try to dislodge whatever that something was on cross.

After Grant had finished eliciting praise from his former pupil, Yuki stood, straightened her suit jacket, and crossed the polished wooden floor to the witness.

She said, "Mr. Miller, did Mr. Grant use his own unpublished work on explosives as a course book?"

"Sure. We learned about all kinds of bombs, from firecrackers to nukes."

"Did Mr. Grant cover any other branches of science?"

"Yes, he covered the basics. Look, I like him. I think he's very smart. But I'm under oath, right? So I've got to say I always thought he was obsessed with explosives."

Grant objected. "Judge, can he just volunteer his opinion?"

Judge Hoffman said, "You opened the door by asking his opinion of you, Mr. Grant. I want to remind you, this is your witness. Go ahead, Ms. Castellano."

"Mr. Miller, could you elaborate on what you mean by 'obsessed'?"

The high school senior looked toward the science teacher and said, "I'm sorry, Mr. Grant, but

I gotta say it." Then, turning back to Yuki, Miller said, "Mr. Grant is single-mindedly all about combustion, or as he has often said, 'The beauty and the power of explosions, the sound and the light, the beginning of creation and maybe the end of it, too.' There were many times when I thought he was fricking crazy."

Yuki thanked the witness and crossed paths with Grant as she returned to her table.

Grant didn't wait for her to sit down before he began his redirect examination of Kenneth Miller.

"Ken, when you say 'crazy,' that's a figure of speech, isn't it?"

Miller said, "I don't think so."

Grant said, "Let me put it this way. You like girls, Kenny?"

The boy stiffened in his chair. "Yeah, so?"

"Are you obsessed with them?"

"Okay. Maybe. Sometimes. Yes."

"Does that mean you're crazy or that you have a passionate interest?"

"Whatever you say, Mr. Grant."

"I'd say that while you might be girl crazy, you're not *insane*. Would you agree?"

Yuki called out her objection. "Leading, Your Honor."

The judge said, "Sustained."

Miller looked up at the judge, who said, "Don't answer."

"Nothing further," Grant snapped, adding under his breath, "Class dismissed."

Yuki didn't care what Grant said under his

breath. Ken Miller had said that Grant was obsessed with explosives, and he'd *detailed* that obsession, including a reference to life and *death*. Nothing Grant could say would negate that.

Yuki knew that she'd scored a big one for the team. Len whispered to her, "Good play, Yuki."

It *was* good. But was it enough?

CHAPTER 45

YUKI'S HAPPY MOMENT faded fast as the science teacher, who looked and sounded as normal as every person in the courtroom, including the judge and jury, got to his feet, straightened his tie, and buttoned his dark-blue jacket.

Connor Grant said, "Your Honor, I'm going to testify in my defense."

Hoffman said, "I suggest you use your adviser to question you."

"Yes, Your Honor. That's our plan."

Grant was on his own witness list, so it was no surprise to Yuki and Len that he would testify. Len had loved, loved, loved the idea of having the opportunity to grill him on the stand. But what they *hadn't* known prior to the trial was that Grant was so sharp, so nimble. Maybe the right word for him was *brilliant*.

Now Len told Yuki he wasn't sure he should cross-examine Grant at all. The defendant was not just slick, he was very compelling.

Grant took the stand and the oath. He adjusted his glasses, ran his hand over his face, and sipped some water as Antonelli approached.

As Yuki expected, Antonelli asked Grant if it was okay to call him Connor, and the next question was to ask how he was feeling. Grant said it was okay and he was feeling fine.

Antonelli proceeded to ask brief questions regarding where Grant had been on the evening of August 3 after leaving the Hotel Slocum. Grant said, "I was walking north along the Embarcadero."

Antonelli asked, "What did you see?"

Grant sketched in the moderate traffic, the perfect temperature, then jumped directly to "the thunderous explosion, the pink light on the flying hail of glass."

"I was absorbed in the entirety of it. I was awestruck," said Grant. "This was the explosion of a lifetime."

And then Grant cut Antonelli off before she could ask another question. He explained earnestly that he had made an offhand remark to the tall, blond-haired woman outside Sci-Tron, not knowing that she was a police officer until she had cuffed him.

Yuki objected that the defendant was ranting beyond the scope of the question, which was "What did you see?"

Hoffman said, "I'm going to let him run with this for another minute or so. Let's hear it in brief, Mr. Grant."

Grant thanked the judge and continued.

"I had been in a state of wonder. I was confused. I just didn't get why she was arresting me," Grant told the court. "Then I find out that she lied about what I'd said and her husband backed her up. I guess that's what married people do. More to the point, I think the jury should see how easy it is for an innocent person to be tried for a crime when people in positions of authority collude."

Antonelli said, "Connor, you've written a book-length manuscript on bombs. When this enormous explosion occurred in front of your eyes, was that a coincidence?"

"Yes."

"Did you bomb Sci-Tron?"

"No, I did not."

Antonelli asked, "Did you know about it in advance?"

"Absolutely not."

"Do you know anything about that explosion that you can tell the jury?"

"CSI director Clapper said that I could have built and set this bomb with my eyes closed. He's totally wrong. This was a very expert detonation. I couldn't have done it if there'd been a gun to my head."

Connor Grant turned to the jury. He looked utterly sincere.

"I feel very bad for the people who were killed and the families who were affected. I am also a victim. My name has been tarnished. I don't know if I have a job when this is over or if I'm going to go to jail for something I didn't do."

As Yuki got to her feet, Antonelli cut off her objection.

"Your Honor, we're done. The defense rests," said Antonelli.

Judge Hoffman said, "Cross, Mr. Parisi?"

CHAPTER 46

LEN PARISI STOOD up and, looking neither left nor right, walked across the floor and stopped a dozen feet from the witness box so that his voice would project and so that Connor Grant would have to speak loud and clear.

Parisi said, "Mr. Grant, do you have a degree in chemistry? Yes or no."

"Yes."

"Do you know how to make bombs?"

"Well, there are bombs and there are *bombs*."

"Yes or no, Mr. Grant, do you know how to make bombs?"

Grant sighed. "Yes."

"Do you know how to make a compression bomb?"

"It's not that hard."

"Yes or no, Mr. Grant."

"Yes."

"Do you have a laboratory at your home?"

"Okay. Small lab in my garage."

"We should take that as a yes?"

"Yes."

"Do you have a Sci-Tron membership?"

"Yes."

"Yes, you have access to Sci-Tron, a home lab, and explosive materials in that lab, and you know how to make a compression bomb, which is 'not that hard.'"

Antonelli stood, said, "Objection. Argumentative."

"Sustained," said the judge.

Parisi kept on rolling.

"Mr. Grant, were you standing within a hundred yards of Sci-Tron when it blew up?"

"Yes."

"Yes. You were right there. I have no further questions for the witness."

Every eye in the courtroom was on Parisi as he turned his back on Grant and returned to his table.

Judge Hoffman told the witness that he could stand down.

CHAPTER 47

I WAS GOING through backlogged e-mail at my desk in the squad room when Claire called.

She said, "Wanna splurge? I'm thinking noodles. Maybe fish."

"Asian Fusion on King?"

"Perfect."

It was the best idea in the world, and there was no one I'd rather have lunch with.

We met at Claire's car, and she drove us to the noodle shop on King Street. There was a line outside the restaurant, but by the time we were standing inside, two seats had opened at the counter.

We ordered tekka maki and spicy sesame noodles, and after the sushi chef placed the seaweed-wrapped raw tuna in front of us, we got to talking.

I told my BFF about taking Julie to see Joe, and she told me about her domestic concern.

Claire's husband, Edmund, plays bass with the San Francisco Symphony.

"He told me he can't stand the hours anymore and his arthritis is getting worse," said Claire. "I think he'd really like to stay home, work on compositions of his own. Rosie would love to have her dad pick her up after school. He'll collect social security in a couple of years. He's not a terrible cook."

"So dinner would be waiting when you got home."

"Dinner. Wine. Living on less, but also a less grumpy husband. Still thinking about it."

Sushi trays were removed and the very hot bowls of savory soup arrived. Between spoonfuls Claire said, "I wanted to talk to you about something else, Lindsay."

"Uh-oh. I think I hear spooky suspense music."

Claire laughed. "Yeah, well, I've been out on the medical examiner spooky music network and found out something interesting."

I said, "Shoot," pouring more tea for the two of us, and Claire went on.

"The pathologist at Metro Hospital took in a fatal heart attack victim a month ago. She thought that the heart attack was suspicious."

"Same MO as the others?"

"Yes. Needle mark in the haunch. No lethal toxins in the blood. Heart wasn't pristine, but didn't look like cardiac arrest. One distinct difference."

"Well, don't stop now."

"The victim was male, homeless, a drug addict. It's a miracle that the pathologist who found this needle prick thought something of it at the time. Made a note on the autopsy report. But no one claimed the body, so that needle mark wasn't investigated. However, there was a witness to the stabbing."

"Really. There was a witness?"

"A do-gooding citizen. A landscaper. Had his earmuffs on and was trimming some shrubbery or something. Saw the victim go down. Saw someone rush away. The landscaper had seen this homeless person earlier, given him a couple of bucks."

"You have contact info for me?"

"I know you're busy, Linds."

"Not too busy."

In fact, my last case had been a man who shot his wife, then dove off the Golden Gate Bridge before I could arrest him. After that I'd kept my desk clear for the trial.

"Good, because I'd like to work this case with you."

"Sure thing."

Claire took out her phone, tapped on the keys.

"Okay," said Claire. "I've sent you the name of the victim, contact info for the pathologist and the landscaper."

"Got it," I said.

"I'm telling you," Claire went on, "some stealthy needle sticker is out there somewhere with a drug that stops hearts and fades very quickly from the bloodstream. Lab tests haven't found the toxin."

"Can the landscaper ID the stealthy needle sticker?"

"You'll talk to him," said Claire. "I can get you pictures of the body. He's already been interred by the city."

"Nothing on missing persons, I take it?" I asked, putting down my spoon.

"Nothing that I found. I need some green tea ice cream. How about you?"

"Red bean for me," I said.

I was already thinking about this possible crime spree. Anything that could take my mind off of Connor Grant's trial was a relief on the order of a blessing.

CHAPTER 48

PARISI STOOD TO make his closing argument. Yuki stared up at him, thinking that with his black suit and red hair, the splash of red tie, he looked like a volcano starting to blow.

He walked toward the jury box and took a position near the rail. He said, "Ladies and gentlemen, this has been a difficult case to hear, and deciding on this case is one of the most important things you'll ever be asked to do.

"Mr. Grant is a very clever man. He's not a lawyer. Yet you're front-row witnesses to how skillfully he defended himself.

"He says he's not proficient enough to build the kind of bomb that destroyed Sci-Tron, and yet he has had years of studying and teaching about explosives, an obsession with bombs—all kinds, according to his own witness, Mr. Miller. Grant had all the materials a bomb maker could need. If he was missing something to make the bomb that could level Sci-Tron, whatever he needed could be found at a home improvement store for pocket change."

Yuki looked at the jury. They were rapt. Even Connor Grant couldn't take his eyes away from Leonard Parisi.

Parisi went on.

"Mr. Grant would like you to believe that his presence in front of Pier 15 at the precise moment the bomb went off was a coincidence. It was not. Mr. Grant told Sergeant Boxer and her husband, a highly knowledgeable former law enforcement professional who has been with the FBI and was deputy director of the Department of Homeland Security, that he blew up the museum. He described the explosion as a thing of beauty and said that he was proud of his work.

"It's awful to hear that, isn't it? I call it diabolical."

Len let his words hang in the air for a moment, then he walked along the jury box, hand on the railing, and he gave the jury his eye-to-eye attention.

Parisi said, "Mr. Grant had the means to build those bombs and the opportunity to plant them in the museum anytime and detonate them remotely. Why did he stand on the sidewalk, totally unafraid, as the crowds fled for their lives? Because he made that bomb. He knew the extent of the bomb's power. And he wanted to witness his homemade big bang, his peak science project and the culmination of his career as a teacher.

"It turns out to be an object lesson for Mr. Grant.

"Remaining at the scene to witness his work caused him to be ecstatic to the point that he didn't realize he was making a confession to a police officer until he was in the patrol car.

"Twenty-five people died as the result of that science project," said District Attorney Len Parisi. "Don't let this man get away with murder."

The judge called on Connor Grant, who went out to the well and stood behind the lectern.

Once again Yuki thought what a natural he was. She could see how a career as a high school teacher hadn't stretched him to his full capacity. Blowing up Sci-Tron, then defending himself in a trial of so much interest to the world, against twenty-five counts of second-degree murder? He was made for this.

"Members of the jury, as Mr. Parisi said, I'm not a lawyer," said Connor Grant. "So I'm talking to you as an accidental defendant, a person just like every one of you.

"You've heard the case against me. While I was still stunned by the force and the effects of the explosion, I supposedly admitted blowing up Sci-Tron. To be fair to Sergeant Boxer and Mr. Molinari, I think they misunderstood my astonishment and took it to be pride of accomplishment.

"They were wrong.

"Homicide lieutenant Brady told you that the police had only one suspect. *Me.* Why didn't they keep looking, when so many people had died and they had such nothing evidence? I'll tell you why. *They needed a patsy.* They needed to clean up the mess, and in a time when bombs are going off all over the world, they sought to calm the city down.

So they nabbed me and they piled on until they had some kind of case.

"It's what's called a rush to judgment."

Grant paused, as if he had been seized by emotion. He cleared his throat, apologized, and picked up where he'd left off.

"The prosecution's forensics expert testified that I could have built and set those bombs based on no evidence linking me to Sci-Tron.

"*There was no evidence. No motive.* Just hypotheticals. Can you believe that? Yes. Believe it. You heard it all right here.

"This case against me is entirely without merit. In fact, I am a victim of circumstance, and this entire case is based on supposition. There is not a witness nor a shred of tangible evidence tying me to this terrible crime.

"Here's the sum total of the prosecution's case.

"One suspect, no evidence.

"I'm asking you not to be swayed by the inflammatory rhetoric and the video of people screaming and the number of people who died in Sci-Tron. I didn't kill them.

"The judge will tell you that if you have reasonable doubt that I committed this terrible, regrettable crime, you must find me not guilty.

"Please. Don't ask me to pay for someone else's crime."

PART THREE

CHAPTER 49

A MAN WITH a slight build, thinning sandy-blond hair, and short arms, who could have been in either his late thirties or his early fifties, depending on the light and the angle, stood over the body on the sidewalk.

The deceased was a real estate broker who had been standing outside his office on Stockton having a smoke when a stranger with a sharp in his hand had come up behind him and jabbed him in the right buttock.

The broker had turned, given the stranger a questioning look, and grabbed at his chest, making a strangled "Whhaaaa" sound before dropping to his knees and falling facedown on the pavement.

The man with the blond hair was Edward Lamborghini, as in the Italian racing car, and was known as Neddie Lambo. Neddie started to laugh when the broker dude fell, but cautioned himself to stay cool until he was actually dead. That might take another minute or so.

Neddie looked around in all directions. No cars had stopped, no pedestrians had walked by, but there were people inside the office waiting for Mr. Homes for Sale to return.

Sadly, Neddie had to go. *Thank you, Mr. Homes. I am free. And you, you're as good as dead. You've got nothing to worry about anymore. Have a good trip.*

Neddie stuffed his weapon into a pocket of his khaki Windbreaker and walked casually away from the dead man, up to the corner of Stockton and Pine. He looked both ways, crossed at the green, and headed west toward home.

The traffic on Pine was moving, and there were even a few pedestrians making the climb up Powell to the cross street. Neddie began to trot as if he were out for a run. His mind was full of endorphins or serotonin—or some natural jet fuel created by his own special brain. As he ran, he exulted in his latest perfect crime.

The exhilaration he felt was like flying a kite in a lightning storm. No, it was like *being* that kite. The risk, the danger, the freedom of flight. He had *earned* his flights. That's why he was not just free, he was untouchable.

As for Mr. Homes, Neddie silently thanked him again for providing this excellent flight of well-being. He ran down the hill of Mason Street, feeling the incomparable rush.

Breathless, he turned the corner onto Bush Street, dashed in front of a couple who were taking their time, and made it to the other side before the light changed.

He began walking at a regular pace. When he was a block from home, he stopped in front of the frame shop on the corner and looked through the windows. There was a tall, gold-framed mirror on an easel, and he could see himself and the traffic flowing behind him at the same time. When he was sure no one had followed him, Neddie made his move.

CHAPTER 50

THE TWIN BRICK towers of the Hyde Street Psychiatric Center, known to the "clients" as the Hyde and Seek Loony Bin, were vine covered, connected by the one-story administrative block and fronted by a spiked wrought-iron fence.

An alley ran along the dark side of the North Tower, ten feet wide by a block long, bounded by the blank concrete wall of the Walgreens next door—the corner of healthy and happy.

Neddie slipped into the alley and went directly to the green metal fire door leading to the Loony Bin's garbage room.

The metal door squealed when he opened it, but he was the only one around to hear it. Commercial garbage days were Monday, Wednesday, and Friday, and this being Sunday, the overflow garbage was piled high in plastic bags, with a narrow path between them leading to the tunnel door.

Neddie unlocked and cracked open the painted wooden door to the tunnel that ran between the Loony Bin and Saint Vartan's Medical Center, the gigantic teaching hospital across the road.

Right away he heard the rattle of trolley wheels and saw the orderly pushing a food cart from the kitchen. Neddie popped inside the tunnel and closed the door behind him, hearing the solid click of the lock.

Another food cart came toward him. The orderly called out, "Hey there, Neddie! How's our Neddie? Lookin' good, Neddie."

He answered in a practiced, high-pitched falsetto, "Hey there, Mr. Larry. Neddie's good!"

He gave the orderly his bright-young-child look, then crossed the width of the fluorescent-lit tunnel and jogged up a flight of stairs to the top landing, which was the lower-level entrance to the North Tower. There was a keypad beside the doorframe, as well as a doorbell. Neddie knew the code to the keypad, but that was his secret. He pressed the button.

He waited a minute, and then the door swung open and Dr. Hoover was there.

Once, after Neddie first met Dr. Hoover, the doctor had given him a quizzical look and asked him, "You're just fooling with me, aren't you, Edward?"

Neddie had said, "Fool-fool-fooling with you." He had grinned brightly, like the brain-damaged, mentally challenged dolt he pretended to be. Hoover had said, "I'll see you in our session tomorrow, same time, okay, Edward?"

Neddie had said, "Same time!"

Dr. Hoover was smart and wary, but that was okay for now. Hoover kept Neddie on his game.

If Hoover ever got onto Neddie's act for real, he would have a surprise heart attack. What a shame. What a loss that would be.

Now Hoover said, "I was just looking for you, Edward."

"I went down for a snack," Neddie said, clapping his hands.

"I hear you. But it's time for dinner now."

As Neddie followed Dr. Hoover down the linoleum-floored corridor, past the dispensary, he sneaked the empty vial and the used syringe out of his Windbreaker pocket and dropped them into the needle disposal can outside the nurses' station.

A second later he ran, catching up to Dr. Hoover's long-legged stride, entering the common room and going from there to the noisy, joyful chow room that fronted on Bush Street.

Neddie squealed "Hellooooooos" and waved various hand signals to other patients, cupped the cheeks of Billy the Kid, saying, "Hiya Billy, Billy good?" He pushed Billy the Kid's wheelchair up to table 6 and took a seat at one end.

Dinner servers came by with the trolley loaded with big vats of food, ladled out the green beans and the mash, slapped down a side of fish next to the veg. Another server came with the jugs of lemonade, pouring it into upheld plastic cups, orderlies watching on the sides, breaking up the fights.

The Hyde and Seek Loony Bin was a zoo, all right, populated with some of the most peculiar people in the city.

Neddie knew how to fit right in. No one would ever suspect him. No one would ever find him here. They thought he was autistic. They thought he had fetal alcohol syndrome or that he'd been dropped on his head. They said he had a low IQ and couldn't live a productive life on the outside. But Neddie knew better.

He had been getting away with perfect murders for years. That—*that* was genius.

He held up his cup for lemonade, and when it was full to the brim, he sucked it all down.

Ahhhhhh. It was good to be Neddie Lambo.

And it was good to be home.

CHAPTER 51

YUKI WAS ON the phone with Brady when Len Parisi loomed huge in her office doorway.

"Jury's back," he said.

"I'll call you later," she said to her husband.

For the last two weeks, sleeping in the same bed with Brady had been impossible. He was the kind of sleeper that could jump awake if the faucet was dripping in the bathroom down the hallway. And she couldn't sleep without flailing, punching pillows, making a cocoon for herself with the blankets, and talking in her sleep.

So she'd "slept" on the couch, her mind poring over every word of the days of testimony and her interpretation of things said, not said, questions asked and answered or not asked at all.

Brady had called this trial her "comeback tour," and it felt that way to her. The Sci-Tron disaster was a big-league crime that would never be forgotten; nor would the horrible, insane defendant, who was as clever as the very devil. And Yuki felt rusty after the year of pro bono small potatoes.

Now Len was waiting for her and within the

next half hour they both would learn if the jury's decision was win, lose, or hung.

Yuki locked up her handbag and followed Parisi out into the busy hallway, threading the maze of cubicles and taking the elevator down to the second floor.

A sheriff opened the courtroom door for them, saying, "Good luck." Yuki smiled, said, "Thanks," and with Len headed up the center aisle, through the filled gallery toward the prosecution table.

As heads turned to look at her, Yuki read the anxiety on the faces of the friends and families of the victims, all of whom had suffered the sudden loss of loved ones and were now hoping for swift punishment for Connor Grant.

Yuki was right there with them.

She and Len took their seats, noting that the defense table was unoccupied, which was reasonable.

Grant's legal adviser, Elise Antonelli, had to bring a change of clothes for the defendant, wait for him to dress, then, along with two armed guards, escort him from the jail on the sixth floor, down the back stairs to the second floor, and through the side entrance to the courtroom.

Was Grant sweating the verdict?

Yuki hoped he was *drowning* in his sweat. She and Len had talked for days about what had gone right and what might have gone wrong in the People's case. Len, who rarely looked back, had questioned his decision to let Grant's statement "One suspect. No Evidence" stand rather than repeat what they had already fully refuted. Now, Len seemed to be having second thoughts.

Yuki had been sure his instincts had been correct and had said so to Len.

On the other freaking hand, reasonable doubt on the part of one juror could hang the jury.

Len checked his watch, and just then Antonelli and Grant breezed into the blond-wood-paneled courtroom through the side door. Yuki noted that Grant had aged in the two-plus months he'd spent in jail. His skin was pale. He needed a haircut. His beard was unkempt, and the scar cutting through his top lip was obscured by the growth of his mustache.

But despite his scruffy appearance, his clothes were clean and pressed and his posture was good. He looked confident.

Judge Philip R. Hoffman came through the door behind the bench. A low rumble of cross talk moved like an oncoming storm from the back of the gallery forward and was shut down hard by a few good bangs of the judge's gavel.

Hoffman said to the bailiff, "Bring in the jury."

CHAPTER 52

AFTER THREE DAYS of deliberation the jurors entered the jury box. Yuki searched their faces for tells. Several of them—the car salesman, Mr. Louis; the software engineer, Ms. Shannon; the elderly, retired haberdasher, Mr. Werner—avoided her gaze.

Len said, "Jesus," so softly no one heard him but Yuki, but that one barely audible word chilled the blood pumping at 120 beats per minute through her veins.

When the main doors were closed and guarded, the bailiff announced that court was in session. The judge said, "I've been told that the jury has a verdict."

The foreman, Dennis Lockley, stood. He was a chain-store pharmacist, forty-two, married, and the father of two boys.

"We have, Your Honor."

Mr. Lockley passed a folded sheet of paper to the bailiff, who carried it to the bench. The room was utterly silent as Judge Hoffman unfolded the paper, read it, and turned it back over to the bailiff, who returned it to the jury foreman.

The judge said, "The defendant will rise."

Grant and Antonelli stood and faced the jury, and Hoffman asked Lockley to announce the verdict.

Lockley read the name and number of the case and then said, "In the first count of murder in the second degree in the above entitled action, we find the defendant, Connor Grant, not guilty."

Connor Grant's face lit up with relief. His attorney clapped him on the back as a dissonance of gasps and shocked exclamations sparked in the gallery, caught fire, and exploded.

The gavel banged repeatedly. The judge issued loud warnings. When the noise quieted at last, he asked the foreman to continue.

Lockley read out twenty-four more not-guilty verdicts in the deaths of the other victims.

Yuki was frozen to the seat of her chair. She stared at the jury foreman, and when he sat down, she dimly heard the judge thank the jurors for their service and release Connor Grant from custody.

But it wasn't over.

A man in the gallery shouted the defendant's name, breaking Yuki's stunned paralysis. She turned to look at the man who'd shouted and saw him jump to his feet. He was in his early forties, Yuki thought, six feet, husky build, his dark hair slicked down tight.

He shouted at the former defendant, Connor Grant, "You did it, you *bastard. You killed my wife.* I'm Master Sergeant Cary Woodhouse. My dear wife was Lisa Woodhouse. Don't forget me. I'm the one who's going to make you pay."

Grant yelled back, "You're crazy. I'm an innocent man. I've always been an innocent man. Maybe *you* set off that bomb."

The judge's voice boomed. "Quiet! Court is adjourned. Bailiff, clear the courtroom."

Hoffman stood and disappeared through his private doorway, accompanied by the clamor of the crowd as they rushed for the exit.

Yuki felt Len's hand encircle her biceps, and she stood up like an automaton. Her mind filled with cases that had gone against her.

"Yuki, this isn't on you. You did a fine job. We couldn't prove what we knew, that's all. Grant is a smart mother. And a damned lucky one."

CHAPTER 53

IT WAS THE day Connor Grant had been found not guilty. Those of us who'd watched it on the squad room TV, which hung from the ceiling, saw the infuriated mobs that sprang up spontaneously downstairs on Bryant.

Reporters cornered men and women on the street and asked for their views on the not-guilty verdict of Connor Grant, and were told that the DA was to blame because clearly Connor Grant had blown up Sci-Tron. Not a smidgeon of doubt could be found.

An old chant was dusted off and repurposed.

"Hey, hey, ho, ho, Len Parisi's got to go."

Cindy Thomas was one of the reporters on the street. She interviewed the jury foreman, Mr. Dennis Lockley, for the *San Francisco Chronicle* and as a stringer for NBC.

Conklin and I were watching her when Brady came out of his office and pulled the side chair out from my desk and straddled it so he had a direct sight line on the monitor.

On-screen Cindy was shouting her questions

over the chaos of horns and chanting around her, and Lockley looked about as comfortable as a man standing in a puddle of gasoline surrounded by chain-smokers.

Cindy asked, "How did the votes break down?"

Lockley said, "It was unanimous for acquittal."

"No one thought he was guilty?" Cindy asked incredulously.

Lockley started to walk away. "I didn't say that," he said.

"Mr. Lockley," Cindy said loudly as he started to cross the street. "What are you saying? People thought he was guilty but couldn't vote that way?"

"Right," said Lockley over his shoulder, while breaking for the opposite side of the street. Jurors had the right to decline post-verdict interviews, and reporters shouldn't pursue them if they didn't want to talk.

Still, reporters noticed Lockley making his getaway and followed him as Cindy summarized her interview for the camera.

"What I'm hearing, David, is that the jury didn't find that the case against Connor Grant had been proven beyond a reasonable doubt."

This story was repeated all day as other jurors were interviewed. At quarter to four Len Parisi gave a less-than-two-minute press conference on the steps of the Hall.

"The verdict was decided by a jury of Mr. Grant's peers. He was found not guilty. I have to accept that. We all do. Thank you, no questions at this time."

I got hold of Yuki, and she filled me in on the whole ghastly post-verdict eruption in courtroom 2A.

"Not guilty on each of the twenty-five counts," she told me. "Then this retired army guy got up and he was livid. Cary Woodhouse. His wife, Lisa, had been killed in Sci-Tron, and he threatened to make Grant 'pay.' That's a quote. I thought everyone in the gallery was going to cheer."

I took the name of the guy who'd threatened Grant's life, went to Brady's office. Brady called Antonelli.

"Your client needs police protection," Brady said.

Antonelli put Grant on the phone, and Brady put him on speaker. Grant said, "I don't want to see another cop for as long as I live. Get me?"

"Someone threatened you, Mr. Grant."

"I'm not worried," said Grant.

Brady threw up his hands. We'd tried. He left for the day at five, which may have been the first time since I've known him. I left a minute or two after that. I had to fight off three reporters' requests for "Just one question, Sergeant" on my way to the car.

At home I cooked your basic spaghetti with marinara sauce and meatballs for me and Julie. We walked our good dog, after which I bathed Julie, read her a book with kittens and ponies in it, and put her to bed.

At eight I was starting to relax. I had shut off the TV and was ready for an early night in bed when Brady called.

There was no acceptable reason to ignore his call.

I said my name into the phone.

He said, "Boxer, here's a no-surprise surprise."

I listened as Brady told me that Connor Grant had called him directly. "He says gunshots were fired through his window. That someone is trying to kill him. He wants protection. You heard me. I told him I had wanted to assign cars to his house."

"I remember vividly," I said.

Brady scoffed. "Well, he's changed his mind. Done a U-turn. Conklin is on the way over to Bayview. You go, too. Maybe now that he's scared, he might blurt out something semi-useful."

I was wearing fluffy socks and my favorite pajamas. I'd been ten minutes from dreamland. "Okay," I said. "Okay, okay."

I hung up with Brady, called the darling Mrs. Gloria Rose. I asked her, "Will you do a shift with Julie, please? She's already eaten. She's asleep."

"When have I ever said no?"

I thanked the number one best nanny in the world, threw on clean jeans and a cotton pullover, jammed shoes onto my aching feet. After Mrs. Rose crossed the hall to my place, I looked in on Julie and told her I'd be home before she knew it. She rolled over and turned her face to the wall.

I told Mrs. Rose I'd call her. Then I booked.

CHAPTER 54

I TROTTED OVER to Twelfth Street, where I had parked my new secondhand Explorer, a newer model than my former beloved ride, which had been shot to pieces while I was behind the wheel.

The new car had bells and whistles I didn't need, but the same comfortable seat height, five-star crash rating, and curve control. Add that to its zippy pickup and quiet ride, and this was the perfect vehicle for me. Before pulling out, I called Conklin.

"I'm about twenty-five minutes out," I told him.

I heard sirens through my phone.

"I'm a block away," he said. "Suggest you step on it."

I gunned the engine and headed to Jamestown Avenue, in Bayview, where Connor Grant lived.

As it had been the first time I came to his place, the tidy wood-frame house, set back from the street and flanked by two concrete buildings, was hemmed in by a formation of squad cars. But now, in the dark, its plain, everyday exterior was animated by cherry lights whirling, flashing, and strobing the landscape.

Conklin was standing on the front steps of the house talking to Grant. I badged the uniforms between me and the front door and joined my partner and the psycho who was officially innocent of all charges.

If the shooter who had shot out his windows was watching, he could be on a rooftop or inside a parked car. To tell the truth, I didn't much care if Grant got picked off while standing on his porch. But I did care about my partner's safety and mine.

I said, "We should go inside."

We followed Grant into his multipurpose living room. I felt creeped out just being in close proximity to him, but still, there was an opportunity here. Everything about Grant seemed to be some kind of act. From the first time I met him, all starry-eyed in the face of death and destruction, to the time he cross-examined me like a professional legal sharpshooter, Connor Grant didn't compute.

I might never get into this house again, but maybe there was something in plain sight that would give me a peephole into the enigma that was Connor Grant.

I crossed the living room and walked through the open doorway to his office. There was an even bigger pile of mail than before stacked on the credenza, and next to his armchair were four plastic tubs of mail the post office had been holding for him.

Grant interrupted my thoughts.

He said, "Well, Sergeant, it took you long enough to get here."

I stifled a snappy comeback that he had rejected police protection and that I wasn't his personal muscle. Instead I said, "Why don't you tell us what happened?"

Grant pointed up to the second floor.

"I was upstairs watching a movie when the window shattered."

He pulled the collar of his shirt away to show us glass cuts on his cheek and neck. I nodded, but I had no sympathy for Grant. The little nicks in his skin only reminded me again of the shower of glass shards flying hundreds of feet in all directions. Lit by sundown for bonus points.

Grant said, "I rolled off the bed onto the floor. When the shots stopped coming, I peeked out the window. I saw a car lurch and head north. I got three letters off the license plate."

I wrote down the letters.

"What kind of car?"

"I couldn't tell. It was dark colored and had a boxy rear end."

"Like a van?"

He nodded. "Could have been."

"How many shots were fired?" I asked.

"Four or maybe five."

"Have you gotten any threatening phone calls?"

"Only three or four an hour on my landline. 'You're lower than pond scum. You should die.' I unplugged the phone."

I told Grant we'd try to get records of incoming calls from the phone company, and I jotted down his cell phone number for the record.

While Grant took Conklin around the small house to do a security check on the doors and windows, I switched on the lamp near Grant's easy chair and turned it so it lit up his library, which wrapped around two sides of the small room.

I had only a couple of minutes, but I gave his bookshelves another look. Scanning the spines, I saw books on law, art history, archeology, astronomy, and notable people from *A* to *Z*. Grant also had a section on guns, about three feet of shelving dedicated to explosives, a section on aeronautics, as well as a top shelf with books on psychology and computer science.

Besides my personal experience with Grant acting as his own attorney, Yuki had told me how he'd distinguished himself throughout the trial. Question: How had he managed to educate himself with law books and retain enough practical knowledge to put on a such a skillful defense against Len Parisi?

I pulled out an intriguingly titled book, *Satan's Advice to Young Lawyers.* I opened it and saw a bookplate: "This book belongs to" and the inscription "Sam Marx." A random sampling of three more law books had the same bookplate and inscribed name, Sam Marx.

Maybe Grant had bought the collection at a tag sale or from a secondhand bookstore. But why?

I heard footsteps on the stairs. Grant was telling Conklin, "I was falsely arrested and tried. My reputation has been trashed. Now I could be assassinated. I was stupid to turn down police protection, but now I demand it."

I left the living room and met Grant and Conklin in the foyer. "We'll get you round-the-clock surveillance for a while," I told him, "but if I were you, I'd move."

"You really have a hate-on for me, don't you, Sergeant?" Grant said. "Do I remind you of someone? Do you have a problem with intelligent men? Do you just like to throw your weight around? You should get over your superiority complex. You're not that superior."

I handed him my card, saying, "We'll check on that partial plate as well as incoming phone calls. Any more shooting incidents, call 911, then call me."

"You mean, if I'm not dead."

Conklin said, "Consider taking Sergeant Boxer's advice about moving. She's usually right."

CHAPTER 55

FIVE MINUTES LATER Conklin and I were sitting in his car in front of the mass murderer's sweet little blue-and-white house.

"I can't possibly say how much I hate that guy," I said.

"You've got good reason," he said. "Linds, just do what you're doing. Stay cool. We do our jobs and maybe some superhero will take him the fuck out."

"If only."

He laughed. My partner, the good cop.

Conklin fed the three letters Grant had given us into the mobile data terminal, while I watched the street. Five squad cars pulled out into the night, leaving two cruisers behind to protect the not-guilty mother of all dirtbags.

Conklin whistled through his teeth as the software ran all the plate combinations with the letters *WXL* in San Francisco.

"Got a Land Rover with a *WYL*," he said.

"Registered to?"

"Cary Woodhouse, of all people. Could be his plate or just pretty damn close to it."

We knew that Woodhouse had lost his wife in the Sci-Tron explosion and had threatened Connor Grant inside a packed courtroom.

"If Woodhouse did the drive-by, he wasted no time," I said. "What can we find out about him?"

Conklin tapped the keys and said, "He's a career soldier. Christ, the guy's an *actual* hero. Desert Storm."

While I stared up at Grant's shot-out bedroom window, Conklin phoned Brady and told him, "Grant got three letters off the probable shooter's plate. Two of them match Woodhouse's vehicle. I'm thinking this was harassment or a warning. If the shooter had seriously wanted to kill Grant, he could have come through the front door. Cheap locks, no cameras."

Brady's voice came over the speaker, telling Conklin he'd put out an APB on the vehicle in question and that he wanted us to drive to the Woodhouse residence.

"Report back," said Brady.

A CSI van rolled up to Grant's house and parked. I got out of Conklin's car, walked over to the van, and spoke to George Campbell, a former science teacher himself and now a CSI on the graveyard shift. We talked about the shots fired, and I asked him to call me when he'd gotten back the ballistics on the slugs.

"Put a hot rush on it," I said. "And Campbell, while you're hunting for slugs, if anything strikes you as weird or out of place, call me."

"I sure will."

I walked back to Conklin's car, thinking that even if Campbell found a notebook with actual hand-lettered instructions on how to blow up Sci-Tron, Grant would still be not guilty. Double jeopardy applied.

Still. I needed to know if he had done it.

Conklin buzzed down his window and said, "Ready?"

"I'll follow you."

I got into my car, switched on the engine, gave it some gas, and was two car lengths behind Conklin as we headed out.

CHAPTER 56

CARY WOODHOUSE LIVED in Parkside on Twenty-Fourth Avenue. The house was of the tiled-roof Mediterranean style that had been popular in the 1930s, and along with the similar homes on this street, it looked fresh and well tended.

Conklin pulled into Woodhouse's driveway behind a boxy, dark-colored Land Rover. I double-parked on the street, and Conklin and I put on our Kevlar vests and our SFPD Windbreakers over them. We approached the front door together.

I rang the bell, and in a minute the door opened.

The guy in the doorway was barrel chested, wearing a blue plaid flannel shirt and baggy cords, standing six feet tall in his bedroom slippers. He had a Bud in his hand.

I introduced myself and Conklin, asked if he was Mr. Cary Woodhouse.

"Yes. What's this about?"

Conklin said, "We'd like to ask you a couple of questions, sir. Better if we come inside."

Woodhouse flung the door wide open and said,

"Come right in. I'm on a streak, so I hope this won't take too long. Some of the boys have to get home to their wives."

I checked out the house as we walked in. Stucco walls, overstuffed furniture, framed photo of Mrs. Woodhouse draped in black hanging over the fireplace. An arched pass-through connected the living room to the dining room, where five men in their forties to midsixties sat around the snack- and beer-bottle-laden dining room table. They were holding cards.

Conklin said to Woodhouse, "We can talk in the kitchen."

"No, just come in and ask what you want. I don't have secrets from my friends and family."

Woodhouse took his seat at the head, named the men at the table, including his father, Micah, and his brother, Jeff. After turning down an offer to "pull up a chair," Conklin asked Woodhouse, "Have you driven your car this evening?"

"Of course. Went out for food and beer. What's this about?"

Conklin said, "About this shopping trip. Were you in Bayview?"

"Bayview? No, I went to the Lucky on Sloat. You didn't answer me, son, and I'm asking you for the third and final time before I kick you the hell out. What's this about?"

"Shots were fired through Connor Grant's windows this evening at around eight. A car was spotted leaving the area that matches the description of your Land Rover."

"Oh, I see. This is because I shouted at that scum sucker. Was he killed, I hope?"

One of the men at the table said, "Eight o'clock? Cary was right here at eight, wasn't he, boys?"

The men around the table agreed: "Yeah," "Uh-huh," "Right here," and "I can vouch for that."

Woodhouse smiled, put down his beer bottle.

"I've got, count 'em, five alibis. Any other questions?"

I said, "What kind of guns do you own, Mr. Woodhouse?"

Woodhouse said, "Oh, come on. I have a lot of weapons, and some of them are recently fired. I used them at the gun club range this morning. If you want to check them out, I guess you're going to need a warrant."

I said, "Mr. Woodhouse, if anything should happen to Connor Grant, you're suspect number one."

"Duly noted," he said, giving me a look that could stop a tank in its tracks. He went on to say, "I can't believe that *you,* of all people, are trying to protect that *maniac.* Please. Show yourselves out."

Woodhouse placed a deck of cards in front of the older man to his right.

"Dad, you're up. Dealer's choice."

Out again on the street, Rich and I said our good-nights. With luck, I'd be back in my favorite pj's in a half hour. As for dreamland, I wasn't sure I still had a ticket.

CHAPTER 57

NEDDIE LAMBO WAS pacing in Ward Six of the North Tower just after lights-out. He walked from window to window, to the bathroom, and back to the bunk room, restless as a man could be.

He thought about Mr. Homes, the broker he'd put down, and the story on *The Six O'Clock News Hour* about Salesman of the Month Bobby Riccardo's heart attack. That he was so young and so well regarded and how much he'd be missed—and it just *pissed* Neddie *off*. Big-time.

Yes, indeed, it was a good thing that Bobby Riccardo had gotten all the attention, but it was maddening not to get any himself. People had thought he was a true moron since he was a little kid, and he'd learned how to work that angle to perfection. But sometimes, like right now, he wished a woman, or even a shrink, would see that someone was home inside of Neddie Lambo. That he was someone very special and very smart.

Neddie paced some more. He looked at his sleeping bunkies, Fred Mouse and Quarter to Ten. He blew on Oscar's face until the old dude flipped onto his stomach. He hid Goose Thomson's shoe in Randy Rockefeller's trunk because Goose would go full-bore insane when he couldn't find his shoe.

But Neddie was getting nowhere fast. Or slow, either.

He had a lot of anger right now, thinking about that damned real estate salesman, and he had to blow it off. He had been at the Loony Bin for thirty-six years and had amassed many privileges. The best of them was not the bunk by the window, the seat at the head of the table, or the title of Dorm Dad.

It was that he could leave the Bin on his own.

Normally, he spaced out these trips abroad. He'd put down the broker only a week ago, but tonight, since the TV coverage of the big funeral for Bob-Bob-Bobby Riccardo, he felt an urgent need to fly.

But where to go?

Neddie knew the vast network of underground spaces beneath San Francisco as if he'd designed those secret places himself.

For one thing, there were the former speakeasies that had been the major entertainment during Prohibition. Along with the speakeasies there had been brothels galore, many of them underground and connected by secret passageways.

Many or even most of the older buildings from that time had storage rooms that went out under the sidewalks and sometimes under the streets, too.

Even ships were buried downtown, and Neddie had seen them, walked through and over them. It was just fantastic. He'd even been to a place under a saloon where sailors had been shanghaied, sold to merchant ships. And then there was the entire Embarcadero, with its wide sidewalk built over a beach and a bay.

It was all true.

Neddie knew where these secret rooms connected and where the tunnels surfaced. He had his own private runways and escape hatches under the buildings and pavement. He had done the cartography in his mind. He'd done it himself.

He was not as dumb and crazy and brain damaged as he appeared to be in the files and folders about him, in the books that the shrinks wrote about their patients, labeled with numbers instead of names, in his reflection in the glassy eyes of the nurses who hardly thought of him at all.

He tickled the feet of the man sleeping in the bunk next to his.

"Mike-Mike-Mike."

"What, Neddie? What do you want now?"

"I can't keep you safe from Meanies tonight, Mikey. I have to fly."

"Go, Neddie. I'm strong. Loud Mike can take care of himself."

Yesssss.

Neddie Lambo, Space-Time Traveler, King of the Underground.

Where should he go tonight?

CHAPTER 58

IT WAS AFTER 9:00 p.m. when Neddie took the stairs down from Ward Six to the basement-level tunnel, which was the corridor to many service rooms, including the kitchen and the laundry. It also ran between the Loony Bin and Saint Vartan's Medical Center.

Neddie wore a black hoodie under a hip-length denim jacket. His weapon of choice was in his pocket, and his most serious running shoes peeked out from the legs of his jeans.

Dodging the few orderlies and maintenance workers using the underground tunnel at that hour, Neddie stuck to the shadows, then exited through the medical waste room under Saint Vartan's and walked a block and a half overland to Jones Street.

Jones had once been a hive of speakeasies with escape hatches into underground hidey rooms, and Neddie knew the whole subterranean network better than anyone.

There, in front of the Wainscot, was one of Neddie's best portals. He sat on the curb and had to wait only a minute for a burst of traffic to pass before removing the storm drain cover at his feet and climbing inside. He smoothly replaced the cover and began his descent down the metal ladder, his eyes quickly adjusting to the dark.

Once he reached the bottom of the ladder, it was an easy sprint along the old speakeasy connector to the manhole at Sixth and Stevenson. Neddie was not only swift, he was nimble. He made the short hand-over-hand climb, listened for a break in traffic, then shouldered open the heavy lid capping the entrance to the tunnel.

Aboveground again, Neddie walked in darkness, making turns along well-traveled streets into narrow alleys, passing strollers and dog walkers in ones and twos in Sue Bierman Park. He kept his hood up, his hands in his pockets, his eyes down, finally taking a pathway at the end of Drumm to the Embarcadero.

Neddie found the Embarcadero, that superwide avenue running along the bay, exhilarating. There was so much traffic here, both car and pedestrian, that no one noticed him.

Several months ago he had made a *perfect* kill beside the Waterside Restaurant. The Beige Woman. But before he'd been able to *see* and really *feel* the thrill of her death, something unimaginable had overshadowed his own sweet success.

He'd been cheated.

Tonight he would take back what had been so rudely stolen from him. Tonight belonged to *Neddie Lambo*.

CHAPTER 59

NEDDIE CROSSED THE Embarcadero at Broadway and proceeded to a small patio with potted trees and benches next to the Waterside Restaurant, where customers had a smoke or waited for their rides.

As he stepped onto the patio, his fading memories of the Beige Woman flooded over him in HD and living color. He could see her now, wearing a beige-colored knit skirt and jacket. She had been deeply engrossed in her phone and was reading out directions to herself.

She hadn't noticed the slight man with sandy hair and deformed arms, so he had said, "Hey, I'm Neddie."

She had turned away, both showing her disgust and giving him a full view of the target.

He hadn't hesitated. He had pulled his fully loaded sharp from his pocket and had stuck her hard in her meaty haunch, pushing the plunger at the same time. She had grabbed at her rear end and swiveled to stare at him.

Neddie had had her attention *then*.

He had stared back into her gray-blue eyes for one long moment. Then she had wheezed, before stepping off the curb into oncoming traffic. A taxi-cab had just brushed her, but she had been off balance and had fallen. She had still been alive. She had been flapping and flailing in the gutter when there had been a boom, like a jet breaking the sound barrier directly overhead.

Neddie had seen the sky change from sunset to a blackout, smothering gray. He had known that he had to run and he had done so, camouflaged by the chaos, disappearing below the surface for long tunnel runs, reappearing on empty streets as if from *nowhere*.

But the loss of his big moment stayed with him.

He hadn't seen the Beige Woman die.

Tonight he would try to claw that moment back. There was no rush, no need to panic.

Before him ranged the whole panorama of promenade and restaurant and patio and sky. He relived the way the Beige Woman had looked at him and actually seen him just before she was hit by the taxi.

Neddie was filling in the missing details, going in for a close-up of her last breath—*when he was interrupted again.*

A police car cruising in a northbound lane pulled up only yards away from where he was standing. Two cops, a man and a woman, got out of the cruiser and headed toward him.

Neddie froze as they approached, blinding him with their flashlights. Why had they stopped for *him*?

"Any problem here?" asked the tall woman cop.

"No problem," said Neddie in his pitchy Nutty Neddie voice. "No problem at all, Officer. I was just looking at the water. Just looking at the *water.*"

The flashlight beam flicked up and down his body. What were they looking for? What did they see? Had someone witnessed his killing right here? Had that witness reported him to the police? Were cops watching this place to see if the killer returned?

Neddie shielded his eyes with a crooked fore-arm.

"Just looking at the *water,*" he said again.

The male cop said, "All right, then. Have a good night."

"Thanks, Officers. I'm going now. Going now. Bye."

By the time he'd crossed back over the Embar-cadero, his rosy and beautiful mood had changed to a menacing gray cloud, just as the sky had changed after he'd made his kill.

He'd been cheated again.

"This isn't fair," he said to himself. "Not fair at all."

CHAPTER 60

NEDDIE WAS WALKING west on Broadway, agitated, muttering, mad at himself for returning to the crime scene. It had been a rookie mistake and he'd gotten exactly *nothing* for it.

Now he had to take a different route home, throw off anyone who might be looking for him. Using the Transamerica Pyramid, directly to the left, as his guiding star, he walked at a normal pace, skirting the tourist magnet of North Beach.

Passing the Green Tortoise Hostel, he approached the intersection of Broadway and Columbus Avenue, all of the neon-blazing North Beach spread out to his right.

Cars sped past him. Crowds of so-called normal people laughed and joked and touched and teased. It was a world he wasn't part of, but—here was a gift—he could move through it *unseen*.

Nutty Neddie, a.k.a. Special Ed, continued on Broadway and hooked a left onto Powell, following it up to the top of Nob Hill, until one of his favorite flight paths was in view.

The cable car tracks turned from Jackson onto Powell, and Neddie waited for the car to rattle to a stop. He grabbed the bar and swung himself up, handed his Muni pass to the conductor.

The conductor looked at Neddie's pass, not his face. He was working, and this was one of six hundred tickets and passes he would check that night. Neddie was onboard, ready for takeoff. He worked his way to the front of the car and mentally urged the car to the crest of the hill—and then the car dropped over the top.

He loved this gliding feeling as the car plunged downward. Union Square was on the left, the Macy's sign was across the way, and the monument to Admiral Dewey stood centered in the square.

Moments later, too soon, the car squealed to a halt, and Neddie jumped off and headed east. His feelings of shame and loss at the cop stop near the patio were abating.

He had made his greatest strides from his biggest mistakes.

Notably, there was the "crime" that had turned his life into *this*.

Blazing light poured through the entrance of the Admiral Dewey Hotel. A taxi pulled up, and a doorman opened the taxi door for a couple dressed for a gala. The doorman walked them to the glass doors and opened them. As Neddie passed the hotel, he was struck by the sight of a woman standing alone forty feet away from the front of the hotel.

She looked to be in her late thirties, with light-brown hair in a long braid. She had a bland face that reminded him of the Beige Woman.

He would give her a test.

He walked toward her and heard himself say, "Hi, I'm Neddie."

Her gaze passed over him as she turned away without speaking.

Her disrespect, her *disgust,* sent a shiver through Neddie, and he saw that this was how he would rectify his earlier mistake. He turned toward the wall and loaded his sharp.

The woman with the braid was staring off into the distance when Neddie jabbed her in the buttock, delivered the payload, pulled out the syringe, and sidestepped out into the street.

He heard a short bark and turned to see the dead woman walking, her arms reaching out as she silently mouthed, "HELP."

"Sorry, no," Neddie said, passing her. "Goodbye," he said. "Almost nice knowing you."

A crowd of people piled out of the hotel, and immediately someone noticed the woman lying in the street. He heard a panicky male voice saying, "Hang on. I'm getting help." Then, "Oh my God. She's gone."

As the crowd dispersed, Neddie glimpsed the dead woman and sighed with pleasure. Job well done. And now, he had to go.

He walked at a normal pace up Stockton Street, crossed Union Square, nondescript in his hoodie and jeans in the dark. He ditched out onto Post Street, only dimly lit at this hour, and then Saint Vartan's loomed. He walked fast but not rushed, and ten minutes later the brick walls of the Hyde and Seek Loony Bin were in view.

The admin block was dark. There was an even darker void between the walls of the North Tower and the Walgreens, and Neddie slipped inside that shaft of blackness. He was as good as invisible. But inside his body Neddie was glowing like a neon-lit night.

Mission accomplished.

Neddie was Safe. And Neddie was Good. Very, Very Good.

CHAPTER 61

I WAS WITH Claire in the autopsy suite, staring down at a human heart in a stainless steel surgical bowl.

The victim, Sarah Summers Nugent, was lying nearby on a table, chest opened from her clavicle down, her face in repose.

Claire was saying, "This heart could run a marathon by itself."

"I'll take your word for it. What do you know about the circumstances?"

"Last night around ten she was waiting outside the Admiral Dewey Hotel for her husband to check out. They had a plane to catch. Going to Chicago. Husband came outside with their bags, saw a crowd in the street and his wife on the ground in the middle of it. First responders arrived within five minutes and found her nonresponsive. Mr. Nugent went with Sarah in the bus.

"Emergency room at Metro made it official. Mrs. Nugent was DOA, looked like cardiac arrest. The husband told the attending physician that his wife was only forty-one. That she had just aced a full checkup. As far as he or she knew, she did not have any indications of heart disease."

I was listening to Claire, looking at the victim's heart, but my mind was roaming over the other so-called heart attack victims whose deaths we had investigated.

There were the first two victims that had aroused Claire's suspicions. Lois Sprague, the female tourist who had been brought in with the Sci-Tron fatalities. Claire had connected Sprague's death to that of a male cabdriver who actually did have heart disease—as well as a needle mark in his left buttock.

Conklin and I had checked into the third known victim, the homeless addict discovered by the landscaper. The landscaper had no information about the attacker, and the victim had no known relatives, which left us with no motive for his murder.

Last week a real estate broker named Robert Riccardo, thirty-six, had left his office for a breath of air when, without warning, he'd dropped dead on the sidewalk. His death would have been chalked up to cardiac arrest if Claire hadn't gotten the word out to the pathologists in all the hospitals in the city. I was thinking of him as victim number four.

Homicide Central Station would be working the Riccardo case, but the lead investigator, Marty Freeman, had called to tell me that he had no idea what happened to the victim. The tox report was normal. The man's heart was normal. The victim had no enemies, no nothing.

"Boxer, this man should not be dead," he told me.

Claire had ruled the manner of death undetermined, knowing full well that she was looking at a murder victim and couldn't prove it.

I was mired in what-the-hell, same as Claire, same as Marty Freeman. There was a pattern that didn't form a picture. What could possibly be the motive for the deaths of these people who had nothing in common?

Cops like to say, "If you know the why, you can figure out the who." The why was a mystery. But the killer—whoever, however, and for whatever reason—was stepping up his schedule.

The first four victims had been killed within several months. Now, with the death of Sarah Nugent, two victims had been murdered in the last week.

I shared these thoughts with Claire and asked her, "What's your report going to say?"

"Manner of death: 'Homicide.' Cause: 'Unknown substance injected into the right buttock.' Mrs. Nugent's blood just went to the lab," she said. "Let's hope for a clue."

She wrote the husband's contact information on her notepad, ripped off the top sheet, and handed it to me.

Carl Nugent, room 982, Admiral Dewey Hotel

"For whatever it's worth," she said.

Actually, Mrs. Nugent's death was our first fresh lead into the needle sticker's case. And that was priceless.

"I'll call you later," I said. I showed myself out.

CHAPTER 62

IT WAS JUST before ten in the morning when Conklin and I entered the open arms of the Admiral Dewey and found Carl Nugent in the nearly empty bar. He was white, midfifties, average height and weight, and looked as though he'd been wadded up and thrown against the back of the circular booth.

I introduced my partner and myself to Mr. Nugent and asked if we could join him, then we slid onto the leather seat, flanking him on both sides.

Conklin told Nugent that we were sorry for his loss.

Nugent's words slurred together when he said, "Yeah, well, nowhere as sorry as I am...useless without Sarry...total mess without my Sarry."

Then he folded his arms on the table, knocking over a largish glass of liquor without noticing, put his head down, and sobbed.

Conklin reached an arm across the man's back and patted him. A waiter appeared with a dishcloth. He sopped up the alcohol and left a stack of paper napkins. Nugent blotted his face and made an attempt to collect himself, but it was clear that he was grieving his heart out. Finally I said, "Mr. Nugent, can you tell us what happened last night?"

"I wish to God I knew."

The waiter returned with a refill for Nugent, asked if we would like anything. After we said no, we asked the widower to talk about the reasons for his trip to San Francisco.

Nugent told us that he and his wife were inventors and had come here to meet with department store buyers. He pulled a golf-ball-size globe with electric prongs out of his pocket, saying it was a night-light they called Smartlight. He explained briefly that Smartlight detected motion, was interactive, and had a wireless hookup to neighbors, the fire department, and the police.

"Sarry's brainchild," he said sadly. "It could save lives."

I asked, "Can you think of anyone who would have wanted to hurt your wife?"

"Over our...gadget? Whoaaaa. What're you...? Sarry had...a heart attack...didn't she?"

"The medical examiner is doing a full workup. She hasn't determined the cause of death." That was pretty much true.

I asked Nugent questions about his travel plans, the state of his marriage, and if either he or his wife had been harassed in person, on the phone, or on the internet.

The bereaved man had no answers, and after he put down his empty glass, he had zero ability to focus. The manager had a bellman take him to his room, and Rich and I talked about the work we had in front of us: checking Nugent's financials, his insurance policies, his internet life. But I didn't see anything in this man that would lead me to think he had killed his wife.

We interviewed the day manager and the door and lobby staff, including the doorman who had been on the scene when Mrs. Nugent went down. He was earnest and professional, and he had called 911—but his back had been to the street when the shouting started.

We headed back to the Hall with plans to return in three hours and interview the night staff.

I said to my partner, "We've got male victims, female victims. Local folks and out-of-towners. Some that were well off and some that were street sleepers. Were they all victims of opportunity? Does the perp just kill at random?"

Rich turned down the radio. I realized I'd been shouting.

I said it again. "Let's run Nugent's name through the computer."

"Copy that, Captain Obvious."

Conklin was laughing when Brady called.

"Boxer, you got Conklin with you?"

"He's right here."

"Good. Our favorite science teacher was beaten up pretty good last night. He's conscious and talking. Why don't you head on over to San Francisco General."

CHAPTER 63

CONNOR GRANT WAS lying in a hospital bed, snoring loudly. His eyes were blackened, his nose was taped, and every part of him that I could see was bruised, contused, or abraded. Looked like after he'd been beaten all to hell, he'd been dragged behind a pickup for a couple of miles.

Conklin said, "Shit."

I grunted my agreement.

Despite my revulsion for Connor Grant, I felt bad for the guy.

But my mind had its own agenda. I flashed on the moment when I saw Joe being evacuated from Sci-Tron on a stretcher. He'd been almost unrecognizable. I remembered his comatose days, when he'd been straddling a wobbly line between life and death. Even now he was in pain because of this man.

I said, "Mr. Grant?"

I touched his arm and he jolted awake, pulling back as though I was going to hit him.

"Mr. Grant, it's Sergeant Boxer."

"Right. I didn't do it," he said. "Hand me my glasses?"

They were mangled, and one lens was cracked across the middle, and when he couldn't lift his left arm, I helped him put them on. Jesus Christ.

Grant asked me for the remote that controlled the bed. I grabbed it, saying, "Tell me when to stop."

When Grant was in a semi-sitting position, I pulled up a chair and Conklin did the same.

I asked the usual first question: "Can you tell us what happened?"

"I had a hot date with a cement mixer," Grant said.

The painkiller in his IV bag was giving him quite the funny bone. I played along.

I said, "Can you describe the cement mixer?"

Grant cracked a giddy oxy grin.

"I think I'm starting to like you."

The feeling was not mutual. I took out my notepad and let Conklin run the interview. Even doped up, Mr. Grant was a blithe fast-talker.

"Last night. I opened the back door and went for a walk. I don't know how they saw me, but a bag went over my head. Made of cloth. A hood, I guess you'd call it. Then I was punched. Thrown down. Kicked everywhere. I screamed. Pretty sure I must have screamed very damned loud," said Grant. "I must have passed out. I woke up a couple blocks up on Hollister Avenue behind some garbage cans. I still had my phone. I called the cops. And here I am."

The jerk had slipped away from the cops assigned for his protection.

I pictured Grant's neighborhood, the featureless buildings, dim lighting, the entire area on the fringe of the vibrant city of San Francisco. This was how and where the science teacher wanted to live—isolated, so that his neighbors wouldn't object to things that went *kaboom* in the night.

Conklin talked to Grant some more. Asked some of the questions over again, looking for discrepancies, locking his story in. He prodded and probed in his disarming way, but there was nothing to learn. The mad science teacher hadn't seen his assailants. They hadn't spoken to him, they hadn't smelled like anything, and they hadn't poked him with a gun.

He said, "For some reason I'm still alive. I think I'm going to be released tomorrow."

Conklin said, "Feel better," and I added, "Please, Mr. Grant. Check into a hotel."

We left a pair of cops at Grant's hospital door and were heading back to the Hall to brief Brady on our "No news, no leads, not much of anything to report, Lieu" kind of day when we reached the elevator bank and the doors opened.

Elise Antonelli stepped out.

"Visiting my client?" she asked.

"It was a professional call," I said.

Antonelli said, "I think he's going to be all right. We've been talking about you, Sergeant."

"Only saying nice things, I guess."

Antonelli laughed. "You'll be hearing from me soon," she said, then she lifted her hand in a wave and headed toward Grant's room.

"What the hell was that?" Conklin asked. He jabbed the elevator button repeatedly and hard until the doors finally opened. We got inside.

"Any idea?" my partner asked.

"I don't know what she was talking about," I said. "And I don't like the way she said it."

CHAPTER 64

IT WAS AFTER lights-out time at the Loony Bin.

Inside the ward, Neddie was in his favorite sleeping position when Mikey said from the next bed, "I can't sleep."

Neddie was so charged up with recent memories, he couldn't sleep, either.

"Tell me the story," said Mikey.

"You want me to start at the castle?"

"Okay…no," Mike said. "Start at the beginning."

"Scooch over," said Neddie Lambo.

Mike shouted, *"Scooch,"* and pushed his bed up to Neddie's and got back under the covers. The traffic outside on Hyde Street splashed the walls with soft streaks of light. Around Mike and Neddie, the other patients in Ward Six were in various stages of sleep.

"Go on," said Mike. "I'm ready, Neddie."

Neddie had told Mikey the story of his life maybe a hundred times. His bunky thought it was a scary fairy tale, because Neddie told it that way.

"Once back in the day, I had a sister," said Neddie.

Mike said, "Uh-huh, uh-huh. Victoria." He sighed deeply and rolled onto his side, facing Neddie.

Neddie remembered his baby sister very well. He had been seven and Vicky four when they were living with their widowed mom on a quiet block in Glen Park. Vicky was very cute and funny, with perfect features and softly dimpled hands.

Their mother called Vicky her "perfect little girl," and that stung Neddie bad because he knew how relieved Mommy was to have a pretty child, with a normal brain, who wasn't doomed to a stunted life that was "too much for any parent to bear."

Neddie said to Mike, "Vicky was twenty kinds of trouble."

"Tell me the kinds."

Neddie listed three, "Noisy, nosy, bossy," and, wanting to move past this part of the story quickly, he said, "She didn't suffer. After she stopped breathing, I had to mess her up a little so that everyone could see that it was her fault for making me so mad."

"Uh-huh," said Mikey. "You cut off her hair. And her fingers. And you stuffed her fingers into all of her bodily cabbities."

Neddie's lawyer, Mr. Paul, had asked Neddie questions in such a way that Neddie knew how to tell the judge that he hadn't known what he'd done to Vicky was *wrong*. That meant he wasn't mentally competent to stand trial.

"Your Honor. He's only seven," the lawyer had said.

Neddie hadn't gone to jail. This had been his first real-life lesson on the value of being a dummy.

Mikey loved to hear about Neddie's Next Stop, Johnston Youth Correctional for the Criminally Insane, which, even at seven years old, Neddie knew was completely hellish and totally wrong.

Mikey said, "Now tell me about the Castle, Neddie."

The prison was an old redbrick building, each floor successively smaller than the lower floor.

"It was big, Mikey. Like a giant red chocolate cake with candles and flags and a dungeon, of course. Mmmmmwah-hah-hah."

Mikey said, "Mmmmwah-hah-hah," then begged for more.

Neddie described the rambling facility in morbidly fleshed-out detail, returning repeatedly to the dark, tiny cells just big enough for a collie. The inmates received random and often experimental medical care, and every once in a while they were hosed down with a power washer. The food was blended mush baked into a "nutrition loaf." The windows were small, high up, and barred. The toilets were execrable. The all-day, all-night screaming was intolerable, and when the two hundred prisoners weren't caged, chained, or isolated in the dungeon, there were bloody fights and suicides. For Neddie, Johnston Correctional was a crash course in survival.

That didn't mean he had to be passive.

Neddie told Mikey, again, that after "someone" had broken a nurse's neck because *she refused to give him a glass of milk,"* Johnston Youth Correctional for the Criminally Insane had been shut down.

He had no regrets. Nursey had reminded him of his mother, who had been both afraid of and revolted by her son, and as soon as he had been locked up at Johnston, she had moved far away, leaving no forwarding address.

Neddie had never heard from her again.

When Johnston was closed, the "youthful offenders" were parceled out to other facilities around the state, and Neddie was bused to Hyde Street Psychiatric. He was twelve by then, and the Hyde and Seek Loony Bin seemed like some kind of heaven in comparison to Johnston.

The food groups were identifiable and often tasty. There were real shrinks and doctors, and they were interested in him, even though they never agreed on what exactly was wrong with Neddie.

Neddie knew. He was a genius. A rare type of genius.

And thirty years ago, when he turned eighteen, he'd gotten privileges.

Neddie told Mikey, "Whoever killed Nursey was an unsung hero. You know what that means, Mike? He never got credit. No one ever knew who killed that horrible old woman."

Silence from the next bed.

Neddie tucked sleeping Mikey's blankets around him and settled himself down. Old show tunes came from the computer in the nurses' station just outside the door. Within this cocoon of safety and comfort, Neddie thought fondly about his life at the Bin.

He was loved and trusted here. Maybe someday Neddie Lambo would get the respect he deserved. Not maybe. He was certain of it.

Because he had *definitely* earned it.

CHAPTER 65

MY PHONE ALARM buzzed, and for a long moment I didn't have the will to get out of bed.

But the choice was taken out of my hands. Martha gave me a sloppy facial, Julie cranked up the first notes of her full-throated cry, and if I didn't move fast, I was going to be late for work.

I sprang from my cocoon and went straight for Julie's room. Once I had her in my arms, Mrs. Rose arrived, and together we launched the morning routine of food for little girl, dog walk, and caffeine with plenty of sugar for me. As Mrs. Rose ran the dishwasher, I checked the TV news.

Elise Antonelli, Connor Grant's attorney, was giving a press conference outside San Francisco General, and her client, who was bruised, bandaged, and deadpan, was standing beside her.

Antonelli was saying, "On behalf of my client, we are filing a complaint against Sergeant Lindsay Boxer with the Internal Affairs Bureau of the San Francisco Police Department. IAB is charged with investigating crimes against citizens or other police officers.

"In the case of Sergeant Boxer, we are claiming unlawful violation of personal liberty, which means false imprisonment.

"We are further claiming that she lied about my client, resulting in his criminal prosecution for twenty-five murders. My client was tried and found not guilty on all counts by his jury, but the publicity generated by this trial resulted in several near-fatal attacks on Mr. Grant's life."

Elise Antonelli put up a hand to block reporters' questions.

"In a conversation with the mayor this morning, we have been assured that Sergeant Boxer will be thoroughly investigated, and if found in the wrong, she will be separated from—that is, fired by—the SFPD."

The press could no longer be constrained. Questions were fired from all sides, but I'd stopped listening. Antonelli's public statement that I was being investigated was too damned real and sent me into some kind of shock. I stared at the tube, openmouthed, fingers tingling, specks floating in front of my eyes.

Mrs. Rose called in from the kitchen, "*What* did she say?"

I shut off the TV and brought Mrs. Rose into the loop on the beating of Connor Grant and how I wasn't surprised that he wanted to hurt *somebody*.

"He's an opportunist, and that's the very kindest thing I can say about him," I told her. "I'll be okay. I'll be fine."

She gave me a look that was both hard and questioning. She knew me well. She knew that I was worried *sick*.

A half hour later, wearing my imaginary cloak of invisibility, I entered the Hall through the back door and ran up the stairs. Brenda, our squad assistant, snagged me the moment I stepped into the bull pen. "You're very popular," she said, handing me a list of one-on-one meetings she'd scheduled for me with Brady, Jacobi, Nash, who is our new head of PR, and Len Parisi. There was also a note from Parisi reading, "Don't speak with anyone but your union rep and the people on the list."

My rep?

I was scared. I had done nothing wrong. But what if I was somehow found responsible for violating Grant's rights? What then? My resources were finite. Joe wasn't working. And after a dismissal for cause, I might never be able to work as a cop again.

I dropped into my desk chair, and I didn't care that he wasn't on Parisi's approved list, I told Conklin all about it. After that I went to my meetings with the brass and I called Joe. We talked for over an hour from my seat in the fire stairs.

By the time Claire called to ask if I was free for dinner with Cindy and Yuki, I was ripping mad.

I said to Claire, "God, yes to dinner. Connor Grant killed twenty-five people and *he's* going after *me*? I want to see all of you, really bad."

CHAPTER 66

AFTER WORK I drove to Susie's Café, our long-time Women's Murder Club HQ. I arrived first, commandeered "our" booth in the back room, and ordered a pitcher of brew.

Yuki and Cindy arrived next, slid into the seat across from me. Cindy said, "Oh, my God, Lindsay, what is the story with Grant filing a complaint against you?"

Yuki poured Cindy a beer, saying, "You're a touch wired, Cin. Not another word until you drink this down."

"Oh, no. You're going to torture me with beer?"

Yuki laughed, which lifted my mood and had a similar effect on the six or seven people within range of her melodious chortle. Cindy looked pleased to get such a big laugh on her small joke, and I refilled my glass. I wasn't yet laughing. I wasn't sure beer could help me.

About then Claire arrived like a stiff breeze, knocking silverware to the floor as she edged between other tables and ours. She apologized, bent to retrieve a spoon, and knocked into another table, scattering more silverware. Our waitress skidded to a halt, balancing full dishes of pulled pork as Yuki scrambled to help Claire in that narrow aisle. Oh, man, everyone was laughing at our clumsy gang.

"We're going to make it easy on you," Claire said to Lorraine.

She ordered the Tuesday Night Special, seven-dollar-a-plate spicy shrimp dinner, all around. And then Claire asked me to tell what I knew about the complaint.

But I wasn't supposed to talk to anyone, right?

"No, I'm under orders from Parisi to keep quiet, so you go ahead," I told Claire.

"You sure?"

"Start talking, Claire, or someone's going to beat you to it."

"Okay, then," she said. "Get this. One of the EMTs who picked up Sarah Nugent outside the Admiral Dewey Hotel remembered something that didn't register at the time."

Claire had our full attention. Forks paused in midair.

"What did he remember?" I asked.

Claire said, "He saw a medical vial in the gutter. So now he and his partner drive over to the hotel and find this empty vial. It's labeled 'succinyl-choline.'"

Cindy asked, "What's that?"

"Sux is a colorless, odorless muscle relaxant, a short-term paralytic used primarily for intuba-tion," said Claire. "It can be administered intrave-nously. It can also be injected intramuscularly."

I said, "I see where you're going. You think the victims were injected with that?"

"It makes sense," said Claire. "If used intravenously, sux works within a minute or two. If you're not on a respirator, you will stop breathing and you will die. Intramuscularly, it takes longer for the paralysis to hit, so you buy another minute or so, but it's the same issue. Without going on a respirator PDQ, you will die."

Yuki asked her, "Why didn't the tox screens pick it up?"

Claire said, "Because sux metabolizes into succinate. That's a naturally occurring substance we all have in our blood, so—very quickly—it's undetectable. I think we've got our smoking gun, Linds. I'm sure of it. The bottle is on the way to the lab. Let's pray that CSI finds prints on it, okay?"

I said, "Sure."

Claire said, "You all think I'm kidding."

She folded her hands and closed her eyes. Right there in Susie's raucous, curry-perfumed Caribbean eatery, with the sounds of steel drums and laughter in our ears, we followed Claire's lead.

We prayed for CSI to find fingerprints on a small bottle that might lead to a serial killer.

We really prayed.

CHAPTER 67

CINDY CAME BACK to the table from the wash-room and found that Lindsay had left.

Yuki said, "She said sorry, but she had to get home."

"Oh, man, I wanted to talk to her," Cindy said.

"You might still be able to catch her if you run."

Cindy said, "Be right back," and bolted out the door and down to Montgomery. She looked in both directions for Lindsay's car and saw her Explorer coming back toward Susie's in the opposite lane.

Cindy waved to her. Lindsay slowed to a stop and said, "I'm racing, Cin. Mrs. Rose has a date with her daughter and has to leave any minute. Call you tomorrow?"

"Okay," Cindy said. "Talk soon."

Cindy had work to do before she slept. And that was putting her into a panic. She had wanted to let Lindsay know she was going to run a story on the sudden deaths that looked like heart attacks and probably weren't. She didn't need Lindsay's permission. Nothing said at the table was off the record, and besides, she already had a good handle on the piece.

Weeks ago Claire had put out a BOLO on the medical examiner's network, seeking information about needle marks on people who appeared to have died suddenly, with no known cause. Other people had access to this network. The *Chronicle* subscribed to it, for instance, and so did the *Daily News*. Cindy had asked Rich for confirmation. Which he had given her.

He hadn't told her anything confidential, but she had known she was onto something when Sarah Nugent, only forty-one years old, died two days ago in front of her hotel—cause of death unknown.

Lindsay was the primary investigator on the case.

It was SOP to get a quote from her, but Cindy didn't need it. What she needed to do was get the story out before another paper ran it. As for the empty vial marked "succinylcholine," she could write that the tip had come from an anonymous source close to the investigation.

But should she? Should she write the story without Lindsay saying, "Sure. Go for it"?

Cindy went back to the restaurant and joined the girls for Key lime pie and tea. "Off the record" hardly applied, as she didn't hear a thing her friends were saying. She was thinking of Lindsay.

With or without Lindsay's permission, she had to write the story. Journalism wasn't a *hobby*. It was a job with a responsibility to the public to write the truth. Plus, it was *her* job.

After the check had been paid, Cindy called

Rich and let him know that she was on the way home. As she drove, she organized the story in her mind and thought she could have it in the publisher's inbox before he got his morning coffee.

When she was a block from home, she tried calling Lindsay, and when she didn't pick up, she left a message.

"Linds, call me, please. I want to run the Sarah Nugent story and talk about the formerly presumed heart attacks. I'm not going to mention Claire by name. But I could sure use a quote from you."

The story was writing itself inside her head. Cindy couldn't wait to start putting the words down.

CHAPTER 68

I WAS MAKING breakfast for Julie, with the TV on in the background, when I heard reporter Susan Steinhardt of Channel 5 say, "This just in. A number of deaths in San Francisco originally attributed to *heart failure* appear, instead, to have been murders."

Say that again?

I dialed down the stove and amped up the volume. Ms. Steinhardt was on set, dark hair perfectly waved, coolly delivering her report, which felt anything but cool to me.

She said, "Senior crime writer Cindy Thomas of the *San Francisco Chronicle* broke this story only minutes ago. She writes that as many as five victims have died from injections of a paralytic drug called succinylcholine.

"According to Ms. Thomas, who gave her sources as 'individuals close to the investigation,' the victims were assaulted on the street and injected with this drug by an unknown attacker," Steinhardt said. "We'll bring you news updates as they come to us."

No way. Cindy had gone *public* with our investigation.

I grabbed my phone and called Cindy, and as soon as she said, "Hello," I went off on her, all guns blazing.

"Cindy, what the *hell?* You put out the sux story? The killer now knows we're onto him. You just made our investigation harder, or *impossible,* so congrats on your scoop and thank you very much."

Then I clicked off. Besides dropping them in the toilet, the worst thing about cell phones is that you can't pound them into the cradle. But I slapped my phone down hard on the counter anyway before returning to Julie's oatmeal.

Just then Mrs. Rose arrived in a cloud of tea rose perfume, calling out, "Girls, I'm here."

When she saw the look on my face, she said, "You okay?"

"Not really."

"Is Julie okay?"

"She's fine."

"I'll be right back," said Mrs. Rose. She leashed a bounding, leaping, squealing Martha and took her out for her walk.

My phone buzzed.

I hesitated. Then I answered it.

"What, Cindy? What?"

"Listen to me, Lindsay," she said. "The days of you telling me what I can and cannot do are officially over."

"Don't give me that."

"I am giving it to you, and if you can't take it, we can't be friends."

I was so stunned by her indignation and her anger, I really had no comeback.

She said, "First, I tried to talk to you, twice. On the street, remember? And then I called and left a message. You didn't get back. More to the point, I'm not a cub reporter anymore. And I'm not your little sister. You know how many crimes I've solved with you and with Rich? Many. Remember? I shot a *killer* who had a gun pointed at *you*. I *killed* someone. I got *shot*."

"I remember," I said. My tone had dropped a little. I wasn't sure she heard me.

"I play by the rules," said Cindy. "I didn't know about the sux until Claire said so, but I didn't use her name, and by the way, I had this story by the *balls* before dinner last night. Claire put it out herself to every ME and pathologist in the state.

"If I hadn't broken it, someone else would have. I did my job. That's all I have to say, Lindsay. I'm done justifying my integrity and my work to you."

I couldn't speak. I was still mad, but shame was starting to heat the back of my neck and direct my eyes to the floor. And then the phone went dead.

I cleaned up my little girl and got ready for work. I tried to ignore my panged conscience, but I couldn't let myself get away with it. I picked up my phone and called Cindy.

She didn't answer.

I left a message.

"Cin, I'm sorry. You're right. I'm wrong. I'll call you later, but I need to apologize now. Don't stay mad. We can work this out. Call me."

CHAPTER 69

NEDDIE FOUND THE newspaper in the basement trash room lying next to the mountain of garbage bags. The headline came at him fast and hard, like a sucker punch.

Stealth Killer Stalks Our City

Was that *him?*

He snatched up the paper and read the story fast. The victim was Sarah Nugent, the woman he'd stuck outside the hotel. There was a photo of her and her husband and quotes from the doorman, and— *No-no-no-no-no*—law enforcement had found the vial of sux. He must have fumbled it when he tried to put it back into his pocket.

The paper shook and rattled in Neddie's hands as he skimmed the second page of the article. Had there been a witness? Had he been seen? He found nothing but the two words describing what he'd done: *Stealth Killer.*

He liked the name. It sounded epic. It sounded like a movie title. William H. Macy would play him, Edward Lamborghini. Oh, man. But as thrilling as the thought was, he was also afraid. Over all this time and so many kills, he'd wished for recognition. Now he might get it.

Was he ready to pay?

"Cool it, Neddie," he said to himself. "Cool your jets."

He put the newspaper back precisely where he'd found it. He thought of the two cops questioning him at the Embarcadero. That was the first warning, and now with this newspaper story, that was warning number two.

Should he stay or should he go?

If he played it safe, if he didn't overreact, he could have a beautiful night flight.

He unlocked and opened the metal door to the alley, leaned against it, and considered his options.

Over the past thirty years he had mapped a three-dimensional schematic of San Francisco in his mind. He had walked the five square miles centering on the Loony Bin above- and belowground. He knew every rusted lock and basement door, every alley and poorly lit path—and then he knew where he would go.

He saw the place in his mind, Washington Square, with its uplifting views of Saints Peter and Paul Church, the roaming homeless and other ragtag people on the grounds. No one ever looked at him in the park. He was invisible there. He was free.

The night was a pleasant sixty-two degrees.

Neddie took some cleansing breaths, then

walked north a block and a half to Joice Street, an alley with a grate where the asphalt met the curb. He had chiseled open this grate on an earlier excursion, and he pried it open now. Metal creaked and he dropped inside a drafty opening, holding on to the curb until he found footing on the metal ladder.

He heard water dripping, and cool air came up to greet him as he entered the new, still-under-construction tunnel for the Central Subway.

The tunnel was enormous. He pulled his penlight from a pocket and flicked it over the heavy machinery parked in the dark—the lifts and the auger and the backhoes. Then he headed north between the just-laid train tracks.

Rats scurried. His running shoes slapped at the low tide. He kept his light on the newly poured concrete walls, looking for the exit, and then his light kissed the ladder on the wall.

Neddie put the end of his penlight between his teeth and climbed thirty feet, hand over hand, finally shouldering open the drain. A moment later he took in the sweet air and the expansive freedom of his night flight. He ran; he pushed off walls and took the peaks and valleys of San Francisco's exciting topography.

He was still flying when he reached Cordelia Street. He slowed and drafted behind three teenage boys, staying back and at the same time with them as they joked and laughed and horsed around all the way to Powell.

Neddie was imagining his entrance to the park, deep in his thoughts, eyes down, when he whumped into something soft and resilient. It was a very large dude.

"Hey. Watch where you're going," said the big man, who looked to Neddie like a grown-old high school football player.

Then he added the zinger, "Are you crazy?"

"I'm *good*. My fault," Neddie said, jacking up his voice to his falsetto range.

The big dude bent to gather up his briefcase, his newspaper, and continued on. Then, as if a new thought had struck him, he stopped and turned to look at Neddie.

Neddie thought he understood why.

That newspaper headline—STEALTH KILLER. And something about Neddie had made the big dude think too much. He had seen the predatory intelligence in his eyes, the look that Neddie always tried to hide. And the big dude was paralyzed by that look.

Neddie thought he'd been recognized. He said it out loud. "Uh-oh."

Quick, his hand was in his pocket, where he wrapped his fist around a loaded sharp. He'd never had a bit of trouble before, but the big dude was looking right at him. This was different. The guy wanted to fight.

He outweighed Neddie by sixty pounds. But so what? Neddie was ready. He looked at the big dude and said, "Game on."

PART FOUR

CONKLIN AND I were working at our desks when Claire came through the squad room door wearing a bloody gown and a cap, her mask pulled down and it appeared that she had something big on her mind.

I said, "You've got a report on that sux vial?"

She said, "I'm still waiting. I need you to come on over to my house. There's someone I want you to see."

"Something wrong with your phone?" Conklin asked my BFF.

"My calls, Inspector, went to voice mail. That would be my calls to the *both* of you."

Oh.

The three of us thundered down the fire stairs, cut through the back door, and strode along the breezeway to Claire's "house," the offices of the chief medical examiner.

We passed through the waiting room, brushing by her gatekeeper and the loosely packed mob of law enforcement officers waiting to see Claire. She put up a hand and didn't skip a step, as good as saying, "Not now!"

We passed Claire's office and continued down the corridor until she stiff-armed the stainless steel swinging doors to the super-chilly autopsy suite. Rich and I stayed with her, stopping at the table with the body lying on it faceup under the lights.

Claire said, "The needle sticker has stuck again. At least, it sure looks like it. Meet Ralph Beardsley, CPA, DOA, RIP."

Mr. Beardsley was a black male, about fifty, heavy-set. "Look here," Claire said, turning the man's head to the side. There was a bite mark in his neck. Claire pulled down the sheet and showed me a bruise with a needle mark centered on his left pectoral.

I said, "Whoa. Is this the first time the needle sticker has struck in the front of the body?"

"To the best of my knowledge."

"So this was a confrontation," I said. "The victim saw his killer."

"No doubt. And they mixed it up."

She bunched the sheet over his privates and showed us the rest of him. She pointed out other fresh bruises, four by my count—one under the rib cage, a big one on his side, one high on his right thigh, and one on his left shin.

"I've got some good news."

I looked up at Claire. I couldn't even guess.

"Some *living* folks saw the killer in action."

Say that again? "There are witnesses?"

Claire said, "Husband and wife saw the hit from their car. They flagged down a cruiser. Here," she said, handing me a scrap of paper. "Fresh contact info, get it while it's hot."

CHAPTER 71

THE WITNESSES, LYNN and Ray Schultz, were in their thirties, owned a liquor store in North Beach, and given the annual stats of liquor store robberies, I was betting that the Schultzes were quite observant.

Conklin and I set them up with coffee in Interview 2, took chairs across from them, and got to work.

Ray Schultz said, "Last night, sometime after nine, we're going home from the store. I'm driving. It's dark and I'm watching the street. Lynn, you tell them, honey."

Lynn Schultz said, "So we were stopped at the light on Union Street."

She drew a line on the table with her blue-polished fingernail.

"I'm staring out the window at some free furniture on the sidewalk. And I see this kinda small, kinda weird-looking guy wearing dark clothes, walking with his eyes down.

"Here." She stabbed a ding in the table at an imaginary point along her imaginary road. "He bumps into Mr. Beardsley, who drops his newspaper and his briefcase."

Lynn Schultz was quite animated now. She said, "The paper blows all over and Mr. Big looks *pissed.* The two of them are, like, five, six feet apart, facing off. I think, *OMG,* and I roll down the window so I can hear. And Mr. Big calls the other one a name. Like 'You crazy little shrimp' or something.

"And the little guy goes, 'Bring it on,' and gets right up into Mr. Big's *face.* I mean, like, aggressive and, yeah, *crazy.* Mr. Big could make two of the other guy.

"And Mr. Big shoves Mr. Little away with his *forearm.*"

The husband said, "I didn't see that, but what Lynn is describing is a football move. Like the way a defensive lineman would push away a blocker. It's called a forearm shiver—"

"And the little one goes down," said Lynn Schultz. "And he gets up slowly, like he's been hurt, and stands there for a second with his hands on his knees, and then *bang,* he leaps at Mr. Big like a tomcat and it looks like he bites him on his *neck,* and that throws Mr. Big off balance and now he's down."

Lynn Schultz was acting it all out now.

"And the small guy, he's on the ground, like, leaning on his elbow, and from that position he launches this sweeping kick and gets the big guy in the shin, right here," she said, patting her leg just below the knee.

"The big guy lands on his back—and in a split second the little one is on top of him, raises his arm high, and looks like he punches Mr. Big in the *chest.*"

Good God. That answered my question of how and why Mr. Beardsley had gotten a needle in his pec muscle.

Ray Schultz was saying, "I'm seeing this now. Mr. Big yowls and he's in trouble. Now the light turns green. Horns are honking. I start to go, but Lynn yells at me to pull over to the curb and 'do something.'

"So I pull over. I get out. The little guy has *gone,* nowhere to be seen. And I run over, get down next to Mr. Beardsley, who's clutching his throat, trying to get his breath. But he can't get enough air. He says, 'Call 911.'

"My phone's in the car, but I run out into the road and wave down a cruiser."

I was thrilling inside. I could see the whole scene going down almost in front of me. These witnesses were *good.*

I asked the Schultzes, "You're sure the smaller man was the attacker?"

Said Lynn Schultz, "Definitely. One hundred percent."

"Okay. If you could, describe him once more, as best as you can," I said.

"Sure. Estimating he could be about five two? Light-colored hair? Like faded blond. He had a collar or a hoodie under his coat. Damned shame I didn't see his face."

Conklin said, "You've given us a lot, Lynn. Our first good lead."

I made notes, including that Beardsley had been carrying a newspaper. If the headline had read STEALTH KILLER, maybe it had sparked Beardsley's curiosity. Had he made the killer, and the killer knew it—so he took Beardsley out?

Conklin was saying, "If you think of anything else, anything at all, call my direct line. Thanks very much for coming in."

We had beautiful, corroborated eyewitness reports and a decent description of the needle sticker. It was, as Conklin had said, our first good lead. It was better than I could even have wished for.

But we needed more. The "weird-looking guy" was volatile and sounded like he was also fearless. He was striking out much more frequently than before—as far as we knew.

How many of our citizens had died as a direct result of this killer?

More than two months after Claire had found a bruise on Lois Sprague's buttock, we had no more idea who the needle sticker was than we had then. Four more people had died.

The killer was on a roll.

CHAPTER 72

CONNOR GRANT'S COMPLAINT to Internal Affairs haunted me all day and cut my sleep short every night as I waited to be interviewed by Lieutenant William Hoyt.

That Monday morning, Carol Hannah, my tough, dedicated union rep, came to Interview 1 and we went over everything I said and did when I arrested Connor Grant and everything I had done or been accused of doing since I joined the police force as a rookie.

Carol said, "I don't see anything to this complaint except that Connor Grant wants revenge. If I'm missing something, please tell me now."

"The whole episode lasted ten minutes," I told my advocate. "I've thought about every second of it and I followed procedure. I'm sure of it, Carol."

Carol said, "If Hoyt goes over the line, I'll intervene."

The way a complaint to IAB was processed was pretty straightforward. I would be interviewed, and my interview would be compared with reports from other sources and my personnel file to see if there was a hinky pattern of behavior. If I'd broken the law, IAB would go to the DA, and if Parisi found that there was cause to try me for these crimes or infractions of police procedure, there would be a trial before the police commission. I would be suspended from my job until the case was adjudicated, but even if the charges were dismissed, my reputation would be permanently damaged. In other words, it would be a living, breathing nightmare that made me sick even to think about.

Connor Grant had thrown me under a steaming pile of bull, and my preparation with my union rep and having her at my side would be my best chance to get out from under it.

That afternoon Carol and I went downstairs to the district attorney's offices, and Parisi's assistant walked us down the hallway to his private conference room, gave us each a bottle of water, and closed the door.

I took a seat. Carol sat down beside me and we waited. Fifteen minutes felt like fifteen years as I watched the second hand tick by on the wall clock. Then there was a tap on the door and Lieutenant Hoyt came in with a man he introduced as Sergeant Kreisler. Hoyt was bald, sharp featured, and about as warm and fuzzy as a hockey puck.

Kreisler had a full head of hair and a rosy complexion. He was a little *too* warm and fuzzy. Like he was enjoying the very idea of this meeting.

Carol set up a recorder and pushed the Play button, and Kreisler did the same.

Hoyt said to me, "Sergeant Boxer, we're going

to cover a lot of ground in this meeting. A complaint against you is a complaint against the entire police force, you understand. So don't take it personally—or take it personally, I don't care. I just want to get to the truth.

"You know the charges?"

"False arrest. Lying. Making up a confession resulting in a trial."

"Good enough," said Hoyt. "Let's begin."

For the next two hours William Hoyt tore apart my career in Homicide, case by case.

The third hour was dedicated to one case in particular: the teenage girl I'd shot to death because I'd had no choice. Warren Jacobi had been my partner then, and that cute young lady had led us on a high-speed car chase through the Tenderloin. As I said, she was cute. Deceptively so. When caught, she got out of her father's sixty-thousand-dollar car and reached for her learner's permit. She pulled out a gun.

She shot me and Jacobi. I was in bad shape and Jacobi was worse, unconscious and bleeding out onto the asphalt.

The young lady was still shooting when I managed to free my gun from its holster and return fire.

A fifteen-year-old would-be cop killer had gone down. Despite my entirely justifiable self-defense shooting, her rich family had sued me for wrongful death, and I'd been tried in civil court.

It was a horrible experience. Those same feelings of frustration and injustice were coming over me now.

I answered Hoyt's questions about the shooting. I had fired in self-defense.

I regretted that I'd had to kill that girl, but the situation had demanded it.

Yes, yes, yes, I had shot several other people in the last few years, and all those shootings had been fully justified and there had been no resulting disciplinary or legal action.

I stayed cool and went on to answer many questions about my critically important first-time meeting with Connor Grant. I said explicitly that I was sure I had heard him correctly when he told me that he had blown up Sci-Tron.

"I asked him to repeat himself. He elaborated on his boasts. I read him his rights and asked him if he understood. He said he did. I turned him over to patrolmen I knew, who brought him to my CO, who was waiting for him in booking.

"Everything I said and did was by the book."

"His word against yours, but we have your husband's sworn statement, and that will be considered," said Hoyt. "I think we have enough for today."

Tape recorders were turned off. Carol and I left the conference room first, and when we were walking up the stairs, she said to me, "Perfect job, Lindsay. You answered honestly and with conviction. I don't see anything here but a dismissal of the complaint."

I couldn't even smile. I remembered when Parisi, Yuki, Brady, and I had had the same slam-dunk feeling that Grant's on-scene confession would convict him. Now I knew what the science teacher could do in a court of law.

If Hoyt wanted to bring the charge forward, he would do it. If Parisi, for political reasons, had to let it go to the police commission, I could be sacrificed for the greater good of clearing the department's name.

I would be fired, made an example of, humiliated, and I would likely never have a job in law enforcement again.

The end.

CHAPTER 73

THAT WEEKEND JOE and I relaxed within the landscaped embrace of Pacifica Rehab's garden patio. He was in his wheelchair, I was stretched out in a high-quality ergonomic lounger beside him, and while we talked together, we were watching Julie.

Our little bambina was in the kiddie pool with three other kiddos, including Joey, a boy of four who had made up a sea monster game. He was in the starring role and had instructed the others to evade and scream. Fearless, Julie sat on the steps, slapped the water, and giggled. Joe and I laughed, too. It was all sunshine with a side of butterflies in the garden, but as I told Joe about my interrogation by Internal Affairs, my mind spiraled down into a darker place.

I said, "I was grilled on a spit, and Hoyt just kept basting me, jacking up the flame. Sorry to even have to tell you about it."

"You'll be okay, and I hope they want to interview me. But I know this is very stressful. I'm here. Tell me everything."

"Okay," I said. "So Hoyt curls his lip and says

to me, 'I don't understand your answer, Sergeant. The scene was chaotic. You're so certain that you remember Mr. Grant's utterance verbatim?'

"I said, 'It wasn't an *utterance,* Mr. Hoyt. It was a speech. It was a brag. It was a confession without coercion.'

"He complimented me on the alliteration. Then he said, 'Sounds a little rehearsed, Sergeant. Let me ask you something else. Have you ever made a mistake on the job? Arrested the wrong person? Shot someone dead? How many people have you killed, Sergeant Boxer? Three? More than that? Fewer than ten?'

"He knew how many, Joe. It was a tactic."

"Of course it was. Keep going."

I took a breath and told Joe what I could bear to remember. "'Why were you demoted from lieutenant to sergeant? Why were you passed over for the job as chief of police? Why should we believe *anything* you say about *anything?*'"

Joe sighed. "Sorry, Linds. Look, the public wants cops to take lunatics off the street, and you did that. Your responsibility stops there."

As we talked about our personal lunatic, I realized that I still hadn't fully accepted what Grant had said to the jurors when he told them that the scope of the Sci-Tron bombing was way beyond the abilities of a ninth-grade science teacher.

So had he really done it?

If so, how?

And how had he managed to annihilate Red Dog Parisi at trial?

We'd never really known Connor Grant. He'd been investigated by the FBI. By DHS. And still, what we knew about the science teacher could cover the face of a three-inch-square Post-it note.

Joe and I had barely touched our sandwiches and chips. He said, "All done?"

"I'll get it, Joe," I said, referring to the remains of our lunch.

He said, absolutely deadpan, "Allow me."

And then the best and most amazing thing happened. Joe got out of his wheelchair and onto his feet as if nothing had ever been wrong with him. He walked. He emptied the remains of our lunch into the trash, stowed the trays in the receptacle, and then he spun around and did a little dance.

Julie flew up out of the pool like a June bug and yelled, "Daddy!" Joe opened his arms and she ran toward him, chirping, "Daddy dance."

They danced. He twirled her under his arm. They made up their own moves. From first step to last, the prancing and twirling went on for only a minute. But it was the cutest damned minute of my life.

CHAPTER 74

NEDDIE WAS STILL hurting like crazy from when that giant son of a bitch had blocked him, making him fall and hit his head on the pavement. His head was still radiating with pain.

He had no intention of letting anyone know.

He went through the whole weekend being Nutty Neddie, playing cards and doing stoopid Neddie tricks, but he was sore in more ways than one.

When he'd been leaving the grown-up football player on Union Street, he'd seen a man jump out of a car at the light and head over to the dead or dying man.

Had the man from the car seen his face? Well, shit, didn't matter. Neddie had gotten clean away.

Now it was after dinner in Ward Six-Six-Six and just before lights-out. Neddie, Mikey, Quarter to Ten, Fred Mouse, and Oscar were going to trade stories.

Oscar was in the bathroom when Mikey leaned over to where Neddie was settling into his bunk and dropped a bombshell.

He said, "I told Dr. Hoover a story about *you,* Neddie. A true one."

Neddie was zapped with a jolt of fear like a lightning strike that ran up his spine to the back of his head, then branched out to his fingertips. He felt dizzy. He tried to focus on Mikey.

"What story?" he managed to ask.

Neddie hoped that Mikey would say that he had told Hoover a Johnston Correctional story; Johnston was fact—published, documented, condemned. No harm could come to Neddie over a Johnston story. But—reality check, Neddie. Mikey hadn't told Hoover about Johnston. Hoover knew all about Johnston.

Mikey said, "I told Dr. Hoover that you go flying at night and stay out until almost morning."

Mikey was smart enough to read Neddie's face and see trouble coming. He started backing up, until he was between two lockers across from the beds. A split second later Neddie sprang off the side of the bed, his shadow rising up against the wall like a bodyguard three times his height.

Neddie closed in. Mikey peed himself.

"Why'd you *do* that, Mikey? What did you *do* that for?"

"Don't hurt me," he squealed. *"Don't hurt me, Neddie."*

Neddie slapped a locker door. Kicked it. Then, as Mikey went into a crouch, Neddie grabbed his hair with one hand, gripped his jaw with the other, forcibly extracting him from his hiding place, then ran him headfirst into a wall. As he fell to the floor, Mikey loosed one long, undulating wail.

"You're going to take it back," Neddie barked into his friend's ear.

Mikey cried, *"You hurt me. You hurt my arm."*

Mike's yowling and the metallic clanking of the lockers had stirred up everyone in and around Ward Six. Fred Mouse was squeaking, "Yip-yip-yip." Quarter to Ten was spinning, and Randy was way under his bed, keening as if his throat had been slit.

And now Nurse Mimi was in the doorway.

From behind her, Dr. Hoover pushed his way into the room.

He yelled, *"Freeeeeeze."*

Neddie stepped away from Mike, who had collapsed in a damp, pee-smelling heap of dummy. Nurse Mimi went to Mike, and he wailed, *"Neddie broke my arm."*

Dr. Hoover loomed above Neddie and said, "Your privileges are suspended, Edward. Effective now."

Neddie joined the big fat baby chorus, crying in his peculiar high-pitched whine.

"He *started* it. I didn't *mean* to hurt him. It was an *accident*. I'm *sorry,* Mikey."

Nurse Mimi said, "Dr. Hoover, I believe him. Neddie never acts up. He's a sweetie, aren't you, dear?"

Hoover said to Mike, "Michael, you're going to Saint Vartan's, okay? Nurse Mimi, get a chair and take Mike to the ER."

He turned back to Neddie and said, "Edward,

you're confined to the infirmary at night until further notice. Give me the keys to the alley."

"Keys? No, Dr. Hoover. Please. The keys are mine."

Hoover stuck out his hand. "Now, Edward."

Neddie took his precious keys, his flight pass, from the hook in his locker and handed them to the doctor.

"Get your pillow."

Neddie plucked his pillow from his bed, and clutching it, he walked ahead of Dr. Hoover down the speckled lino hallway, past the nurses' station to the men's infirmary.

"When can I come out, Dr. Hoover? When can I have my privileges back?"

"Behave, Edward. I'll come for you in the morning and we will have a talk. Leave everything else to me."

"Yes, okay, okay, Doctor."

Neddie sat on the edge of the bed, assuming a posture that made him appear as meek and as harmless as a small, middle-aged loony tune could look. The infirmary door closed and locked.

He waited for the peephole to open and close, and once he was finally alone, Neddie held on to his head, and when he couldn't suppress the pain, he raged around the very small room, which was four times the size of the dog kennel he'd slept in at Johnston. He knew that his situation had hit a patch of bad weather. Dangerous winds. Electric thunderstorms. Isolated tornados. None of that would get in his way.

Did Hoover think that he was such a dummy that in all these long years at the Bin, he'd never gotten spare keys? If Hoover knew where he'd gotten the sux, he'd probably kill himself.

Neddie flapped his arms and raged and made plans.

CHAPTER 75

I WAS HALFWAY into my drive to the Hall through morning rush when Claire called.

"I've got good news and I've got bad news."

I couldn't read her tone of voice. I jerked the wheel, left-right, to avoid a pothole and continued up Masonic Avenue.

"Bad news first," I said. "Give it to me straight. I can handle anything and I prove it every single day."

Claire laughed. "You're my hero, Lindsay."

"Yeah, yeah, hit me, Butterfly."

"Ready? There were no usable prints on the run-over, crushed-to-powder sux vial and no DNA on it, either."

"Oh, great. I'm having a hard time imagining the good news."

"Brace yourself. I know where that vial came from. The lot number told me so."

"Ya-hooo."

This wasn't a case of good news. This was a case of fantastic, groundbreaking, possibly case-breaking news.

"You're *my* hero," I said to Claire.

"Oh, shut up," she said. And then we both laughed.

As soon as I arrived at the squad room, I briefed Rich and Brady, who stood up, clapped his hands together, and said, "Get on outta here. Don't forget to phone in."

Rich and I stopped at Claire's office for a photocopy of the vial label with the lot code. And then we took off.

Saint Vartan's is a big, well-respected teaching hospital that takes up the whole block between Pine and Bush. When I say it's big, I mean fourteen floors, three hundred beds, 180 physicians, and a thousand employees.

That big.

After my partner and I cleared the expected bureaucratic steeplechase, we met with Dr. Merrilee Christianson, the director in charge of the hospital's in-house pharmacy.

Dr. Christianson was a tightly wrapped sixty-something woman, all business, moderately defensive as she explained the storage and dispensing system at Saint Vartan's in-house pharmacy. She ticked off the protocols, including the passwords, key cards, and required records every time a unit of medication was moved from locked drawers and cabinets to mobile carts.

Conklin said, "Dr. Christianson, we're trying to track the source of a vial that was sold to Saint Vartan's and was found on the street. It may be evidence in a murder. Please take a look."

I handed her the copy of the sux vial label, with its ten-number code highlighted in yellow.

"Can you wait?" she asked.

She left her desk and returned only ten minutes later.

"This product expired last year. This lot was destroyed."

I said, "All except for this vial?"

"Naturally," she huffed, "I can't account for individual vials, but what remained of this case lot is on our 'Destroyed In-House' list."

Conklin, the best guy with women I've ever met, pushed his brown hair out of his eyes and asked a number of questions: "Where and how are expired drugs destroyed?" "Was it possible for those vials to be stolen after they left the pharmacy?" "Could they have been lifted, for instance, from the OR?" "How long is sux effective after its expiration date?"

Dr. Christianson replied in depth.

No one could have stolen the vial from the dispensary without leaving a trail, and no such trail had lit up the tracking software. That went for the surgery unit, too. Saint Vartan's had a facility in the basement, an incinerator cleared by the DEA, that was dedicated to destroying expired drugs. Records were meticulously made and maintained, of course.

"Of course," Conklin said.

Christianson went on, "Sux would still be effective for five to eight months after expiry. After that the potency would be diminished."

"But it would still paralyze an individual who was injected with it?" I asked.

"Of course. But we would never use a drug after the manufacturer's expiry date, okay? I've got to get back to work," she said with finality.

Conklin asked to see the drug disposal facility so we could complete our report. Christianson made a call, and Kelly Caine, a young pharmacy assistant, took us down to the B Level.

The elevator doors opened.

I wasn't prepared for my first look at what lurked beneath Saint Vartan's. The basement wasn't just huge. It sprawled. It had high ceilings and many Alice-in-Wonderland doors.

It had the look of an underground city.

CHAPTER 76

I TRIED TO take in the vast, humming, industrial-grade basement level under Saint Vartan's.

The off-white painted walls were notched at intervals with intersections and blue doors that led to the boiler room, cooling apparatus, maintenance services, kitchen facilities, laundry. Pipes and tubes scaled the twenty-foot-high ceilings, which were paneled with fluorescent lighting that bleached this mechanical underworld and polished it to a high shine.

Along with the thumping of the major pumps and the chopping of fans, there was traffic aplenty: maintenance workers, kitchen workers, and orderlies pushing wheelchairs and gurneys. Electric carts streaked past.

Let me just say that the almost futuristic, machine-driven quality of the place was a little creepy.

I looked to Conklin to see how he was taking it and saw that Kelly Caine had fixed her big brown eyes on Inspector Hottie and had sidled up inside his personal zone.

I butted in.

"The incineration facility?" I reminded her.

"Right this way."

We followed the young woman down the main corridor, came to an intersection, and turned right down a spur of hallway to a door marked FURNACE ROOM. We peered through a window in that door and saw a large, blocky furnace in use. A maintenance worker opened the adjacent storage room for us.

A logbook was prominently positioned beside a computer on a long table. Shelves wrapping around three sides of the room were stacked with drugs that had been consigned to the fire. There were locks on both doors, and an operator was present "*most* of the time," according to Kelly.

I asked, "What does 'most' mean?"

"Eighteen hours a day. But the doors are always locked, a hundred percent."

But maybe the man with the key took a break now and then. My excitement over tracking the sux to its last known whereabouts had cooled. What now?

As we walked back toward the elevator, Kelly was saying to Conklin, "You're here about that Stealth Killer, right?"

He said, "Could be. Any thoughts on that?"

"Well," Kelly said, blinking up at my partner, "I probably shouldn't say this, but I saw an aide sneaking around down here a couple weeks ago after the storage room was closed for the day."

"Really?" I said, my enthusiasm warming up a touch. "You know the name of this aide?"

"Doreen something."

"What does Doreen look like?"

Kelly said, "About my height, blond, hippy."

We had been looking for a man, but could the woman Kelly described have passed as a "weird-looking" dude?

She said, "Doreen works at the Loony Bin. That's the psych ward? It's across Hyde and around the corner on Bush. Redbrick compound with a wrought-iron fence out front? There's a shortcut to the Bin through our basement, you know?"

"Didn't know," Conklin said. "That's very interesting, Kelly."

"Yeah, this corridor goes directly to Hyde Street Psychiatric," she said, pointing over my shoulder. "Psych patients are transported from the hospital to the Bin and vice versa. Like, Doreen could have come from the Bin to the furnace and no one would know. Ready to go back upstairs?" she asked.

Conklin said, "I think we'll take the Hyde Street detour. Thanks for your help. We appreciate it."

As my partner and I struck out along the underground route to the psychiatric hospital, the little voice in my head was pleading, *Doreen Something, are you our killer? Please, God. Give us a sign.*

CHAPTER 77

I HAD BEEN feeling that we were playing beat the clock with the Stealth Killer, that this maniac could be winding up for another random hit. Was it possible that he was close by, that he worked at the Hyde Street Psychiatric Center?

Conklin and I found Dr. Terry Hoover in the common room of the Center's North Ward. He was tall and bespectacled, wore his tie loosely knotted and his shirtsleeves rolled to the elbows. He waved us into his glass-walled office, which had a 360-degree view of the busy corridor that ran past Ward Six and the nurses' station. He kept his eyes on all 360 degrees as we spoke with him.

I downplayed our reason for this sudden visit by the SFPD, telling Dr. Hoover that Conklin and I were investigating illegal use of succinylcholine, that an empty vial of sux found near a murder scene had led us to Saint Vartan's.

I explained that the vial had come from an expired lot that had been marked for destruction in the hospital furnace.

"While we were at Saint Vartan's we were told that one of your nurse's aides had been seen poking around their drug incinerator."

"One of *our* aides? I don't understand. Wait, this isn't about those murders I read about?"

"We just have to check it out," I said to the doctor. "What can you tell us about a nurse's aide, first name Doreen?"

"Doreen Collins. She's been with us for about four years. A very kind woman. I can't imagine why she would be anywhere near the furnace," said Hoover. "Does she need a lawyer?"

"No, no," said Conklin. "We just want to ask her a few questions."

"Let me talk to her," said Hoover.

Conklin and I went with the doctor down the long hallway to a busy ward where Doreen Collins was massaging a patient's hands. She looked to be about thirty, wide through the hips, not more than five two, with short, choppy blond hair.

Hoover said to the patient, "I'm sorry, Mr. Fritz. I need a few words with Doreen."

The nurse's aide came over to us and she looked terrified. Why?

Hoover asked, "Doreen, these are police officers, looking into missing succinylcholine. Do you know anything about that?"

She shook her head vigorously and said, "No, I don't know anything. Why would anyone want sux? Why are you asking me?"

Hoover said, "Apparently, someone saw you hanging around the furnace in the basement."

The woman's hands went to her face and she dissolved straight into tears.

"I'm diabetic," she said. "I'm sorry, Dr. Hoover. I was looking for insulin. The door was locked. I punched in my code, and when it didn't work I left. I didn't take anything."

"Please don't do that again, Doreen. Stealing drugs will get you fired. Expired insulin could get you killed. Do you understand?"

Hoover took his eyes off Ms. Collins, flicked them past the crowd of patients and staff who were slow-walking past the doorway.

He said, "Sergeant, Doreen is, in fact, diabetic. She has a perfect performance record at Hyde Street Psych. Is she a suspect?"

Doreen said, "I only did this once. I swear to God, I didn't take anything. I swear to *God*."

CHAPTER 78

CONKLIN AND I questioned Ms. Collins in an exam room down the corridor from Dr. Hoover's office. She accounted for her whereabouts at the time Mr. Beardsley was killed. She said she had been here at Hyde Street Psychiatric, had reported to the nurses' station at four in the afternoon, and had worked with patients and other staff members, not leaving the center until midnight, when she punched out. She took us to her locker, opened her handbag, and showed us her time card. And while we were there, she gave us a go-ahead to search her bag and her locker.

In short, she had a solid alibi for the time of Beardsley's death. I took her contact info, as well as that of her mother and roommate, gave her my card, and asked her to call us if she had any ideas that might help the SFPD.

Conklin and I returned to Dr. Hoover's office. He was distracted, and after we gave him our cards, he was done.

"I don't see how I can help you further," he said with finality.

We left Hoover in his office and edged through a swarm of milling patients in the common room, one of whom came up to us. His hair was silver-shot blond. I made him to be five four, 130, and possibly in his fifties. He had an awkward stance, proportionately short arms, and an overall gnome-like appearance.

"I'm Neddie," he said in a high-pitched, cartoonish voice. He grinned at me. "I'm good. Are you good?"

I smiled back at him and said, "Hi, Neddie. Everyone is good."

I looked around at the other patients in Dr. Hoover's ward and saw people with obvious challenges and others who looked as normal as anyone in any crowd. Some of the patients wandered, some played games, one sang "The Star-Spangled Banner" while lying in the intersection of two corridors. Another group watched *Dr. Phil* on TV.

There was noise all around, but my internal alarms were quiet. What I now knew about Saint Vartan's and this psych center led me to conclude that we had both too many suspects and none whatsoever.

Conklin and I made our way out of the labyrinthine Hyde Street Psychiatric Center. Out on the street I said to my partner, "I hate square one."

"Let's grab lunch," Conklin said. "I think better when I'm not half starving."

"Copy that."

CHAPTER 79

NEDDIE WATCHED THE two cops talking to Doreen Collins and heard her crying, "I'm diabetic. I'm sorry, Dr. Hoover. I was looking for insulin."

Neddie was paralyzed by panic. Cops were *here*. *Right here*.

He didn't get it at all.

What had brought them to the Bin, and why were they grilling *Doreen*?

The vial of sux he'd stupidly dropped. That was coded. They'd traced it to the hospital. And the rest of it came together in a horrible, stinking flash.

He'd been *seen*, either when he stuck the woman outside the Admiral Dewey—or maybe when he stuck the football-player dude. He had gotten careless. *Someone* had seen him and described him to the cops.

This was bad.

He'd known Doreen casually for four years, but now he saw that they resembled each other in the grossest, most general way. Both of them were short and blondish.

But Neddie was pretty sure that once the cops talked to Doreen, they'd know how stupid she was, too thick to pull off murder under any circumstances. And elegant murders? Never.

Another thought struck him.

Mikey had told Hoover about his night flights. Would Hoover tell the cops that he disappeared sometimes all night long?

He went cold and numb just thinking about that.

Hoover was very smart, but he was arrogant. Neddie had been the perfect idiot for so long, would Hoover even consider that Neddie was a killer? No. No, no, no. Never.

Or was this his own arrogance speaking?

He had to check on this to be sure. He wanted to see Hoover's expression. He wanted to see the cops' eyes when they looked at him. It was compulsive, he knew, but he'd learned many lessons during his lifetime in lockup. One of those lessons was how to read faces.

He would know if he was a suspect when he looked into the eyes of those cops.

Neddie cut through the little gang of gawkers outside Hoover's office and approached the two cops, a man and a woman who could have been the two cops who had stopped him on the patio outside the Waterside Restaurant.

"I'm Neddie," he said in squeak mode. "I'm good. Are you good?"

Hoover's voice boomed. "Neddie, Carlos, Tommy, please clear the hallway. Thank you."

The tall, blond woman cop looked Neddie in the eyes, checking him out, maybe asking herself, *Is this one a killer?* Then she smiled at him, dismissing Neddie as everyone always did.

"Hi, Neddie. Everyone is good," she said.

Could he count on that?

He still had his spare keys. They hadn't found the sux he'd plucked from the cart in the electro-convulsive unit at the end of the hall. The cops had nothing on him.

He could run.

Where would he go?

CHAPTER 80

CONNOR GRANT HUMMED and sang along with Pavarotti over his sound system as he packed for his liftoff to obscurity.

His ribs ached. The right side of his jaw was still shades of green and blue, but his week-old beard disguised the remains of the beatdown, and he was moving around just fine.

He came down from his bedroom with the bag that he had packed with a few basics—enough for about four days—which he would ditch as soon as he got overseas.

Inside his office, with the tenor keeping him company, he swung open the hinged bookcase and tapped the digital code into the wall safe behind it. He removed a banded stack of currency, a half dozen credit cards embossed with assorted names, several passports, and a one-way first-class plane ticket to Zurich. He slipped the ticket and chosen passport into the inside breast pocket of his "cheerful" blue jacket.

The small fireplace was working on some notebooks he'd piled in pyramid fashion, and the blaze was at a nice steady burn. He grabbed a few files from his desk drawers and fed them to the flames. It was time to get rid of all his souvenirs, the clippings of the original fire back in Maynard, Wisconsin. His memories were vivid enough. He'd started a grass fire that had traveled across the small yard, lighting up a propane tank, which blew up the small wood-frame house, killing everyone inside: mother, father, and little brother Lane Kingsley.

Ninth grader Adam Kingsley had set the fire. He watched the shattering of glass and the explosion and the inferno that burned until nothing was left. Even the human remains were unidentifiable. He'd never cared for his family, and they hadn't cared for him, either. As a breeze blew across the cinders and ash, he saw an opportunity to become someone else. Someone better.

He hitched to Michigan, took on a new name, dummied up a birth certificate, and convinced Ann Arbor Senior High to let him into the eleventh grade. The next year he got a driver's license at the DMV. He started college that year, and four years later, when a car bomb killed three kids in the senior class and he was presumed to be a fourth person in that car, he took on a new identity in a new town.

By the time he graduated from the University of Miami School of Law as Sam Marx, he had perfected his methods of switching lives: missing persons, dead babies, unidentifiable victims of fires and explosions that he'd set—all became his cash flow and the framework for new lives.

When his pièce de résistance, the Sci-Tron explosion, sucked up all the available fire and rescue manpower in San Francisco, no one thought about the apartment fire in Nob Hill that burned up the remains of a bachelor, Jonathan Bishop, as well as several other people living in that building.

The real Jonathan Bishop had been an investment banker, and although his body was ashes now, his life story would carry on. "Connor Grant" gathered up his folder containing documents of Jonathan Bishop's life and dropped them into his bag.

Jonathan Bishop's history was filling his mind, his career path and family history, the well-planned and fortunate life of an elite one percenter in America.

And so, what to do with his own remains?

Grant crossed the small room to the photo gallery over the credenza. He lifted the few framed photos down from the wall: pictures of himself as a child; the seductive shot of his third ex-wife, RIP; the only picture he had of the Kingsleys; and in the back of the frame, behind the cardboard, was Sam Marx's diploma from the University of Miami.

They had to go.

He removed the photos and the diploma from their frames, then put them into the fire. Jonathan Bishop wouldn't need them in Zurich.

Grant stirred the fire with a poker. Then he took all his backup CDs and broke them up. He had already wiped his hard drive; it was sparkling clean and would come with him overseas.

Bye-bye, Connor Grant.

He was panting a little, sweating from the heat of the fire, when he made iced tea. He took the glass back to the easy chair in his living room and sipped tea until the guttering flames died.

As an afterthought he pulled a book on international banking from the bookshelf and tossed that into the bag and zipped it up.

The man still known as Connor Grant was elated to be leaving town. But he wouldn't ship out without giving San Francisco a great big kiss good-bye.

CHAPTER 81

GRANT LEFT HIS blue-and-white little granny house through the kitchen door and stepped out into the driveway. His large canvas duffel bag was where he had left it on a luggage trolley beside his old Hyundai.

He tossed his travel bag into the front seat, carefully loaded the duffel into the trunk, and folded up the trolley, which he fit into the trunk on top of the duffel.

Reaching behind him, he took his semiauto handgun out of his waistband and secured it under the driver's seat.

Done, done, and done.

He walked over the gravel drive and out to the front yard.

The uniformed officers were parked in their patrol car at the curb, coffee containers in hand, car radio on full blast. Officer Brad Jamison was a rookie. His partner, Ray Baxter, was an old-timer. The two of them together didn't have the brainpower of a mosquito. This was San Francisco PD's idea of protection.

"Officers," he said. "I'm taking Sergeant Boxer's advice. Leaving my house and checking into a hotel for a while. My insurance company is paying for it."

"Well, that's fine, Mr. Grant. You should let Sergeant Boxer know where you're off to."

"Already did it," said Grant.

"You need any help with your luggage or anything?" Officer Baxter asked.

"No, no thanks."

"So where are we going?"

"Not we. Just little old me. Like I told the sergeant, I won't be needing protection for a couple of weeks. I'll stay at the Marriott while I look for a new place."

Jamison said, "Okeydoke. You should also fill out a form at the post office so they hold your mail."

"Good idea. So thanks for—uh, thanks."

It was noon when Grant turned out of his driveway and headed toward Bayshore Boulevard. He drove carefully. No mistakes now. No traffic stops. No license checks. No ironic moments. He was on track with his well-wrought plan for a carefully executed and beautiful metamorphosis.

Soon he would be in another country, playing an even greater role on an even grander stage. And the memories of all his past roles would continue on inside him.

God, he loved his life.

CHAPTER 82

CONKLIN AND I were parked in front of the red-brick Hyde Street Psychiatric Center, lunching on egg salad sandwiches.

"It was always a long shot," my partner said to me. "All we had was a label *this* big with no trace, no nothing on it."

"You know what I hate?" I asked him.

"Yep, I do. You hate square one and egg salad with pieces of shell—"

"I hate waiting now for another murder so we can hope for another chance at this—"

"Look," Conklin said, pointing past my nose and out the side window.

"What am I looking at?"

"That guy. He's a patient. What's he doing outside?"

I saw him now. His name was Neddie. He was coming out of an alley that ran between the brick face of the psych center and a blank concrete side of the Walgreens. His hands were in his pockets, eyes down, and his posture and gait were purposeful, entirely different from the awkward movements he'd exhibited just a half hour ago.

My partner and I exited the car and began following Neddie from a distance. I wasn't ready to question him until I knew what he was up to.

He was directly ahead of us when he took a right turn onto Jones Street. We were so close to him that I was shocked when we turned the corner and he was just not where I thought he should be. In fact, I didn't see him anywhere. Not in the shade of the smoke shop awning, not buying a paper from the newsstand, not crossing the street. It was as if he'd stepped through a portal into a fourth dimension.

"Oh, come onnnn. Rich, where'd he go?"

"He wasn't carrying a knapsack, right? Didn't have a bag?" Conklin asked.

"No. Hands in pockets. Nothing on his shoulders or in his hands, I'm sure of it," I said.

"Then he'll be back."

My mind was doing flip-flops. Even if we hadn't lost Neddie, what could we charge him with? Leaving the psych center? Maybe he was allowed to go to the post office or whatever. Were we making shit up out of pure desperation?

We looked up and down Jones, peering into shop windows, and didn't see Neddie. We split up. I went up Geary, and Richie took O'Farrell. We checked in with each other by phone, and fifteen minutes after losing Neddie, Conklin and I met back at the car. We took our seats and kept our eyes on the alley. Damn it to hell! How did we freaking lose that guy?

And then—*Neddie walked right past us.* His eyes were still down and he was talking to himself.

I heard only a few words: "…need some cash."

I said to Conklin, "Now."

We sprang out of the unmarked car and walked up on Neddie as he turned into the alley.

We were ten feet away when he saw us and started to *scream*. He unlocked the green metal door that led to the building and disappeared inside. I heard the door lock behind him. I pulled on the handle anyway, but it was secure.

I let out a few loud curses.

Conklin pulled his gun and shot out the lock.

CHAPTER 83

CONKLIN PULLED OPEN the metal door, and we rushed through the doorway into a garbage room piled high with bulging construction bags. The room was about fifteen feet square and was bracketed by two doors.

We'd come through the first, the metal door that connected the trash room to the alley. Neddie was crouched against the wooden door in the far wall, which led to the underground corridor—and he was screaming, "I'm *good*. I'm *good*."

At the same time he was trying to fit a key into the door lock and was having no luck. His height and the short length of his arms and his fear were preventing him from inserting the key.

I took very quick stock of the situation. Neddie was crying and wailing, and yet I'd seen him walking normally. If what he was doing now was an act, it was a very convincing act of a man playing with half a deck.

My gun was in my hand when I said, "Neddie. Give me your keys."

He was making terrible whimpering sounds, like a small animal caught in a trap. I wondered what the hell I thought I was doing, holding a gun on a mental patient armed with a set of keys.

Did I seriously think I would shoot him? For what?

Was this the "weird-looking guy" who might have killed a half dozen people or more? Or was he just what he seemed to be, a mental patient on a walkabout? I couldn't know. And I couldn't take any chances.

Conklin said, "Neddie. I'm Richie. No one's going to hurt you. See?" He showed Neddie his gun, then opened his jacket and slipped the gun into his holster.

"My partner, Lindsay, will put her gun away, too."

I did it.

Rich went on, "Sorry to scare you, Neddie. Sorry about the noise. Let's go upstairs so we can talk."

Bags rustled behind me. I spun around and saw a maintenance worker hiding between the garbage bags and the wall, his hands over his ears, trying to make himself invisible.

Neddie said to Conklin, "Talk. Just talk, right, Richie?"

Rich reassured him, and Neddie said, "I give up, I give up."

Neddie was holding a small bunch of keys above his head, and Rich reached for them. Neddie ducked under Rich's arm and threw himself face-down on top of the orderly.

What is this?

Neddie said to the man, "Lawrence, we're leaving here together."

Lawrence said, "Neddie, leave me out of this. Go or don't go. It's no business of mine."

"It is now," said Neddie.

The squeal in his voice was gone. Neddie had a straight-up normal voice and there was something in his hand. Conklin and I saw it at the same time. It was a syringe, and Neddie had positioned the needle so that it pricked Lawrence's neck.

One minute we had been trying to disarm a suspect with a set of keys. Now we had a hostage situation that couldn't be more unstable. This had to be handled with competence and grace, or people were going to die.

I used my soothing hostage-negotiator tone. "Neddie. Tell me what you want so we can keep everyone safe."

Neddie angled for a more comfortable position on his bed made of Lawrence's body and the garbage pile. I could see the dimple in Lawrence's neck where the needle penetrated flesh. Blood beaded up on his skin.

If Neddie pushed the plunger on the syringe, Lawrence would become paralyzed, and if he couldn't breathe, he would die. We were only a short sprint from the hospital, but as I understood the effect of sux, we might as well be on Mars.

"Neddie," I said. "Tell me what you *want*."

"I'm working on it," he said. "But while I figure that out, put your guns down on the floor. If you call for help, if you let anyone through either door, my friend Larry is a corpse. I guarantee it."

CHAPTER 84

I WAS STILL stunned by the changes in Neddie. His high-pitched, singsongy speech was gone. When he fixed his eyes on mine, I saw cool resolve. He was cornered and he was willing to kill. He might also be willing to die.

Ten feet away from where I stood, Lawrence breathed loudly and stretched his neck minutely in an attempt to move it away from the needle.

Neddie adjusted his position correspondingly, pressing down on Lawrence with his full weight, sending the needle in deeper.

I said, "I think I understand what you want, Neddie. No guns. No one comes in and no one leaves. What's on your mind?"

He said, "I've killed eight people. Larry is lined up to be number nine, but here's the thing. I don't like odd numbers. If I kill him, I've got to kill one of you. I admit that would be hard to do. So here's the deal:

"Take your guns out with your fingertips and kick them over to me. I'll leave and lock the door behind me. Anyone comes after me, I'll shoot.

After I'm clear of this shithole, you'll never see me again."

"We can't do that," I said. "It's got to be our way. Put down the needle, Neddie. Live to see another day."

"Oh, Lady Cop, do you really think I'll just give up and let you put me away? I've been locked up for my whole life. Isn't that enough?"

We were in a freaking standoff from hell. Adrenaline had red-lined my heart rate. I was fully aware that Neddie could pump Larry full of sux before I got my gun out of my holster.

I said in the calmest tone I could muster, "I hear you, Neddie, and here's my counteroffer. Let Larry go. My partner and I will work with the DA and tell your side of the story. The abuse you've suffered. The extenuating circumstances that brought you to this point. He'll listen to us."

Neddie remained in a crouch only yards in front of me. It wasn't going well for Larry. He whimpered and said, "Neddie, man, I never did anything to you."

Neddie said, "Shut up, Larry." It looked to me that he was weighing his options. I was weighing mine. Could I dive onto him? Knock the needle out of his hand?

I was gauging the distance when Neddie spoke.

"If I give up," he said, "you have to tell the media in your own words. Make sure they understand that I'm a genius who fooled everyone. You have to make it clear that in your professional opinion, Edward Lamborghini is one of the most brilliant serial killers—of this century. Do that. Give me your word."

I didn't trust *him,* but I needed him to trust *me*.

I said, "Okay, Neddie. That's a deal I can live with. You have my word. Now slowly toss the needle down."

A dreamy smile came over his face. What was this psycho thinking? He locked his eyes on mine. And—no! He pushed the plunger.

At the same time I heard the shot.

Conklin!

Neddie shouted and the needle jumped out of his hand. He gagged, rolled off Lawrence and the mound of garbage bags, and lay still.

Conklin went to Lawrence, who clasped the side of his neck and gasped, "He…stabbed me."

I grabbed the keys off the floor and jammed one after the other into the lock in the basement door. On the third try the key twisted easily and the door creaked open. I ran into the cavernous and well-traveled basement corridor.

I saw a medical team conveying a patient on a stretcher toward Saint Vartan's. I flashed my badge and I yelled, "*We need help*. Two men are down. One needs a respirator, NOW. We need an emergency unit, NOW."

CHAPTER 85

NEDDIE HADNT MOVED since he was shot, but Lawrence Janes was gasping the shallowest of breaths.

I held his hand. I was thinking that the sux was old. There was a chance Neddie hadn't shot the full dose into Larry before he went down. If sux was injected into a muscle, rather than an artery, it took longer for the drug to paralyze the body. That was good for Larry.

I fanned a small flame of hope and stayed with him, telling him, "It's going to be okay. You're going to be fine. I'm here. We're getting help. Hang in there, Larry. Hang in there."

An emergency team blew through the doorway. "He was injected with sux," I said.

The medic didn't ask any questions, just went straight to work and bagged Larry right there on the floor. Seeing his chest rise and fall gave me such relief that tears came into my eyes.

Another doctor attended to Neddie. He listened to his heart and announced, "He's gone." With his body limp, spread out on the pile of garbage bags, Neddie looked deceptively young and innocent and *good*.

I took Richie's gun and I called Brady.

"It was a good shoot, Brady," I said. "Conklin had no choice."

"I'm on the way," said Brady.

I told the medical personnel to leave Neddie's body just as it was. That the police were coming. That everything in this room was ours until further notice.

I opened the alley door and stood in the doorway with Richie, looking out at the blank concrete wall.

I said to my partner, "Neddie had no way out and so he chose suicide by *you*, Rich. He said he didn't want to spend another day in lockup. He knew we were armed. He wanted to go out on murder victim number nine. You saved Larry's life, and he's going to have a great story to tell his grandchildren. You did what you had to do. And you did it perfectly."

He nodded. He said, "Thanks," but he was hurting. And then he said, "You know what I hate?"

"I do."

He hates to shoot someone. He hated that he'd taken a life. I told my partner that I'd be back in a second, then wandered out into the alley, out of earshot from Rich, and called Cindy.

"I've got something for you," I said. "The Stealth Killer is dead, and yes, that's on the record. Give me a couple of hours, I'll get Brady to give it to you officially and with quotes."

"That would be tremendous, Lindsay."

"Right now, though, can you call Richie? I think he really needs to talk to you."

CHAPTER 86

CINDY WAS IN her office at the *San Francisco Chronicle* polishing her story, headlined, "The Stealth Killer's Last Stand."

Lindsay had told her about the shooting death of Edward Lamborghini, a.k.a. Neddie Lambo, by an unnamed homicide inspector and how close the victim had come to taking the life of hospital employee Lawrence Janes. Lindsay had also put Brady on the phone to confirm her story, after which Cindy had spoken with Dr. Terry Hoover, director of the Hyde Street Psychiatric Center.

According to Dr. Hoover, Neddie had had "privileges." Chief among them was that he had permission to leave the facility alone during daylight hours as long as he returned by dinnertime curfew.

The dazed Dr. Hoover allowed that Neddie had been well liked, a friend to all, and that it seemed to him in retrospect that this patient had been wildly underestimated.

"It's possible, I suppose," said Hoover, "that Edward could have had access to drugs here at the psychiatric facility, to the pharmacy at Saint Vartan's, and to the whole of San Francisco. But did he commit any crimes? The Neddie Lambo I knew could never have done that."

But he had.

After speaking with Hoover, Cindy had researched Edward Lamborghini's background, and while she couldn't unseal his criminal record, she thought he had to have committed a horrific crime to be sent to Johnston Youth Correctional when he was only seven years old. When Johnston had closed, Neddie was transferred to the Hyde Street Psychiatric Center, a next-to-zero-security hospital. She thought the facility would be tightening up their "privileges" policy. PDQ.

Cindy scrolled to the top of her page. Under the headline was her lead paragraph.

Edward Lamborghini, a patient at the Hyde Street Psychiatric Center on Bush Street at Hyde, was shot to death today by a homicide inspector of the SFPD.

Sergeant Lindsay Boxer, who was present at the scene during the incident, said, "Mr. Lamborghini confessed to killing eight people. He was armed and holding a bystander hostage. He refused to drop his weapon and attempted to kill his hostage with a lethal injection before he was brought down."

Lindsay's quote was perfect. Richie hadn't been able to speak to her on the record about his takedown of Neddie Lambo, but he'd given her background color that had made the writing pop:

descriptions of the signage in the trash room, the smell of garbage, the look of the cavernous underground tunnel.

The story was good. Vivid. Accurate. Moving.

Cindy reread the entire four-thousand-word piece again, tightened it up in a few places, spell-checked everything.

Then she sent her story to the editor in chief, Henry Tyler.

While she waited for him to read it, she called Richie. When she left him that morning, he'd been in deep sleep getting the rest he deserved and needed.

"I'm doing good, babe," he said to her. "I'm having chocolate chocolate chip ice cream and coffee with heavy cream. You only live once, right?"

"Totally right."

"And now I think I'll go back to bed."

Cindy smiled, just picturing him. "See you later. I love you," she said.

"I love you, too, Cin."

Tyler buzzed her.

She punched a button on her console. "Henry?"

"Great job, Cindy. Fire away. Let's meet after lunch and discuss your follow-up on this."

Cindy sent her "Stealth Killer" to the copyeditor and sat back to enjoy the moment.

Tyler loved the piece. And people who had been afraid of "the Stealth Killer" would now feel safer out on the street.

Cindy tidied her desk, then went to the cafeteria for a late breakfast. When she returned to her desk and opened her mail, she saw that her inbox was overflowing. The e-mails all voiced variations on the theme, *What great news! Thank God it's over*.

Almost buried in that avalanche of e-mail was one from Lindsay reminding the members of the Women's Murder Club that they had a meeting tonight, not for laughs over a spicy meal but a working get-together at the Hall of Justice Homicide squad room.

Lindsay was hoping that if they pooled their resources and gave the Connor Grant files a thorough thrashing, they might come up with something damning enough to counter his unjustified, vengeful, and just plain evil complaint against Lindsay.

If it was possible, Cindy was sure that the four of them could do it.

CHAPTER 87

I HAD COMMANDEERED the break room for our meeting because it had a long, well-used table and four folding chairs. There was also a coffeemaker close at hand and a big tin of oatmeal cookies on the counter, courtesy of Inspector Samuels.

I'd asked the property room to bring up the dozens of boxes we'd taken from Connor Grant's garage laboratory before his trial; he had never asked for their return. They were stacked now in a line against a wall, twelve across, eight high.

Conklin and I had gone through about half of the boxes before the trial and marked the ones we'd ransacked with an *X*. Nothing we'd found rose to the level of evidence against the science teacher. No. The boxes were neatly filled with papers related to classwork, but no material on bombs, mass murder, GAR, or any antigovernment activity, like we'd hoped to find.

We'd given up after the fiftieth box, owing to the press of work and shortage of manpower. Tonight the WMC was going to dig through the rest.

"Why bother with this?" I asked the girls rhetorically. "Because his complaint to IAB calls me a liar and could cost me my job and my career. Also, and probably more importantly, I think the guy is guilty. He told me that he bombed Sci-Tron. Why?"

"My theory," said Claire, "is that he's like an arsonist. He was elated at having pulled off the explosion. He was high. So he bragged to you, and then reality set in when he was booked."

Yuki said, "Or he wanted to up the stakes. Blow up Sci-Tron and also beat the justice system."

I said, "I like both theories. Connor Grant is the human equivalent of a switchblade. He acted as his own—brilliant—lawyer and he got off. In my opinion, that just does not comport with the personality of a career high school science teacher. Yuki, you agree?"

"In spades. He was smooth and tricky and sympathetic at the same time. Hey, he beat our pants off."

I said, "I keep asking myself, who is this masked man, anyway? Granted, going through his boxes could be yet another dive into ninth-grade science, but if there's a clue in here…"

"…we'll know it if we see it," said Cindy.

"Exactly," I said. "I'm hoping for dirty pictures, sketchy bank accounts, warrants for previous misdeeds, and of course his plans for blowing up a big public venue. Or, hey, Mr. Grant, surprise us. It would be a genuine bonus round if we found evidence of a crime that he was never charged with.

"But for tonight, as a minimum, I'd just like to find something ugly that will scare this guy and get him to retract his complaint against me."

We did a four-way fist bump and divvied up the boxes.

Claire likes to work with music. She fired up her smartphone and tuned in to something classical. Then she grabbed a filebox, lifted out a fat sheaf of paper, and set it down on the table in front of her. Yuki and Cindy worked as a team, each sorting through a box at a time, showing various bits of paper to each other as they went.

I watched everyone and worked on my own box as well.

I was scraping the bottom of my third box when a name that I had seen before jumped out at me.

I shouted, "Yuki, there's a paper here on litigation written by a Samuel Marx, U. of Miami. I found law books in Grant's place with bookplates saying they belonged to Sam Marx."

Yuki said, "Looking up Samuel Marx now."

She tapped on her laptop, then said, "He was a lawyer in Skokie, died about ten years ago in a house fire."

I said, "If you type *Sam Marx* plus *Connor Grant,* what do you get?"

She shook her head. Nothing. Had Grant known Marx? Had he bought Marx's books at a tag sale? It was a connection between Grant and the law, but it added up to nothing. Yet.

CHAPTER **88**

WE WORKED FROM six until ten, when Claire said, "Let's air out our brains, okay?"

She cued up one of her husband Edmund's orchestra pieces, the Double Bass Concerto in D Major, by Vanhal. The music absolutely lightened our moods. Coffee cups were topped up and we polished off the tin of oatmeal cookies, including the crumbs. Cindy, Claire, and Yuki texted their significant others and I called Mrs. Rose, telling her that I'd be home in a couple of hours. "I hope so, anyway."

But unopened boxes were calling. After the break we began sifting and sorting again.

Mainly, we had found photocopies of newspaper clippings about explosions, randomly interspersed between tests on astronomy, paleontology, and basic chemistry, papers we'd set aside for further discussion.

When all boxes had been searched, we talked back and forth about our findings. For instance, I had something in my hand that was pretty shocking.

It was a copy of a Wisconsin newspaper article about a house fire thirty years ago in which a family had died. According to the story, a backyard grass fire had lit up a propane tank, destroying a suburban home, flattening it to rubble. Four people had lived in that house, and they were so burned up, the bodies couldn't be identified.

It seemed significant, so I opened it up to the floor.

"Is this the beginning of Connor Grant's story? Did this gas explosion get him thinking about the power and the glory of bombs? Why else would he save it?"

Claire said, "He may have known the family?"

She googled the name of the town and Connor Grant's name, then said, "I got zippo."

We took a few more spins around the internet, and the search for *Connor Grant science teacher* produced small-time science fair pieces on Grant going back a dozen years.

"They could be real stories, or they could be planted," Cindy said. "It's not too hard to post something about yourself in a chat room or on a blog, start a website, write an article for a small-town paper. Then it gets picked up by other publications, not fact-checked, and then it shows up multiple times on Google."

"Listen to this," Claire said. She read from the article. "William Tilley officiated at a memorial service for his friend Connor Grant, a climate scientist who was killed in a plane crash."

Claire looked up. She said, "This Connor

Grant's body was never recovered from the burned wreckage."

"Is there a picture?" Cindy asked.

There was. But the dead-in-a-plane-crash scientist Connor Grant didn't look anything like our Connor Grant. I stared at the photo of the chief mourner, William Tilley. He wasn't Connor Grant's twin, but I thought he looked more like our Connor Grant than the dead man.

I googled Tilley's name and four thousand *William Willy Bill Billy Tilley*s popped up.

So where were we? We had a collection of articles citing the violent, fiery deaths of several people who didn't actually link up. What did these people mean to Connor Grant?

Why did he collect stories of this type of tragedy?

Were they his victims?

We weren't going to be able to chase down all these deaths tonight. After six hours of dedicated hard work, we'd crossed off every last box, found semi-intriguing tidbits that added up to not much of anything and certainly not a dirty bomb to drop on my enemy.

"Thanks for the really good try," I said.

The girls said that they were sorry, and we hugged all around before cleaning up and leaving for home.

I thought about Grant on the drive back to Lake Street. Had we been looking for something that didn't exist? Was Connor Grant exactly who he said he was—a high school teacher with a deep and far-reaching mind? If so, why did I persist in feeling that he had scammed all of us by getting away with mass murder? Was Grant a mystery that would never be solved?

He still had me in the stocks with his IAB complaint, but as for what I had on him?

I *still* didn't have even a clue.

CHAPTER 89

THE MAN WHO was spending his last twenty-four hours as Connor Grant counted out his cash. He had forty-five dollars in fives, eight singles, and some loose change. He wanted to use all of it before he got on the plane.

He had been staying inside his suite at the middle-of-the-road businessmen's Travelers' Inn for the last two days. No one knew where he was—not his lawyer, not the cops, not the school. He had wanted this little cushion of alone time in order to rest up before his big farewell to the City by the Bay.

He had spent the time well, lying in the middle of the big bed, listening to his playlist of favorites on his iPhone. Room service on demand. Memories on demand, too.

He took his time and reviewed the five years he'd spent in San Francisco. He thought about the kids in his classes at Saint Brendan, and by count, he remembered every one of them.

He remembered meals with ocean views, cable car and ferry rides, books he'd read by the fire in his little house. He thought of women he had slept with and their stories, and he didn't skip over the conversations or the good-byes.

He sipped his Scotch and played his music, un-spooled the images in his mind. He wanted to save the best for last, and then it was there. He re-membered building the compression bomb with a fire extinguisher, filling it with gas, adding the perchlorate, leaving the bomb under the skirts of the space travel exhibit, which was a few yards from the spiral staircase that went up to the dome.

He remembered packing the fistful of C-4 with a timer into the cyborg exhibit at the front of the Welcome Gallery, so that the doors would blow twenty-five minutes after the big compression bomb detonated.

And he thought about that girl he'd paid for a couple of hours earlier that day. Irish, he thought. Reserved. Modest, even. She'd needed the money and he had needed her. Win-win.

While the sunset came on outside his windows, "Grant" let the rest of that evening play unedited through his mind. He remembered with crystal clarity that he had been standing on the Embar-cadero not far from Pier 15 as the timer set off the compression bomb. The size and scope of the blast had been beyond his expectations. The shower of glass seemed to turn the air to ice, freeze it so that it reflected the light and the roaring magnificence as the building fell to its knees.

Images overlapped: the destruction still unfurling, overlaid with the screaming of fire engines and of the crowds, so many people. That explosion was one of the pinnacles of his life.

The two months in jail had passed quickly as he prepared for the trial. He had relished the planning of it, and it had exceeded his dreams in the execution. It had been so easy, and even hilarious to watch the faces of the prosecution as he turned the jury into his best friends.

Too bad he wouldn't be here for Lindsay Boxer to get the boot from the SFPD. The humiliation would devastate her, but for him, the complaint had just been a distraction while he planned his next move.

Grant finished his Scotch and looked at the room service menu. He ordered, and while he waited, there was one thing he wanted to do before checking out tomorrow. He wanted to thank his friend Dylan Mitchell, the great Haight himself. He picked up his burner phone and composed an e-mail.

Haight, I'm a leavin', on a jet plane. Thank you for your guidance, inspiration, encouragement. Couldn't have made glass rain under a setting sun without you.

Grant

He sent the message, and it was answered immediately.

Grant, you've left your mark on the movement. I am glad to have helped you birth your vision. Thanks for the gift of your notebook. Burn your phone. AN

AN, "Apocalypse Now."

Grant sighed happily. No more souvenirs. He took the chip out of the phone and flushed it down the toilet. Then he opened the door all the way for the room service waiter and his double cheese-burger.

CHAPTER 90

I WAS WORKING late at my desk, moments from shutting off the computer, when Jacobi appeared in front of me.

"Glad I caught you."

"Only good news, please, Jacobi."

"Task force needs you."

"No, no, no, they don't. I'm wiped. I'm done."

Jacobi continued talking as if he hadn't heard me, and I was quite sure there was nothing wrong with his hearing.

"Do you know of a Dylan Mitchell, goes by the name of Haight?"

"Hate?" I said. "What's that? Some kind of tag?"

Jacobi said, "H-a-i-g-h-t. Like the street."

I shut down my computer. Drank down the dregs of my coffee, threw the container into the trash.

"Don't think so. What about him?" I asked.

"He's a big player in the terrorist underground. He grew up on the flower-power down-with-the-government revolution and has turned into a cheerleader for the new suicide bomb generation."

"I'm not sure I'm following."

Jacobi laughed. "My fault. See if you follow this. This guy Haight is a pot stirrer. He disseminates videos on the so-called inevitable breakdown of the system. His motto is 'Power to the people by any means,' especially violent means. He's shrewd. Has a quick delivery. But we know where this leads. Bloody hell. Problem is, he just informs and rants but doesn't dictate or advise. So technically what he's doing is not illegal."

"I'm waiting for the punch line."

"Patience, Boxer. I'm briefing you on your assignment."

"If I choose to accept it."

He ignored me. "DHS went through J.'s computer, which he attempted to scrub and left behind in that tenement in the Tenderloin. Also, DHS went through Yang's computer. Ingleside. They found a connection between those two and Haight."

Now I was interested. Very.

Said Jacobi, "J.'s computer and Yang's have something in common, what the gearheads call hash code. Like a fingerprint, showing contact with Haight's computer, which the Feds have been hacking forever."

"But is it a crime that these three were in contact?"

Cops all around me were leaving for home. I said good night to Chi. Waved at Cappy. Samuels said, "Do you need help here, Boxer?"

"I'm okay."

Jacobi sat on the corner of my desk.

"Boxer."

"I'm listening."

"Good. Because this is where I get to the point. This really is going somewhere. Haight is in the spotlight because two known terrorists contacted him. Now DHS just got a hit on Haight's computer. Connor Grant e-mailed Haight and he wrote back."

"Really?"

"Really," said Jacobi. "This is the key fact. Grant thanked Haight for his support. Guessing that the support was for Grant's attack on Sci-Tron. Grant says to Haight that he's leaving town. Didn't say when, and we don't know where Grant is, but DHS wants to pick up Mr. Flower Power and question him. He could be a co-conspirator in a terrorist act that killed twenty-five citizens of our city."

I was stunned. I'd just about given up on Grant, and now it sounded like he had finally left a virtual fingerprint on the Sci-Tron disaster and had implicated an even bigger catch.

"SWAT is out front waiting for you. Conklin is on the way. I wish I could go," said Jacobi. "Now get out of here."

CHAPTER 91

HAIGHT WAS IN his studio watching the sky go cobalt blue beyond the reinforced glass. After his brief exchange with Connor Grant, creator of the Sci-Tron bomb, Haight changed his IP address. It had been a mistake to write to Grant, the first time he'd ever written back, but he had to say goodbye to his prize pupil. He'd always enjoyed Grant's clearheaded intelligence, his scientific mind.

He finished cleaning up his hard drive and he planned his evening. He was baking root vegetables, and while they cooked, he would post a podcast. Some audacious lone-wolf bombings had taken place this week in New York and several cities in Europe.

It was very important that he cheer on the loyal soldiers everywhere. It was important to send out a message to motivate others.

He was making his notes, gathering his thoughts for his podcast, when he saw a line of cars coming down Twentieth Street toward his factory.

Oh. Shit.

Haight heard the chopper blades as cars filled

the parking area below. He ran upstairs to the roof and put up his hands, yelling ineffectually, *"Don't shoot."*

Goddamnit. Of course he'd been hacked. No surprise but one little mistake, 122 characters, immediately deleted and cleaned to death.

And still the fucking net had closed.

"Don't shoot."

CHAPTER 92

I WAS RIDING shotgun in the lead car with tactical force commander William Niles as we bumped over the broken asphalt in the industrial section of Dogpatch. Choppers were lending air support, and Niles was on the radio, instructing his team.

As bright lights from the helicopters lit up an old factory, our assault vehicles pulled into a line, blocking the roadway and providing cover.

A man was standing on the roof of his factory home with his hands up, but when the blinding lights hit him, he ran back into the building.

Niles was out of the car and on the bullhorn.

"Come out, Mr. Mitchell. You're surrounded."

Conklin and I got out of the vehicle.

What was Haight going to do? On Niles's go, the tac team ran forward and took positions on all exits, and two men rammed in the front door.

Flashbangs lit up the windows.

And a moment later the spear tip of our counterterrorism task force went in. I found a stunned Dylan Mitchell, a.k.a. Haight, sprawled out on his bed, barely conscious.

Niles filled a pot with water and splashed it on the man who was stirring up crazy anarchists in America and the rest of the world, then yanked him awake and into a sitting position.

"What?" the man asked.

"We're arresting you for conspiracy in recent bombings and other acts of terrorism. I have federal warrants to search your premises and to confiscate your electronic devices, including your phone and your computer. Your ass belongs to the DHS until further notice."

"I haven't done anything. I posted a *blog*."

"Okay, well, we say you conspired with Connor Grant in the bombing of Sci-Tron and are implicated in the deaths of twenty-five people. That's for starters."

"I don't know any Connor Grant. And that's the truth."

Conklin was looking at something that was all but hidden under the bed on wheels. He reached under and with a gloved hand pulled out a fat notebook that looked to be handwritten and dog-eared.

I knew what it was. In fact, Conklin had found this notebook or one just like it in Grant's garage laboratory.

He read the title out loud. "'How to Make a Bomb: For Twenty-Five Dollars in Twenty-Five Minutes, by Connor A. Grant.' Bedtime reading, Mr. Mitchell?"

Looked like Haight swallowed the ordinary and stupid protest *I don't know what that is or how it got there*, but he wore the hangdog expression of defeat.

A man in black relieved Conklin of the notebook and bagged it. Niles turned to me.

"Sergeant Boxer? Will you do the honors?"

Conklin was right there with me when I spoke to the man sitting on his bed.

"Dylan Mitchell?"

He looked into my face and broke out into a smile.

"Oh, my God," he said. "I lived long enough to actually see lipstick on a pig."

I said, "I'll take that as a yes."

Conklin walked behind him and cuffed him tightly.

"Mr. Mitchell, you have the right to remain silent, understand?"

I read him every one of his rights and stepped aside as he was dragged to his feet and out the door to an assault vehicle.

He was yelling now.

"You'll never get away with this. I guarantee it."

"Tell it to your lawyer," I shouted back. "I've had a long day."

CHAPTER 93

I SLEPT WELL that night, and the next day was shaping up beautifully.

Haight—guru to the kill, torture, and explode movement, a man who had reinvented hate speech and who hid behind the name GAR—had spent the night in federal custody. One could only hope and pray that taking him out of circulation, eliminating the incendiary posts he sent out to the four corners of the planet, would have some slowing effect on homegrown terror everywhere.

In other news, there was a letter on my desk when I got to work that morning.

Conklin said, grinning sheepishly, "I read it. I couldn't help myself. I'm a detective, you know."

I said, "All right, all right. I love you anyway, you snoop."

The letter was from Lieutenant William Hoyt, IAB, formally dismissing the complaint against me on the grounds that there was "no reason for further investigation." Hoyt wrote, "You did your job by the book and went above and beyond. We're lucky to have an officer like you on the force."

Parisi stopped by with cupcakes and gave me a hug. When Parisi hugged me, I *knew* I'd been thoroughly hugged.

I called Joe from work and said, "How about dinner at our place?"

It was a big step, and I thought I was ready for it. I left work at six without anyone throwing spike strips in front of me and got home without incident.

I didn't have much time, but I dressed for the occasion, wearing tight distressed jeans and a loose white shirt, and let my hair down, the way Joe likes it. I topped off my act with aqua-blue toenails, which I showed off by going barefoot.

Joe rang the doorbell at seven on the dot and was greeted by everyone—Julie, best dog, and me. And wouldn't you know, even on short notice he brought imported sauce from a small town in northern Italy, dessert from b. Patisserie, and a bottle of Brunello, a varietal from Tuscany, which he'd bought at the liquor store down the street. I'm pretty sure that bottle cost an extravagant hundred bucks.

Joe looked like the Joe I loved and had known in so many ways: lover, husband, companion, father of my child, and secret keeper who'd sworn to make things right. His dark curls had grown out, so I asked to see his scars so that I could put my hands in his hair.

And then I was in his arms.

He kissed me, and it felt like the first time years ago when we'd worked a case together, him with the FBI, me a lieutenant with the SFPD, and there had come a moment when we both just knew— this, the two of us, it was going to happen.

Joe said, "I knew Grant's complaint was going nowhere."

"I didn't. But I couldn't make a plan B. I didn't want a plan B."

"I'm really happy with plan A."

"Me, too."

He kissed me again, and I almost forgot the pasta on the stove and a darling little girl who looked like her dad, who was underfoot, and so was Martha. We stole another kiss. And the promise was made without words.

There would be more.

Joe stirred his special red sauce, and I made the salad with radicchio and romaine, escarole, and ripe Campari tomatoes. I whipped up a balsamic vinaigrette, spiced per Joe's own recipe.

And as we cooked, we talked about bringing down Haight, of course. And we talked about Julie, how bright she was, how talkative, how she wanted a bed "without fences," and we laughed at that. Soon she would be going to kindergarten, but not yet. There was plenty of time before Julie went to school. Family time.

I set the table, and Joe brought Julie over to her chair. I was trying on the thought of asking Joe to stay the night. It was up to me. It might be better to let dinner go with kisses and hugs and have another date next week. But I knew and he knew that I missed him. Julie missed him. So much time had passed and so much had happened since we'd split up, it was crazy to obsess about the past. Right?

Joe was dishing up dinner for Julie and me when my phone buzzed, rattling the glass top of the coffee table, far away in the living room.

Joe said, "Don't take it, Linds."

Then the landline rang.

"I'd better," I said. "I'll make it quick."

I answered the wall phone in the kitchen, where I could watch Joe cutting up spaghetti for Julie.

"Right *now*?" I said to Jacobi. "Okay."

I switched on the living room TV and called my husband over.

"Joe. Look."

He stood up, came over, and focused on what I couldn't believe I was seeing. A retina-searing blast had lit up the television screen. The newsman was saying that this explosion had happened in front of City Hall.

I pressed the phone to my ear.

"Oh, my God. Warren, please tell me again what he said."

He talked and talked, and I listened even though I kept saying, "Oh, my God. Oh, my God."

CHAPTER 94

CONNOR GRANT DOUBLE-CHECKED the room for anything left behind, placed fifteen dollars on the dresser for the housekeeper. He strapped his big duffel onto the trolley, hung his travel bag over his shoulder, and headed down to the front desk.

Connor Grant's credit card was currently in good standing, and after the charges that would never be paid were rung up, he rolled his duffel bag through the doors and out to the front of the motel.

A cab was waiting.

The driver was a woman built like a jockey. She wanted to help him with his bag, but he said, "No, no. Please just open the trunk. I'll handle this."

He got into the cab, telling the driver, "Two stops, please. First, City Hall. And then SFO, international departure."

The driver said, "Okay, boss," and flipped the meter.

The man wearing the blue cap leaned back and enjoyed the ride. His plans were vivid in his mind.

He wanted his good-bye kiss to be incendiary and unforgettable. City Hall was an architectural masterpiece. Inaccessible, of course, but he had scoped out a vulnerable spot. There was a short ramp off McAllister Street that led to a valet parking area just below street level.

There would be no valet there at night, and as he saw it, he could simply leave the duffel with the timer set for when he was high above the clouds.

The driver's name was Minnie.

She was a careful driver and he liked that. She didn't speed, wasn't aggressive, and even used turn signals. They drove along McAllister, lit up and with a modest amount of traffic. Passing the intersection at Polk, they approached City Hall, and Grant leaned forward and spoke to the driver.

"Just pull in over there."

"Valet parking, you mean?" Minnie asked. "I can't. That's not allowed."

"It's okay. Completely okay," Grant said. "We're only stopping for half a minute."

She looked into the rearview mirror, caught his eyes. He smiled encouragingly. She put on her directional signal, crossed McAllister, and stopped at the top of the short ramp.

"Okay, this is good," Grant said. He could walk his duffel down to the entrance. "Just open the trunk latch for me."

"Why?" she asked. "We're still going to the airport, aren't we?"

"Yes. I'm just getting something out of the trunk."

"No, sir. I can't do that. Please understand, I've

had people run off without paying the fare. You owe me thirteen dollars fifty cents."

"Open the damned latch," he said, barely keeping his anger in check. "I'm not bolting on the fare."

He got out of the cab and walked toward the trunk. Then he saw her hand out.

"Goddamnit."

His wallet was in his travel case, inside the car. Thirteen fucking dollars.

Swearing, he opened the rear door again.

CHAPTER **95**

MASTER SERGEANT CARY Woodhouse was part of a three-man vigilante team made up of his father, Micah; his brother, Jeff; and himself.

When Connor Grant had put the jury under a spell and gotten away with twenty-five counts of murder, including that of Cary's dear wife, Lisa, he'd stood tall in the courtroom and promised Grant that he would pay for what he'd done.

Those weren't just words. It wasn't a casual promise.

Jeff had been watching Grant's house when that sicko pulled out of his driveway on Jamestown Avenue and took Route 101 to the Travelers' Inn on Lombard Street.

Jeff had waited for Micah to take the next shift, and Cary had called the motel, asked to speak to Mr. Grant—what was his room number again? He had sweet-talked the operator, said he only wanted the room number so he could send a Priority letter. That he'd tried, but the courier service would not accept the front desk as an address.

The operator had caved.

"Don't tell anyone," she said.

"I promise," Woodhouse said, and hung up his phone.

After that the three Woodhouse men took eight-hour shifts watching Grant's window from where they'd parked across the street on Lombard, in front of the Gala Restaurant and Lounge. They knew when he was sleeping. They knew when he was awake. And Cary was on watch when Grant left the Travelers' Inn carrying two bags. One hung by a strap over his shoulder. The other was a large duffel bag, which he loaded into the cab's trunk himself.

Cary Woodhouse pulled into traffic and stayed four cars back from Grant's cab. When it headed into town toward the Civic Center, five by six blocks of majestic old granite buildings surrounding a treed plaza, Woodhouse felt some alarm. City Hall was the focal point of the Civic Center, with its huge gilded dome, which was taller than even the dome topping the Capitol Building in DC.

The Civic Center Plaza was always open. It was a public square, but why would Grant be coming here at night? Cary Woodhouse continued following the cab along McAllister, crossing Polk. The cab reduced speed and signaled for a left turn. It looked like the taxi was taking the short ramp in front of City Hall that led down to a valet parking area below.

Then the cab stopped at the top of the ramp.

Woodhouse pulled his car into the fire lane, out of the way of sparse traffic, and watched Grant's cab from fifty feet away. He called Micah and Jeff, told them what he'd seen and that he was pretty sure what was on Connor Grant's program for the night.

What Grant had done to Sci-Tron had described his character in full, and a man's character didn't change. Woodhouse felt strongly that Grant was looking for another high-value target. The valet parking area was as close as a vehicle could get to the north entrance of City Hall, a beautiful and historic building, the jewel in San Francisco's crown.

The cab was still poised at the top of the ramp, not moving. He tried to anticipate Grant's next move. As he watched, the cab's left-side rear passenger door opened and Grant got out. He leaned down toward the driver's window, seemed to be demanding that the cabdriver open the trunk. It also seemed to Woodhouse that the driver was refusing. He had his hand sticking out the window, the universal sign for *Give me the money*.

Woodhouse took it that the driver wanted to be paid and that he wasn't taking the cab any farther. Maybe he'd gotten a whiff of nutcase stink off his passenger.

Woodhouse, a former military officer, didn't need to wait for this dispute to be settled. He opened his car door and placed his Ruger 10/22 rifle on the doorframe. He took a bead on Grant's temple and said softly, "This is for you, Lisa."

He fired.

A split second before Woodhouse's gun went off, Grant reached into the backseat of the cab. The crack of the rifle shot was loud enough to shock both Grant and the cabdriver.

The driver leapt from the cab and ran. It was a woman, skinny, fast, and she just vamoosed. *Good,* thought Woodhouse. *One less thing to worry about.*

Then he noticed that Grant had taken a position behind the cab's rear passenger door. Grant fired his pistol at Woodhouse. He got off three quick shots. The first one hit Woodhouse in the shoulder, and the other two went through his windshield.

Woodhouse fired back, but the pain and the bleeding from his shoulder threw off his aim. Instead of blowing a hole through Grant's head, his shot hit the trunk of the cab.

The last thing Cary Woodhouse expected to happen under that black, starry sky was for something loud and as bright as the sun to obliterate everything.

CHAPTER 96

I HUNG UP with Jacobi and tried to tell Joe what I could barely understand or believe.

The TV was on mute and the explosion was on a short loop. It kept playing again and again, with a crawl at the bottom of the screen reading, "Bomb goes off at Civic Center. Area is closed while bomb squad, fire dept., police contain the perimeter."

Joe said, "What did Jacobi say?"

I said, "It was about Connor Grant. Jacobi told me that Grant was trying to blow up City Hall."

"How does he know that?"

Joe asked me to repeat every word of what Jacobi had told me. We were in the living room, out of Julie's earshot.

I told Joe, "A man called the police station right after the explosion and asked for the chief. His name was Micah Woodhouse. He was the father-in-law of Lisa Woodhouse, one of the Sci-Tron victims. Micah told Jacobi that his son Cary had been watching Grant, making sure that he didn't blow up anything again.

"According to Micah Woodhouse, Cary had

followed Grant to the Civic Center and had called his father to say he was suspicious. And then a taxi blew up in front of City Hall.

"Micah thinks his son was killed in the blast."

Joe and I turned back to the TV, and watched as new images came on. It appeared that the roads had been torn up, a few vehicles had been overturned, and City Hall had taken some damage, not yet assessed. But the many iconic buildings were still standing. The body count wasn't yet in, but when Joe picked up his phone to access the Twitterverse, he told me that it was confirmed: the passenger in the cab was dead.

I tried not to show Julie that I was shaken when I put her to bed. Had Cary Woodhouse foiled Grant's plan? Or was Grant's entire escapade meant to end in a suicide car bomb?

Connor Grant.

Still a mystery to the final freaking *kaboom*.

CHAPTER 97

WHILE I QUELLED the fierce bedtime protests from our bambina, Joe took Martha for a walk. When he came back through the door, I realized I didn't have to say anything about date nights anymore.

I disabled the ringers on all the phones.

Joe took me into his arms.

We went to bed. I was full of so many feelings. That Connor Grant was no longer in our lives. That we were safe. That Joe was home.

Joe was *home*.

Joe and I held each other for a good long time before kisses turned up the heat and our clothes came off fast. Making love with Joe wasn't the homey tumble of the last time we'd been together so long ago, and it wasn't the desperate passion we'd felt when our story first began.

This was both making love with my *husband* and the release of the anger and resentment I'd harbored for so long. I told him I loved him, and he told me he loved me so much.

"I'll never let you down again," he said. "I'll never let you go."

We spent the rest of the night talking like we used to do.

We never slept, and we heard Julie calling out for me as the sky began to lighten.

I went into her room and grabbed her up over the "fences" and carried her into our bedroom. She crawled in between Joe and me, turned her head to look at each of us.

"Nice," she said.

"Isn't it?" I said, grinning at our adorable, blue-eyed, curly-haired child. It was better than nice. This was all that mattered.

ACKNOWLEDGMENTS

Our thanks to Captain Richard Conklin, BCI commander, Stamford, Connecticut, PD; to Humphrey Germaniuk, medical examiner and coroner, Trumbull County, Ohio; and to Chuck Hanni, IAAI-certified fire investigator, Youngstown, Ohio, for sharing their wisdom and expertise. We are also grateful to attorneys Philip R. Hoffman and Steven Rabinowitz of Pryor, Cashman, NYC, for their wise legal counsel. And many thanks to the home team, John A. Duffy, Mary Jordan, Lynn Colomello, and to our amazing researcher, Ingrid Taylar, West Coast, USA.

ABOUT THE AUTHORS

James Patterson holds the Guinness World Record for the most #1 *New York Times* bestsellers, and his books have sold more than 350 million copies worldwide. A tireless champion of the power of books and reading, Patterson created a children's book imprint, JIMMY Patterson, whose mission is simple: "We want every kid who finishes a JIMMY Book to say, 'PLEASE GIVE ME ANOTHER BOOK.'" He has donated more than one million books to students and soldiers, and funds over four hundred Teacher Education Scholarships at twenty-four colleges and universities. He has also donated millions to independent bookstores and school libraries. Patterson invests proceeds from the sales of JIMMY Patterson Books in pro-reading initiatives.

Maxine Paetro is the author of three novels and two works of nonfiction as well as more than twenty bestsellers coauthored with James Patterson. These include the Women's Murder Club, Confessions, and Private series as well as *Woman of God* and other books. Paetro lives in New York with her husband.

BOOKS BY JAMES PATTERSON

FEATURING ALEX CROSS

The People vs. Alex Cross • *Cross the Line* • *Cross Justice* • *Hope to Die* • *Cross My Heart* • *Alex Cross, Run* • *Merry Christmas, Alex Cross* • *Kill Alex Cross* • *Cross Fire* • *I, Alex Cross* • *Alex Cross's Trial* (with Richard DiLallo) • *Cross Country* • *Double Cross* • *Cross* (also published as *Alex Cross*) • *Mary, Mary* • *London Bridges* • *The Big Bad Wolf* • *Four Blind Mice* • *Violets Are Blue* • *Roses Are Red* • *Pop Goes the Weasel* • *Cat & Mouse* • *Jack & Jill* • *Kiss the Girls* • *Along Came a Spider*

THE WOMEN'S MURDER CLUB

16th Seduction (with Maxine Paetro) • *15th Affair* (with Maxine Paetro) • *14th Deadly Sin* (with Maxine Paetro) • *Unlucky 13* (with Maxine Paetro) • *12th of Never* (with Maxine Paetro) • *11th Hour* (with Maxine Paetro) • *10th Anniversary* (with Maxine Paetro) • *The 9th Judgment* (with Maxine Paetro) • *The 8th Confession* (with Maxine Paetro) • *7th Heaven* (with Maxine Paetro) • *The 6th Target* (with Maxine Paetro) • *The 5th Horseman* (with Maxine Paetro) • *4th of July* (with Maxine Paetro) • *3rd Degree* (with Andrew Gross) • *2nd Chance* (with Andrew Gross) • *1st to Die*

FEATURING MICHAEL BENNETT

Haunted (with James O. Born) • *Bullseye* (with Michael Ledwidge) • *Alert* (with Michael Ledwidge) • *Burn* (with Michael Ledwidge) • *Gone* (with Michael Ledwidge) • *I, Michael Bennett* (with Michael Ledwidge) • *Tick Tock* (with Michael Ledwidge) • *Worst Case* (with Michael Ledwidge) • *Run for Your Life* (with Michael Ledwidge) • *Step on a Crack* (with Michael Ledwidge)

THE PRIVATE NOVELS

Count to Ten (with Ashwin Sanghi) • *Missing* (with Kathryn Fox) • *The Games* (with Mark Sullivan) • *Private Paris* (with Mark Sullivan) • *Private Vegas* (with Maxine Paetro) • *Private India: City on Fire* (with Ashwin Sanghi) • *Private Down Under* (with Michael White) • *Private L.A.* (with Mark Sullivan) • *Private Berlin* (with Mark Sullivan) • *Private London* (with Mark Pearson) • *Private Games*

(with Mark Sullivan) • *Private: #1 Suspect* (with Maxine Paetro) •
Private (with Maxine Paetro)

NYPD RED NOVELS

Red Alert (with Marshall Karp) • *NYPD Red 4* (with Marshall Karp) •
NYPD Red 3 (with Marshall Karp) • *NYPD Red 2* (with Marshall
Karp) • *NYPD Red* (with Marshall Karp)

SUMMER NOVELS

Second Honeymoon (with Howard Roughan) • *Now You See Her* (with
Michael Ledwidge) • *Swimsuit* (with Maxine Paetro) • *Sail* (with
Howard Roughan) • *Beach Road* (with Peter de Jonge) • *Lifeguard*
(with Andrew Gross) • *Honeymoon* (with Howard Roughan) • *The
Beach House* (with Peter de Jonge)

STAND-ALONE BOOKS

Fifty Fifty (with Candice Fox) • *Murder Beyond the Grave* • *The Patriot*
(with Alex Abramovich) • *Home Sweet Murder* • *Murder, Interrupted* •
The Family Lawyer (with Robert Rotstein, Christopher Charles, Rachel
Howzell Hall) • *The Store* (with Richard DiLallo) • *The Moores Are
Missing* (with Loren D. Estleman, Sam Hawken, Ed Chatterton) •
Triple Threat (with Max DiLallo, Andrew Bourrelle) • *Murder Games*
(with Howard Roughan) • *Penguins of America* (with Jack Patterson
with Florence Yue) • *Two from the Heart* (with Frank Constantini,
Emily Raymond, Brian Sitts) • *The Black Book* (with David Ellis) •
Humans, Bow Down (with Emily Raymond) • *Never Never* (with
Candice Fox) • *Woman of God* (with Maxine Paetro) • *Filthy Rich* (with
John Connolly and Timothy Malloy) • *The Murder House* (with David
Ellis) • *Truth or Die* (with Howard Roughan) • *Miracle at Augusta*
(with Peter de Jonge) • *Invisible* (with David Ellis) • *First Love* (with
Emily Raymond) • *Mistress* (with David Ellis) • *Zoo* (with Michael
Ledwidge) • *Guilty Wives* (with David Ellis) • *The Christmas Wedding*
(with Richard DiLallo) • *Kill Me If You Can* (with Marshall Karp) •
Toys (with Neil McMahon) • *Don't Blink* (with Howard Roughan) •
The Postcard Killers (with Liza Marklund) • *The Murder of King Tut*
(with Martin Dugard) • *Against Medical Advice* (with Hal Friedman) •
Sundays at Tiffany's (with Gabrielle Charbonnet) • *You've Been Warned*
(with Howard Roughan) • *The Quickie* (with Michael Ledwidge) •
Judge & Jury (with Andrew Gross) • *Sam's Letters to Jennifer* • *The Lake
House* • *The Jester* (with Andrew Gross) • *Suzanne's Diary for Nicholas*

• *Cradle and All* • *When the Wind Blows* • *Miracle on the 17th Green* (with Peter de Jonge) • *Hide & Seek* • *The Midnight Club* • *Black Friday* (originally published as *Black Market*) • *See How They Run* • *Season of the Machete* • *The Thomas Berryman Number*

BOOK**SHOTS**

The Exile (with Alison Joseph) • *The Medical Examiner* (with Maxine Paetro) • *Black Dress Affair* (with Susan DiLallo) • *The Killer's Wife* (with Max DiLallo) • *Scott Free* (with Rob Hart) • *The Dolls* (with Kecia Bal) • *Detective Cross* • *Nooners* (with Tim Arnold) • *Stealing Gulfstreams* (with Max DiLallo) • *Diary of a Succubus* (with Derek Nikitas) • *Night Sniper* (with Christopher Charles) • *Juror #3* (with Nancy Allen) • *The Shut-In* (with Duane Swierczynski) • *French Twist* (with Richard DiLallo) • *Malicious* (with James O. Born) • *Hidden* (with James O. Born) • *The House Husband* (with Duane Swierczynski) • *The Christmas Mystery* (with Richard DiLallo) • *Black & Blue* (with Candice Fox) • *Come and Get Us* (with Shan Serafin) • *Private: The Royals* (with Rees Jones) • *Taking the Titanic* (with Scott Slaven) • *Killer Chef* (with Jeffrey J. Keyes) • *French Kiss* (with Richard DiLallo) • *$10,000,000 Marriage Proposal* (with Hilary Liftin) • *Hunted* (with Andrew Holmes) • *113 Minutes* (with Max DiLallo) • *Chase* (with Michael Ledwidge) • *Let's Play Make-Believe* (with James O. Born) • *The Trial* (with Maxine Paetro) • *Little Black Dress* (with Emily Raymond) • *Cross Kill* • *Zoo II* (with Max DiLallo)

BOOK**SH🔥TS**
Flames

Sabotage: An Under Covers Story by Jessica Linden • *Love Me Tender* by Laurie Horowitz • *Bedding the Highlander* by Sabrina York • *The Wedding Florist* by T.J. Kline • *A Wedding in Maine* by Jen McLaughlin • *Radiant* by Elizabeth Hayley • *Hot Winter Nights* by Codi Gray • *Bodyguard* by Jessica Linden • *Dazzling* by Elizabeth Hayley • *The Mating Season* by Laurie Horowitz • *Sacking the Quarterback* by Samantha Towle • *Learning to Ride* by Erin Knightley • *The McCullagh Inn in Maine* by Jen McLaughlin

FOR READERS OF ALL AGES

Maximum Ride
Maximum Ride Forever • *Nevermore: The Final Maximum Ride Adventure* • *Angel: A Maximum Ride Novel* • *Fang: A Maximum Ride Novel* • *Max: A Maximum Ride Novel* • *The Final Warning: A Maximum Ride Novel* • *Saving the World and Other Extreme Sports: A Maximum Ride Novel* • *School's Out—Forever: A Maximum Ride Novel* • *The Angel Experiment: A Maximum Ride Novel*

Daniel X
Daniel X: Lights Out (with Chris Grabenstein) • *Daniel X: Armageddon* (with Chris Grabenstein) • *Daniel X: Game Over* (with Ned Rust) • *Daniel X: Demons and Druids* (with Adam Sadler) • *Daniel X: Watch the Skies* (with Ned Rust) • *The Dangerous Days of Daniel X* (with Michael Ledwidge)

Witch & Wizard
Witch & Wizard: The Lost (with Emily Raymond) • *Witch & Wizard: The Kiss* (with Jill Dembowski) • *Witch & Wizard: The Fire* (with Jill Dembowski) • *Witch & Wizard: The Gift* (with Ned Rust) • *Witch & Wizard* (with Gabrielle Charbonnet)

Confessions
Confessions: The Murder of an Angel (with Maxine Paetro) • *Confessions: The Paris Mysteries* (with Maxine Paetro) • *Confessions: The Private School Murders* (with Maxine Paetro) • *Confessions of a Murder Suspect* (with Maxine Paetro)

Middle School
Middle School: Escape to Australia (with Martin Chatterton, illustrated by Daniel Griffo) • *Middle School: Dog's Best Friend* (with Chris Tebbetts, illustrated by Jomike Tejido) • *Middle School: Just My Rotten Luck* (with Chris Tebbetts, illustrated by Laura Park) • *Middle School: Save Rafe!* (with Chris Tebbetts, illustrated by Laura Park) • *Middle School: Ultimate Showdown* (with Julia Bergen, illustrated by Alec Longstreth) • *Middle School: How I Survived Bullies, Broccoli, and Snake Hill* (with Chris Tebbetts, illustrated by Laura Park) • *Middle School: My Brother Is a Big, Fat Liar* (with Lisa Papademetriou, illustrated by Neil Swaab) • *Middle School: Get Me Out of Here!* (with Chris Tebbetts, illustrated by Laura Park) • *Middle School, The Worst Years of My Life* (with Chris Tebbetts, illustrated by Laura Park)

I Funny

I Funny: School of Laughs (with Chris Grabenstein, illustrated by Jomike Tejido • *I Funny TV* (with Chris Grabenstein, illustrated by Laura Park) • *I Totally Funniest: A Middle School Story* (with Chris Grabenstein, illustrated by Laura Park) • *I Even Funnier: A Middle School Story* (with Chris Grabenstein, illustrated by Laura Park) • *I Funny: A Middle School Story* (with Chris Grabenstein, illustrated by Laura Park)

Treasure Hunters

Treasure Hunters: Quest for the City of Gold (with Chris Grabenstein, illustrated by Juliana Neufeld) • *Treasure Hunters: Peril at the Top of the World* (with Chris Grabenstein, illustrated by Juliana Neufeld) • *Treasure Hunters: Secret of the Forbidden City* (with Chris Grabenstein, illustrated by Juliana Neufeld) • *Treasure Hunters: Danger Down the Nile* (with Chris Grabenstein, illustrated by Juliana Neufeld) • *Treasure Hunters* (with Chris Grabenstein, illustrated by Juliana Neufeld)

OTHER BOOKS FOR READERS OF ALL AGES

The Candies' Easter Party (illustrated by Andy Elkerton) • *Jacky Ha-Ha: My Life is a Joke* (with Chris Grabenstein, illustrated by Kerascoët) • *Give Thank You a Try* (with Bill O'Reilly) • *Expelled* (with Emily Raymond) • *The Candies Save Christmas* (illustrated by Andy Elkerton) • *Big Words for Little Geniuses* (with Susan Patterson, illustrated by Hsinping Pan) • *Laugh Out Loud* (with Chris Grabenstein) • *Pottymouth and Stoopid* (with Chris Grabenstein) • *Crazy House* (with Gabrielle Charbonnet) • *House of Robots: Robot Revolution* (with Chris Grabenstein, illustrated by Juliana Neufeld) • *Word of Mouse* (with Chris Grabenstein, illustrated by Joe Sutphin) • *Give Please a Chance* (with Bill O'Reilly) • *Jacky Ha-Ha* (with Chris Grabenstein, illustrated by Kerascoët) • *House of Robots: Robots Go Wild!* (with Chris Grabenstein, illustrated by Juliana Neufeld) • *Public School Superhero* (with Chris Tebbetts, illustrated by Cory Thomas) • *House of Robots* (with Chris Grabenstein, illustrated by Juliana Neufeld) • *Homeroom Diaries* (with Lisa Papademetriou, illustrated by Keino) • *Med Head* (with Hal Friedman) • *santaKid* (illustrated by Michael Garland)

For previews and information about the author, visit JamesPatterson.com or find him on Facebook or at your app store.

JAMES
PATTERSON
RECOMMENDS

Don't tell Alex Cross and Michael Bennett this, but I might have a bit of a soft spot for Lindsay Boxer and the Women's Murder Club. Why? Because Lindsay, Cindy, Claire, and Jill always get their man. And by "man," I mean the criminal they're hunting. As some of the most respected professionals in the San Francisco justice system, they were sick and tired of tip-toeing around their male bosses to get the job done. So they banded together, shared information, and closed more cases.

Meet the first ladies of crime fighting: the Women's Murder Club.

"Patterson has mastered the art of writing page-turning bestsellers."
—*Chicago Sun-Times*

JAMES PATTERSON

1ST TO DIE

#1 NEW YORK TIMES BESTSELLING AUTHOR

A WOMEN'S MURDER CLUB NOVEL

1ST TO DIE

Three sets of murdered newlyweds, bureaucratic red tape, and a truly terrible diagnosis from the doctor—Detective Lindsay Boxer has her hands full in 1ST TO DIE, the book that launched the Women's Murder Club series. She's one tough cookie, though, and a heck of a character to get to know: fierce, determined, smart, and unstoppable. In short, she's my kind of woman. She'll need to keep her wits—and her WMC friends—about her, though, because the killer is the last person anyone would ever see coming.

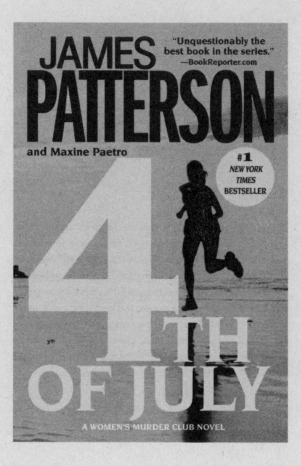

JAMES
PATTERSON

and Maxine Paetro

4TH
OF JULY

A WOMEN'S MURDER CLUB NOVEL

4TH OF JULY

As an author, I love shaking things up and seeing how characters grow—or, in my books, if they even make it to the end of the story. The most interesting thing to test? Loyalty. Lindsay Boxer has dedicated her life to upholding the law. But after a routine arrest goes terribly wrong, she finds herself facing judge, jury, a very public trial, and a brutal murderer slashing through her sister's once-peaceful hometown. I turned Lindsay's life upside down in this book. And that's not all of it. Read what happens because I put a twist in this book that's pretty killer.

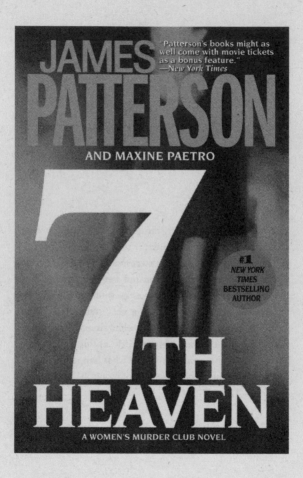

JAMES
PATTERSON

AND MAXINE PAETRO

7
TH
HEAVEN

A WOMEN'S MURDER CLUB NOVEL

"Patterson's books might as
well come with movie tickets
as a bonus feature."
—*New York Times*

#1
NEW YORK
TIMES
BESTSELLING
AUTHOR

7TH HEAVEN

San Francisco. Beautiful weather. Beautiful people. Beautiful architecture. It's the perfect setting for everything to go wrong. And, boy, does everything go terribly wrong. Lindsay and the WMC face two of their biggest cases yet: the politically charged disappearance of the mayor's son and a string of devastating fires that destroy some of the city's most iconic homes—with their wealthy owners inside. When the pressure is on, the WMC is at its best, and that's what they need to be in this book. Because when everything converges in 7TH HEAVEN, it's nothing short of explosive.

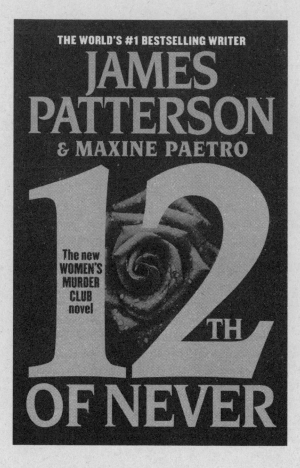

THE WORLD'S #1 BESTSELLING WRITER

JAMES PATTERSON

& MAXINE PAETRO

12TH

The new
WOMEN'S
MURDER
CLUB
novel

OF NEVER

12TH OF NEVER

When I think of a newborn baby, I think "nesting" and desperately trying to sneak in a few moments of precious sleep. Lindsay Boxer, detective and newly minted mom, doesn't experience any of those in 12TH OF NEVER. After only a week of baby bliss, a string of murders pulls Lindsay out of the nursery and onto the streets of San Francisco. I've always been amazed at how working moms juggle families and careers. But on top of finding lost socks, Lindsay also has to find a missing body from the morgue. And that's just the beginning. The shocker I have lined up at the end? Mind-blowing.